MISSING CLAYTON

A single mother searches for her missing child

Bev Irwin

Irwin Press

Reviews

KUDOS FOR *MISSING CLAYTON*

Irwin does a brilliant job of portraying her villain. I once heard a psychologist say that no one thinks of themselves as evil. No matter how evil they are, they always justify their deeds to themselves. Well, that is certainly true in the case of the villain in Missing Clayton. Irwin has done an excellent job of making the villain seem real. In fact, all of her characters are completely three-dimensional and believable. The plot twists and turns kept me reading to the very last page. I gave up emails, dinner, and television to finish the book. – *Taylor, Reviewer*

The story starts out in the boy's POV, and though he is a little precocious for five-almost-six, he is still well-developed and three-dimensional. All the characters are extremely well done. The thing I liked best about the book is the ring of truth it has. It feels so authentic it makes me wonder if Ms. Irwin hasn't been through exactly the same thing herself. From the moment she discovers that Clayton is gone, Jenny's life is turned upside down. The cops are called in—but how much can they really do—and Jenny and her ex become the prime suspects, at least for a time. Meanwhile, as the cops investigate and the search for the boy goes on, Jenny's hope for his safe recovery diminishes as her terror at his fate grows. My heart went out to her. As it did to Clayton and to Steve. The ex and Jenny's mother, not so much. In fact, I wanted to brain the both of them. And it takes a good writer to get me that involved in the characters. – *Regan, Reviewer*

A child is missing and a mother who doesnt give up looking. A story filled with suspense. You really care about the characters. I highly recommend it!   Janet Scott

Great story. Read the entire book on a flight from Las Vegas to Boston. I couldn't put it down. Very well written.   Kelly

Missing Clayton kept me wanting more. The suspense kept me on the edge in hopes that Jenny would find her child before it was too late. And when she was taken to the morgue to identify a child's body, it had me holding my breath. This is an experience that has to be one of the hardest things a parent can do and go through.   Martha Cheves

Missing Clayton by Bev Irwin is an excellent thriller. I was touched, terrified, and delighted, not only in the same book, but often in the same scene. The story revolves around the disappearance of five-year-old Clayton from his home one morning. His mother Jenny panics, naturally, and goes looking for him, searching the neighborhood. The neighbor Steve (the love interest) sees her tearful state and runs to help. When they can't find the boy, the police are called in. Irwin does a brilliant job of portraying her villain. I once heard a psychologist say that no one thinks of themselves as evil. No matter how evil they are, they always justify their deeds to themselves. Well, that is certainly true in the case of the villain in Missing Clayton. Irwin has done an excellent job of making the villain seem real. In fact, all of her characters are completely three-dimensional and believable. The plot twists and turns kept me reading to the very last page. I gave up emails, dinner, and television to finish the book.   Taylor, reviewer

I received this book and agreed to give it an honest review. I so need to know what happened next!! Jenny Kingsley left her abusive husband and controlling mother to live in Scottsville with her five-year-old son, where her son could grow up in a community that was better than in the city; she even had an accounting job for Lawson Manufacturing where she could work from home.
Once she discovered her son was not playing in his sandbox, was he playing hide and seek? It was his favorite game and he promised to never play the game again until he did it again. Jenny was out of her mind with worry as she'd searched all

over and still couldn't find him. Then she noticed the gate in the backyard was open, and she hurried out of the game to look down the street to see if he was there.   Nancy

This is the first book written by Ms Irwin I have read. Bev Irwin has a knack for writing very realistically and emotionally from many points of view, even the protagonist. It is a story of loss and pain from the mother's perspective that grips you and leaves you praying for her and her son's safe return. I was riveted. I look forward to her next book.

I so thoroughly enjoyed this book. Yes, if you read the blurb, it's about a little boy who goes missing whilst he is outside in his safe fenced-off back garden playing in his sandpit. His mother has just popped into the kitchen to prepare some lunch for them both, just some sandwiches and a drink. In that short period of time Clayton goes missing.

This is not just some massive search for a kid, no, it opens into much more than that. I'm not going to spoil this story by telling you too much about this, but at the end when they find out who abducted Clayton, I thought "hey, this is going to be make or break time now" and WOW the missing pieces all fitted in.   Marcia

I have never read a book by Bev Irwin before, she was asking for reviews for a couple of her books in our facebook 2 friends promote group, so I do have another book written by her which I am looking forward to reading, she is really a good author IMHO and one I am going to be watching.   readalongwithSue

First of I was given a copy of this book in exchange for an honest review, but I'd gladly pay the price for the chance to read this amazing book. This is my impression of the book. Spoiler alert!!!

Missing Clayton by Bev Irving is a thrilling story about a five-year-old boy taken from his backyard in the middle of the day. We are taken for an emotional as well as nail-biting ride along with his mother, Jenny, who is caught up in the whirlwind of hell. She will stop at nothing to find her boy dead or alive. With the boy's disappearance, the entire town (a small community) seems to relive the horrors of their own, and everyone knows something but is reluctant to say it. Media has a field day, bringing out the worst of Jenny's life, accusing her of harming her own child then claiming he's gone missing. Police officer on the power trip harasses the usual suspect, Jenny's neighbour Steve, and her one light point and rock to lean on. The reader also gets to see the horror little Clayton is experiencing shoved inside the dugout hole beneath the shifting boards. And while his kidnapper has no intention to really hurt him as long as he is co-operating, one can't help but shudder in fear.

Bev Irvin has managed to capture the mentality of a small town in the middle of the farming county so well, every character jumps off the page and becomes alive, even the bloodhound Missy hot on the trail of the missing boy. I highly recommend this book to all and especially parents and grandparents.   MicaMaca

I'd like to thank the author Bev Irwin for gifting me a copy of "Missing Clayton" in exchange for a fair and honest review.

I found this a great read, a change to the usual missing child novels I have read before, fresh and uplifting.

However, I did find the story very repetitive in places, and this got a bit frustrating at times! As for the tea towel Jenny (the mum) was holding and wringing constantly for quite some time ~ I just wanted to take it out of her hands and fold it up and put it down for her!!

The characters were well-rounded and mostly likable. I enjoyed the way how they all connected and formed relationships with one another. I look forward to reading more from this author as I love a good suspense story and this author writes it well.   Beathag

Whatever you do, do NOT miss reading a Bev Irwin book! I received Missing Clayton for my review. This is the 2nd book of Ms Irwin's I have read and I cannot wait to read another one! Missing Clayton kept me spellbound and I couldn't wait to find out what happened! After I finished I was sad that I didn't have more! This book, as with Ms Irwin's other books will keep you on your toes throughout the entire book! Her writing style pulls you into the book where you can feel this mother's pain and fear in searching for her son. I don't want to give a spoiler on this book, so Go, Get this book NOW and read it! While you are at it get another

Bev Irwin book! This book along with her others are heading for best sellers! I can also see movies in the future! Keep up the wonderful reads, Bev!   Kraftyvada

Bev brings the most terrifying situations to life with compassion and thoroughness. You could feel a mother's angst and terror over losing her son. How often do we see an Amber alert and think - oh how terrible - but not realizing how the family feels. Her characters are so well written you think you know them. I cannot imagine how losing a child would feel but learned an inkling by reading this book. As with her other books this was very well written, fast paced and easy to read. I would highly recommend.   Kindle Customer

Missing Clayton is about a child's abduction and the related trauma.
I had a sort of love/hate relationship with this one as it was just too realistically horrible and painful experiencing so much through the mother's and the son's eyes. However, this does show how well-written the book is.
Overall, it is a very vivid, fast-paced ride!   Monica

Missing Clayton by Bev Irwin was a fascinating read. Having your child kidnapped is a parent's worst nightmare, especially since the child is so rarely returned home safely. So, being a parent myself, it was easy for me to identify with Jenny when she discovers her son is gone. Irwin did a brilliant job of showing us Jenny's felling of terror, love, and guilt as the story progresses. The story starts out in the boy's POV, and though he is a little precocious for five-almost-six, he is still well-developed and three dimensional. All the characters are extremely well done. The thing I liked best about the book is the ring of truth it has. It feels so authentic it makes me wonder if Ms. Irwin hasn't been through exactly the same thing herself.   Reggie

This is an amazing book. Jenny and Clayton's story could have been snatched from the news. The book really brings to life every parent's fears. Bev Irwin brings us a very intense story and keeps it rolling throughout the book. I really loved this book and couldn't put it down. Great job!   Miss Lyn

Bev Irwin has captured the essence of a parent's worst nightmare. Kudos to Bev; great work!
A must-read novel. Nada

BLUrB

Five-year-old Clayton Kingsley was in his backyard building a sandcastle two minutes ago. Now the sandbox is empty, so is the swing. And the gate that kept the world at bay is open...

His mother, Jenny, recently divorced, has left behind a controlling mother and an abusive husband, who thought more of his buddies and the bottle than being a father to his son. Now that son is missing. Is Jenny's ex really the distraught parent he seems or is he the culprit?

As the days go by with no sign of Clayton, Jenny searches frantically for her son. Who could have taken him? If not his father, could it be her sexy, secretive neighbor, a man suspected in the disappearance of another child? Or is there a serial predator in the serene bedroom community that Jenny thought would be the perfect place to raise her son?

Acknowledgements

There are so many wonderful people who go into the making of a book. I thank everyone who helped bring MISSING CLAYTON to fruition.

Special thanks go out to Jane Gloor for her help with the bitter end, to Michael Rieder for his initial critique and for planting a seed dream that MISSING CLAYTON would be a great movie. To a wonderful team of first readers and editors: Tina Gowing, Sue Atchison, Cathy Mott, Nicole Dietze, and Jacqueline Nestler. They have all been a huge part of making my dream come true.

And to Joseph Clement of Sault Sainte. Marie, Ontario, for the questions he answered and the information he provided on Bloodhounds and their amazing ability to track people long after other dogs have lost the trail.

Such a great team. Hats off to you.

Dedication

I dedicate this book to all the mothers who have lost children, be it for a moment or forever.

TO MY READERS

Thank you for reading my book. There are excerpts of my other novels at the end of this one. If you enjoy my writing, I would greatly appreciate it if you would consider leaving an honest review. A short line would do. Recommending my books to others would also be awesome. Reviews are invaluable for authors and help us to do what we love to do, and what we hope you enjoy.

CHAPTER 1

I *don't like it here. It's dark. It's cold. Why doesn't Mommy come and get me? She knows I don't like the dark.*

"Your mommy has to find you," the man had said.

Where is she?

"It's a game," he said.

He grabbed my arm. It hurt. It's not a good game. He's not nice.

I called her, but he put his smelly hand over my mouth. I wanted to bite it. Mommy doesn't like biting. But he's mean. I don't like this place. Will she find me here? She will. She's good at hide-and-seek. I hope she finds me soon.

The boy sat cross-legged in the cave-like space, a mat of blue tweed his only protection from the damp dirt floor. Putting his head in his hands, he felt the mud coating his hair. He'd screamed when the man rubbed it on his head.

"My mommy doesn't like my hair dirty. She'll be mad at you."

The man laughed. Not a nice laugh, either. He sounded like the Joker in Batman. The laugh reminded him of his father when he got angry.

He had to be good. There was no closet to hide in here.

The thick mud covered his blond hair. Clawing at his head, he broke off bits of clay. He remembered that morning and his mother brushing his hair. She said it shone like the sun.

They were going to his new school, and she wanted him to look nice for his teacher. If Mommy didn't find him in time, would he have to stay in kindergarten? He scrubbed at his head until his hands hurt, yet the dirt remained. He didn't want to cry, but tears slid down his face and merged with the dirt. They ran into his mouth, the mixture stung his tongue, and he spat it out. More tears ran down his face. His mother didn't like spitting.

He clenched his fists and pounded at the rug beneath him. It wasn't long before his hands throbbed. He stopped pounding and began tearing at the ragged fringes along one end of the rug. When his fingers slipped beyond it, he felt earth—cold and hard and damp. He shivered.

After what seemed like forever, curiosity overcame his fear, and he began to investigate. His eyes, adjusted to the dimness, saw a few feet beyond the rug. A dirt wall, like the one behind him, ended the open space in front. He stretched out his right arm and his fingers felt the dampness of another wall of dirt. To his left, the area stretched into a black space.

He peered into the darkness. Several wooden crates—each containing differently shaped objects too blurry to make out—filled the space. Above him, he saw the wooden door he'd been shoved through. He counted four wooden rungs leading up from the crawl space. The trap door allowed only a sliver of light to enter the space.

I don't like the dark.

Mingling scents of mold, dampness, dried animal droppings, closed in on him. It made his throat tight, and he coughed.

He stretched a hand above his head. Sticky strands closed around his fingers. He jerked his hand back, scrubbed the spider webs onto the rug, and retreated to the safety of the woven mat. Maybe it was better not to explore. Sitting Indian style, he cradled his arms around his chest and rocked back and forth. Beyond where he sat, the cave was jet-black. He tried to hold back his tears. Soft scuffling sounds came from the corners of the dugout. He knew they weren't human. The rhythm of his rocking increased.

When is Mommy coming? I'm going to curl up here and sleep until she finds me. There's just enough room. If I close my eyes, I won't see how dark it is. It will be as dark inside my head as it is on the outside.

He curled into a fetal position. Somewhere close he heard the scurrying of tiny feet. Stuffing his fingers in his ears, he made himself think about playing in the safety of his backyard. Anything to drown out the wild pictures crowding his head.

He remembered building the castle in his sandbox. He was scooping out the moat when someone called his name. The man came into the backyard.

"I have a surprise for you."

The chocolate was soft and gooey. "More in the truck," the man said. But he didn't have any more. He lied.

He remembered the smelly rag being pressed into his mouth. He remembered the bandana tied over his eyes. He remembered the man grabbing him, running with him. He remembered being shoved in the back of a truck.

"We're playing hide and seek," the man said. "Your mommy has to find you."

The smell of gas and oil stung his nostrils as a blue tarp landed on top of him. It shut out the sun. He heard a door slam, an engine start, wheels squealing, and the truck sped away.

How is Mommy going to find me? Maybe he lied about that, too.

Earlier that day:

"Clay, lunch is ready."

Jenny Kingsley took a loaf of bread from the breadbox. Sunlight streamed through the open kitchen window catching the embossed pattern of fuchsia and sapphire roses on the box's lid. Her gaze drifted to the matching canister set and she traced the edges of the delicate flowers. She'd spied the set at Stockley's Variety Store last week and had to have it. It matched perfectly with the wallpaper she'd recently hung. Jenny couldn't resist splurging on it. She couldn't remember ever having a matched set of anything.

Buttering the bread, she plastered peanut butter on top. A quick lunch, but they had things to do. They had to be at Manor Park School in forty-five minutes to register Clayton. Jenny couldn't believe how quickly time passed, she couldn't believe her baby was old enough to be going into the first grade.

As she glanced around the newly decorated kitchen, she smiled. The old wall-paper, with its faded olive vines and tarnished brass teapots, had been replaced. The chipped and stained cupboards, painted a dull mustard when she moved in, now had a fresh coat of white paint.

Anything was better than yellow. She detested that color—too many reminders of her mother's kitchen perpetually painted some ugly shade of yellow or beige. Jenny shuddered. How many times had she entered that kitchen, her mother's domain, quivering in fear, never knowing what mood she'd be in?

Jenny thought she'd left that behind when she married Ray. But she'd only moved from one black hole to another, even to the apartments they rented—neutral colors she couldn't change. But no more. No more yellow, and no more living under a veil of fear.

Everything in this house looked bright and cheerful. Just like her life.

She'd made the right decision. Now, she and Clayton had a place of their own, a safe place—a place free of Ray's fits of anger, his drinking, his abuse. A place where she didn't have to listen to her mother's suggestions on how to live her life.

With a population of under thirty thousand, Scottsville was a good choice. It had enough business to provide the inhabitants with work yet was close enough to Columbus if people wanted more. And at a fifty-minute drive from Dresden, it afforded Jenny a comfortable distance from both Ray and her mother. Not much chance of them popping in to remind her she'd made a big mistake leaving Ray and moving away.

Jenny forced the nagging voice of uncertainty into submission. It had taken months of weighing the consequences to formulate a plan, but it was worth it. Finished with people pushing her around, she could make her own decisions, make her own mistakes. Her fingers caressed the black-and-white photos posted on the fridge. Last week, at the movies, Clay had seen the photo kiosk and begged to have their picture taken. She traced the line of his toothless grin.

Jenny executed a pirouette in the center of the room, then laughed at her foolish antics. Picking up the knife, she layered strawberry jam on top of the peanut butter. Yes, it had been the right decision. They were both happy and out of harm's way.

After moving into the house three months ago, she'd tackled the kitchen first. Having never painted or wallpapered, it took her countless hours to strip the layers of old wallpaper, and many more to refinish the woodwork. She glanced at her nails. They were still chipped and broken. But it was worth it. She loved it—the Wedgwood walls, the ceiling border of fuchsia and blue flowers, and the white paint on the cabinets. Even the kitchen table gleamed with a new coat of white enamel. Fresh paint, fresh colors, fresh kitchenware—a good first step toward building a brand new life.

Jenny leaned toward the window. "Clay, get in here."

Crossing the room, she placed the peanut butter and jam sandwiches on the table. While she waited for Clay to run in, she stroked the delicate new tea set. It must be a sign her life was finally changing, finally getting on a positive track.

Everything was falling into place. She'd found this house at an affordable price and had landed a great job. So what if her accounting teacher had pulled a few strings? Doing the books for Lawson Manufacturing at home meant she didn't need a babysitter for Clayton. She glanced at the pile of papers she'd been working on earlier. When they got back from the school, she'd finish tallying the accounts for this month's sales. Maybe Mr. Lawson would recommend her to some of his associates. With Clay in school full-time, she could take on more clients.

Ray had forbidden her to take the accounting course but, thank God, she'd stood her ground. She'd worked hard and graduated with honors. Once Clay started school, she'd enroll in an advanced accounting course.

Jenny picked up a towel and wiped off the teapot before placing it on the table. She glanced at the clock. Eleven-forty-five. *Where is he?*

"Clay, we have to eat. We need to go to your new school." She'd give him one minute to get inside.

Standing on tiptoes, Jenny leaned against the counter and peered through the window. It afforded a partial view of the fenced-in yard. She scanned the lawn. At the back of the property, overgrown shrubs lined the chain-link fence. She saw the swing set beside the fence and part of the red plastic slide. She saw the sandbox where Clayton was building a castle.

It was empty.

Throwing the tea towel over her shoulder, Jenny walked to the back door. She looked through the screen toward the sandbox—the castle abandoned, his red shovel cast off in the shimmering platinum sand. Rusty hinges creaked when she shoved the screen door open.

Jenny swatted at a mosquito attacking her calf. With the July heat, the insects were out in droves. Movement caught her eye. She glanced at the swing. Empty, it swung in the breeze as if recently occupied. Her gaze paused briefly before continuing over the expanse of lawn.

She expected Clay to run in and demand his lunch, demand they go now to his new school. Jenny called again. The yard was silent. There was no demanding child. Her voice mushroomed several octaves. "Clay, where are you?"

Stepping onto the porch, Jenny let the wooden screen door slam behind her. She used the tea towel to swat at the onslaught of mosquitoes taking advantage of the open door. She hurried down the three worn plank risers to the grass. Was he hiding at the side of the house? The tea towel swung on her shoulder as she skirted the vinyl-sided building. Her voice rose, partly in annoyance, partly in concern. "Clayton, come here now!"

I hate playing hide and seek.

She thought of how Clayton would hide behind some bush or piece of furniture and then jump out to scare her. She'd scold him. "It frightens me when I can't find you." He'd giggle at her panic. With pouting lips and a downcast head, his mischievous blue eyes would peek out of his angelic face. He'd promise never to do it again—until the next time.

The side of the house was empty. She looked behind and inside the shed. A wheelbarrow stood in the middle of the lawn where Weigelia bushes awaited planting. Maybe he was hiding behind it. Jenny circled the wheelbarrow, but he wasn't there. Could he fit under it? He wasn't very big. She moved one of the bush-filled buckets and looked underneath. Nothing.

"Darn it, Clayton, where are you? This isn't funny."

Jenny hurried to the back fence, her heart beating faster with each step. Branches scratched her forearms. She thrust them out of the way. He wasn't hiding there. A lump clogged her throat. She gasped for air. It hurt to breathe. She scrutinized the fence skirting the perimeter for holes Clayton might have slipped through. There weren't any.

She turned and inspected every inch of the yard. It was as vacant and desolate as an uninhabited planet. Hot air escaped her lungs. The lump in her throat shifted, going deeper into her chest. Jenny rushed to the porch.

He's here. He's just hiding, playing one of his tricks on me. "Clayton, come out, right now!"

She was screaming, but she didn't care. Nothing mattered as long as Clayton heard her and came running. She just wanted to see his towhead popping out from under a bush, or from behind a tree. But she'd already checked every bush, every tree, every possible hiding spot.

Do it again, whatever you need to do. You have to find him. Under the porch. You haven't checked there yet. He wouldn't be there, he's afraid of the dark. Check it anyway.

Racing to the wooden porch, she scrambled to her knees and peered into the darkness. Nothing. No small shape, no hiding child. Only darkness. The tea towel fell from her shoulder. Involuntarily, she picked it up and wrung the linen between her sweat-soaked palms.

Check the front yard. He's not allowed to play there. Check it anyway.

She darted toward the front of the house. Dirt and grass clung to the bottom of her floral sundress. The front yard lay before her, manicured, peaceful, deserted. Tears trickled from the corners of her eyes.

A freshly painted, white picket fence enclosed the small, neatly mown lawn. But the yard held no bucket, no shovel, no play cars, no tricycle, and no blond-haired little boy. Something caught Jenny's attention. A movement. A sound. She turned.

The white gate, the gate that kept the world at bay, was open—a gaping hole to another sphere. She watched in horror as the gate swung gently back and forth, back and forth. It screeched on rusted hinges, trying to latch with each sweep.

She felt as if she'd fallen into a bottomless abyss—twirling out of control, spinning in a place where light no longer existed. Her breath wedged in her throat, like a swollen seed, engorging, distending, obstructing her wind-pipe. She felt as if she might never take another breath. It seemed a lifetime before a strangled cry edged its way out of her constricted throat.

"Clayton."

Her gaze darted up, then down the street. No Clayton. She raced to the corner and checked both directions on Willow Street, then ran back down Elm, peering into every backyard as she made her way to the next block.

All along Chestnut Street she saw pristinely painted houses with manicured lawns—a perfect, safe neighborhood—not one where a child would go missing out of his own backyard. Jenny searched the rows of sedate houses. The streets were empty except for three boys doing wheelies in the middle of the road.

"Have you seen a small boy go by here in the last few minutes?"

One of them spun his bike close to the curb. "Nope."

"He's about this high." Jenny held her hand a few inches above her waist. "He's blonde."

As if picking up on her hysteria, they skidded to a stop and leaned tanned arms on their handlebars. After darting glances between them, they shrugged. "No, ma'am. We haven't seen him."

Her knees wobbled like Jell-O, but she forced them to keep moving. Maybe he's still in the backyard. Maybe he's playing hide and seek. Jenny rushed back through the open gate, screaming his name. Again she checked behind every bush, every tree. Her mind tormented with inconceivable possibilities, she raced to the front of the house. She looked up and down the street, screaming her son's name.

Silence the only response.

Jenny sagged against the fence—the barricade to their safe haven. Her body went as limp as the damp dishtowel she clutched in her fingers. Shattered words slid over her parched lips.

"Clay...Clay, where are you?"

CHAPTER 2

J enny, are you okay?" Steve Townsend called from his front porch.

The voice sounded muffled, as if filtering up through a fathomless mine-shaft. Jenny tried to lift her head. It weighed a hundred pounds. She struggled to turn toward the voice. Like a car stuck in neutral, her mind raced, but her body refused to respond.

Her neighbor bounded down his porch steps.

"Help ...me...please. Clayton's gone."

A vision of Clay's small body, twisted and lifeless, bombarded the empty spaces of her mind. Jenny slumped to her knees. Hugging herself, she couldn't stifle the banshee shriek that rose unbidden from somewhere deep inside her soul.

Strong arms enfolded her. They pulled her upward until her body came to rest against his broad chest. The subtle scent of citrus and cedar clung to the soft fabric of his T-shirt. His head leaned close and she heard his soothing words. She tipped her head toward the voice. His intense blue eyes, and the determined set of his jaw, slowly came into focus. A face she could trust. She let her body slump into the security of his arms.

"Clay's gone." Her voice broke.

"Are you sure? Maybe he's just hiding. I drove my mom crazy playing hide-and-seek. I'd watch her run around like a chicken with her head cut off looking for me."

"No." Jenny stepped back and stumbled—her legs transformed into trick canes that wouldn't snap into place. She sagged against Steve for support. "I've looked. He was playing in the backyard ten minutes ago. Now he's gone."

"Let's get you into the house. Mom's visiting, you stay with her, and I'll have a look. I'm sure he's here somewhere." Turning toward his house, Steve yelled: "Mom, can you come out here?"

"I want to go with you."

"No. I can go faster on my own. You stay here. He'll be upset if he can't find you when he comes out from hiding."

Too weak to answer, Jenny allowed herself to be led toward the house.

"You have a nice cup of tea. I'll be back before you know it."

The screen door flew open and a small, gray-haired woman burst through the door. "What's wrong, Steve?"

"Clay's hiding from his mom. She's got herself in a state looking for him. Can you make her some tea while I have a look?"

Jenny's eyes pleaded with Steve. Unable to form words, she uttered a low, keening groan.

"Now, hush." Myrtle Townsend's arm wrapped around her shoulder. "I know you've checked, but let Steve look again."

Jenny caught the look of unspoken concern pass between Myrtle and her son. They were trying to reassure her but their silent communication made her shudder.

"I'll check with the neighbors. He can't have gone far."

"He might be over at the Sawyer's," Myrtle said in a cheery lilt. "You remember how excited he got the other day when he saw their new puppy."

Jenny turned to Steve. "Do you think he might be there?"

"I'll run and check. You have a cup of tea."

Jenny wanted to protest but couldn't find the energy to speak, let alone make it to the Sawyer house.

With Myrtle's aid, she stumbled up the front steps and into the house. From some far-off place, Jenny heard the woman chattering and wondered which one of them she wanted to reassure. Jenny tried to pay attention, but the voice faded as visions of Clayton lost and alone filled her brain.

In a daze, she followed Myrtle down the hall. Lowering herself onto the kitchen chair the woman held out for her, Jenny sat, stiff and silent as the piece of furniture beneath her.

CHAPTER 3

Steve ran to Jenny's backyard, his mother's words echoing in his head. He tried to block the thoughts tumbling round and round. He'd seen the concern in his mother's eyes. It mirrored his own. It couldn't be happening again. No. He wouldn't even think it. Clayton had to be somewhere close by. Steve sent up a silent prayer.

Through the open kitchen window, he heard his mother's voice—firm, kind, calm, as she reassured Jenny. He needed her reassurance too. But there wasn't time to stay and listen. He had to find the child before anything happened. He hurried to the backyard, scanning the fenced area and the empty expanse of lawn.

Where would a boy hide?

Steve saw the sandbox, the red pail, and the shovel discarded along with several plastic cars. He saw the empty swing and noticed the way it swayed as if a child had recently leaped off. But he knew it was only the slight breeze that gave it momentum.

Was he in one of the pine trees bordering the lawn? He checked. Nothing. His gaze caught sight of the back porch. He could be under there. Steve rushed toward the porch.

Crouching at the side of the porch, he peered through the dimness. The shadows made it difficult. He lay on his stomach and squirmed under the spider-web-covered boards. Rotting pieces of wood littered his way. Did he hear something? "Clay?"

He crept farther under the porch. There was room to hide. "Clay, are you here? Your mother's looking for you."

Steve inched his body over the damp ground. Something lay against the house. It was three feet long, light-colored, shapeless. Could the boy have fallen asleep? Wouldn't he hear his mother calling, or me? Steve knew he was grasping at straws, but that was all he had right now. His mind refused to believe it could happen again.

"Clayton, is that you?"

No answer. No movement. The form remained still.

Steve slid farther under the porch. His heart paused as he stretched out his hand and his fingers grazed a rough piece of cloth. He grabbed it. It came away in his hand, weightless and empty. A dirt-coated T-shirt. An adult T-shirt, not a child's. He sighed, partially in relief, partially in disappointment.

Shifting his body, Steve inspected every dark recess under the porch. He heard movement and turned toward it. A rodent scurried away. Crawling backward, Steve guided his body between the wooden support beams. It took him several seconds to adjust to the bright sunlight.

Jenny had checked the backyard already, but he circled the perimeter, examining the fence for any gaping holes. None. He checked under the branches of the forsythia and dogwood bushes. Nothing. And nothing behind or under the evergreens. Reluctantly, Steve admitted Jenny was right. The boy was not in the backyard.

He hurried back to the front of the house, looking up and down the street. There was no blond-haired boy on any of the front lawns; in fact, there was not one child on the street. He ran to the Sawyer's house. Maybe his mother was right. Maybe the boy went to see their new puppy.

There was no car in the driveway, and the front door was closed. Getting no response to his knock, Steve looked over the five-foot wooden fence. A chain snaked through the grass, but there was no dog attached. The yard was empty.

Steve raced back to the street. Five doors away, Mrs. Hawthorne weeded her front garden.

"Mrs. Hawthorne, have you seen Clayton this morning?"

"Don't know any Clayton."

"Clayton Kingsley. He's six. They moved into the McLaren place three months ago."

"I haven't seen anybody. Nobody bothers me, and I don't bother anybody."

The crispness of her tone failed to dissuade him. "His mom can't find him. She's worried."

"I don't know any Clayton Kingsley. You know I don't let the little brats near my lawn. They run all over, digging up my flowerbeds, knocking over my ornaments, tearing up the grass. As soon as I fill the bird bath, they tip it over." Her voice rose to a shriek as her garden claw pummeled the inky soil. "The little buggers, none of them brought up with any manners. Now, in my day—"

"Are you sure you didn't see him?"

"Told you I didn't."

Steve shook his head and walked away. He made his way up the street, knocking on every door, questioning anyone who answered. No one had seen Clayton. It was time to widen his search.

Clayton was a bright, pleasant child. Steve liked how he paid heed to his mother, never cussing or talking back. Not like many of the young ones running wild in the park. Springbank Park. That's where he is. But the park was several blocks away.

Steve didn't think Clayton would roam that far without his mother. From what he'd seen, he kept pretty close to her.

Steve thought about his neighbor and their budding friendship. At first, he'd tried to deny the effect she had on him, but today, he only wanted to find her son and protect them both from the world.

He hurried to his car, relieved his keys were in his pocket, relieved he didn't have to go back into the house, relieved that he didn't have to face demanding eyes when he had no answers. He feared what those answers might end up being.

Letting the blue Chevy roll down the driveway, Steve prayed nothing would happen this time.

CHAPTER 4

Myrtle Townsend sat Jenny on one of the wooden chairs facing away from the side window, one with no view of the driveway. Jenny wouldn't be able to see the car if Steve came for it, and maybe if she kept talking, she wouldn't hear it either.

The boy might be hiding. Or maybe he went to a neighbor. All the kids like the Sawyers' golden lab. Maybe he's there. That's it. The young lad's gone to play with the dog. Steve will find him and have him back here before we've finished our tea.

Myrtle filled the kettle, set it on the stove, and prayed. Reaching up to the cupboard, she pulled out tea bags and sugar. Her plump hands shook. She put the bowl down, spilling white grains on the counter. She wrung her hands. The shaking continued.

Getting the tea organized kept her hands busy, yet her mind raced. She tried to shut out the voices in her head. She told them to go away, but they wouldn't.

It's happening again. The police are going to come. They'll ask questions. All the same questions. They won't give us any peace. They might not believe us this time.

The whistling kettle drowned out the purr of the Chevy's engine—almost. Out of the corner of her eye, Myrtle watched the hood of Steve's car fade out of the driveway. The kettle screamed through the small kitchen. She reached for the china mugs. Steam misted upward, forming a vapor on the cupboard above. She pulled the kettle off the element, silencing its scream mid-flight.

Had Jenny heard the car? She continued to stare at some spot ahead of her. There was no indication she'd noticed anything, including Steve's car leaving. By rote, Myrtle poured the boiling water into the china teapot, discarding the first filling. She added three bags and poured more bubbling water into the pot. She placed it on the table and added the matching pitchers of milk and sugar. Only then did she sit, adjusting her chair to provide a view of the driveway. With only a slight shift of her head, she would see the car return.

While the tea steeped, Myrtle shuffled the morning papers lying on the table—anything to keep busy, anything to keep the voices silent. She maintained a one-sided conversation, all the while watching the young woman. Barely in her mid-twenties, she had the weight of the world written in indelible ink on her ashen forehead. Myrtle wondered what unspeakable fears hid behind that blank stare.

Please, God, don't let it happen to this one.

The cup of tea sat on the kitchen table in front of her, lukewarm, barely touched—not forgotten, but unreachable. Jenny wanted to stretch her hand out to grasp the cup and let the liquid warm the cold, empty spaces in her body. But her hand refused to follow commands, refused to reach out and hold the cup without shaking so violently that the contents would spill all over the table.

She took two sips before the tremors made holding the cup impossible. Putting it back on its saucer, she folded her hands and laid them in her lap. There, it didn't matter if her fingers trembled uncontrollably. There, no one would see them, not even herself.

She slid her hands under the stained tea towel where the dampness of the material crept through her skin, making her hands even colder. But she couldn't move them. Neural pathways were in overload. The transmission of further sensations no longer accepted. Her hands stayed frozen in her lap even when she heard Steve's car pull back into the driveway.

Jenny watched as Myrtle rushed to the door, spinning the chair in her haste. She tried to rise, but her body felt weighted down as if she'd donned a suit of armor. A suit that increased its mass tenfold when Steve came into the house alone. She slumped back into the chair and sat in silence as he listed the places he'd looked and the people he'd talked to. The outcome was unchanged. He hadn't found Clayton.

Neither Steve nor Myrtle seemed to notice when her fingers took a death grip on the cotton tea towel, her knuckles drained of blood. And Jenny barely noticed. She stopped feeling her body at five minutes before twelve—the exact moment she realized Clayton was missing.

Jenny listened, stone-faced, while Myrtle called 911. She heard the woman talking from somewhere, some other zone, some other planet. She saw herself sitting in Steve's small, bright kitchen. She saw the dark oak cupboards lining the two opposite walls, the sparkling white appliances, the large sunflowers climbing the wall behind the kitchen table. Jenny heard Myrtle stating her address. She saw, and she heard, yet none of it computed in her brain. She stared at the bright yellow paper flowers that gave no sunshine to this day.

Her mind was in a catatonic state. Unable to open her mouth, she listened to the clinical reporting of events as if they were happening to a stranger. If Clayton was still missing by six o'clock, he'd be on the evening news. Her mind drifted away, enveloped in a hazy mist.

The fog was cool and safe. The heat of the July day didn't penetrate there. She didn't feel the fine sweat on her brow, or the dampness at her armpits forming an amber semicircle on her sundress. Even the fly buzzing around the kitchen, landing occasionally on her bare limbs, went unfelt. She saw Steve batting at the fly and vaguely wondered why he bothered. Myrtle shooed it away with her open hand. Jenny kept her hands folded in her lap. Her gaze focused on the fuzzy brown center of one very large sunflower.

"Jenny. Jenny."

The gnarled hand shaking her shoulder was irritating. Jenny tried to nudge it away, but the hand remained. She wanted to tell it to leave her alone. The words didn't come. Reluctantly, she left behind the security of the sunflower. Her gaze met a pair of compassionate gray eyes.

"Jenny, the police need to know what he was wearing."

Jenny stared blankly ahead. The words sounded familiar, but she couldn't connect them.

"Jenny, Jenny."

The hand continued to shake her. Myrtle's eyes pleaded for her to come back from wherever she was hiding. Gradually, the words penetrated the fog and collated into a recognizable form. She forced her brain to work. She remembered the previous evening and laying Clayton's clothes on his chair—a pair of blue shorts, blue socks, and a white T-shirt. A white T-shirt with brown puppy dogs embossed on the front.

Her voice sounded foreign and mechanical as she repeated the list. She didn't recognize it as her own, but she knew it had to be, she felt the stiff shift of her lips as she uttered each word.

"They need his birth date."

It came automatically. "October nineteenth, two thousand six."

He would be six in a couple of months. Going into grade one. Her baby. It seemed like yesterday she gave birth; yesterday he took his first step. Yesterday, life was normal, and her son was safe in her arms.

"How much does he weigh?"

"Forty-nine pounds."

Myrtle covered the receiver with her hand while waiting to relay the information to the Deputy. "How tall is he?"

Jenny's hand jerked up to a spot in the air where Clayton's head would reach if he were standing in front of her. She tried to convert it into feet and inches. She tried to remember the last measurement on the giraffe growth chart taped to the kitchen door. Her head shook, her hand stuck in the air, but no numbers came.

"He's about four feet tall," Steve said. "Mom, tell them he's just under four feet."

Jenny's hand fell back into her lap as Myrtle relayed the number. She looked at Steve; her lips turned up slightly at the corners, wordlessly thanking him for his help. Then the tight mask slid back and her mouth became a thin line again.

Myrtle hung up the phone. Putting a hand on Jenny's shoulder, she gave it a gentle squeeze. "A deputy is coming straight away."

"Tell him to hurry," Jenny sobbed.

Mentally, she went over and over the morning. When had it gone wrong? How could she have lost her child? The most important thing in her whole life. She shouldn't have left him alone. She should have made him come in with her when she made lunch. She should have...

It seemed as if hours past while they waited. Several times, each of them glanced at the clock, discreetly monitoring how many minutes since the last time they'd looked. Peering over their teacups, they shuffled the cream and sugar containers on the table, not wanting to draw attention to the slowly passing minutes, but painfully aware of each one.

They were on their third cup of tea when a loud knock sounded at the front door. Myrtle rose quickly. Jenny, like a startled doe, jumped up to follow. Her chair, unbalanced by the abrupt movement, teetered backward and spun toward the floor. She grabbed for it, but a large, calloused hand reached first.

Jenny's hand recoiled to the safety of her body. Steve's eyes smiled gently as he righted the spinning chair. He nodded his head slightly. Turning away, she hurried out of the kitchen and down the hall. Myrtle's hand reached for the doorknob.

The knocking on the oak door echoed through the house, penetrating its every crevice, then found life again as it bounced off the paneled walls. To Jenny, it sounded like the explosive thunder of a summer tempest. She wanted to cover her ears and block out the roar, but it took every ounce of her strength simply to put one foot in front of the other. The booming continued. It added to the throbbing pain in her head.

Myrtle pulled the door open. A long-limbed policeman stepped into the hall. "I'm Officer Charlton. You called about a missing child?"

The small measure of light penetrating the dim hallway faded as his bulk obliterated the sun. Jenny's throat constricted. Would he have news that would take her pain away? Maybe someone had already found Clayton.

Jenny strained through the dimness, attempting to read his face, but he stood in the shadows. Dwarfed by his looming presence, she shrank backward, her shoulder slamming against the wall. She didn't flinch from the pain that shot through her, she could only watch mutely as Myrtle led the officer down the hall into the sun-bright kitchen.

He had a young face, one that had probably only experienced the tug of a razor for a couple of years. A nape of short-cropped, blonde hair jutted out beneath the stiff edges of his blue hat. His uniform was unstained, unwrinkled. The crisp bright blue material and brass buttons, shining and untarnished, shouted new uniform, new cop. Innocent blue eyes barely beginning their life's career. How much pain and horror had they witnessed? What did he know of the trauma she was going through?

In slow motion, she followed. Steve helped her back into her chair while Myrtle motioned to the policeman to sit beside her. He nodded and pulled the chair away from the table. The sound of it scraping on the linoleum grated like fingernails on a chalkboard. His hand flew to his head, snatching off the hat he self-consciously laid on the table. He frowned apologetically for not remembering the courtesy earlier, then shifted uncomfortably. He leaned his tall frame forward and placed a black spiral notebook on the kitchen table beside the hat.

Jenny stared at the glaring white page—her name, the time, missing child—nothing else. Her heart sank. He had no news. He didn't know where Clayton was. It had been over an hour now and Clayton was still missing. An hour! Her baby, not even six yet. Where could he have gone? Myrtle told her the police would find him. But this man knew nothing. She raised her head until her gaze met his. She begged him to tell her more than what she saw on the blank page.

He averted his eyes. He had no answers. It was easier for him to focus on his notebook, hoping for something to magically appear, anything to ease her pain.

He'd probably taken all the required courses where psychologists and social workers stand in front of a class and lecture on how officers are supposed to deal with people's grief. Empathy—the abracadabra word. He looked sensitive and compassionate—he'd have no trouble dealing with difficult situations. It sounded grand, noble, honorable, in a classroom. But here he was, face to face with her crisis. No cardboard character with practiced lines and simulated tears, her grief written across her face for the world to see. She didn't want his damn empathy—she just wanted her son back. All the empathy in the world couldn't change that.

Officer Charlton stared at the blank page, as if willing it to give him the answers, as if he was trying to remember what he'd learned in those classes. Jenny watched his face go blank and knew he wanted to resort to the time-worn adage, "Just the facts, ma'am, just give me the facts." Maybe if he kept his distance, he'd avoid the anguish written in capital letters on her forehead. He focused on the page, trying to ignore how she sat, pale and stiff and silent.

Her hands worked the dirt-stained tea towel into a tight ball, jumping when he spoke.

"Ma'am, we have to go to your house. I need to look around. More officers are coming to help with the search."

"He's not in the house...he's gone..."

Like stones dropping into an empty well, her words echoed through the room. Officer Charlton rose and waited for Jenny to accompany him.

She stood awkwardly. Steve slid his arm around her and she leaned against him. Together they led the policeman to her house—her vacant, silent house. The damp tea towel remained clutched in her bloodless knuckles.

CHAPTER 5

Filled with a mix of horror and shock, Jenny sat in her living room. She watched as one by one they came. Without knocking, they plowed through the front door, leaving it to slam behind them. There were five of them now, and more to come. Three of them wore standard police blue, the other two wore dark, off-the-rack suits.

Myrtle wanted Jenny to stay with them, but she insisted she had to be home. "I have to be there. Clay will be scared when he comes home and can't find me."

Steve stayed. They sat, stiff and uncomfortable on the worn living room furniture, their conversation no more than monosyllables. Invading every shadowed corner, officers overwhelmed the small house. Despite their meticulous search, the house gave up no mislaid child.

The two suited detectives approached. The first had salt and pepper hair with bushy sideburns that no longer boasted any pepper. He towered over his partner by four inches, over Jenny by more than a foot. The partner was younger, his ruddy complexion and the tinge of salmon behind his heavily freckled face suggested recent overexposure to the sun. The detectives paused by the arm of the sofa.

They glanced at Steve, seated beside Jenny, then back at her. The taller man introduced himself as Detective Jarvis, his partner as Detective Mahoney. Jarvis settled his wiry frame in the vacant chair across from her. From there, he had a view of both Jenny and Steve. Mahoney sat at the far end of the sofa. The seams of his suit threatened with each movement of his stocky frame. Turning sideways, he kept Jenny and Steve in his range of vision. Jarvis extracted a black leather notebook and silver pen from his pocket and laid them on his knee. Nodding slightly at his partner, also with pen and paper ready, he began the questions. He stopped occasionally to make notations, Mahoney kept his pen moving.

"You're Mrs. Jennifer Kingsley?"

Her acknowledgment barely a whisper, Jenny met the steel gray of his eyes—her own begging for his help. His gaze locked with hers—no promises made. He turned quickly away, unwilling to let her pain reach any deep recess of his heart.

Jarvis turned to Steve—examining, watching. Years of training, anticipating the revelation of some hidden shame, some secret, some forthcoming confession. "And you are?"

"Steve Townsend. Mrs. Kingsley's neighbor."

Jarvis nodded. Apparently satisfied with the answer, he turned his attention back to Jenny. "While we're talking, my men are checking the house, inside and out. The child may be hiding somewhere. We have deputies searching the immediate area."

Jenny nodded. She didn't tell them she'd already checked every place she could think of. She heard them in the basement—the banging of the dryer door, the scraping of furnishings being moved, the thud of heavy footsteps as they inspected every potential hiding spot. Other uniforms were in the bedrooms. They overturned and examined everything she owned, including the furnishings rented with the house. If they could find him, she didn't care if they turned the house inside out.

"Tell me what happened this morning."

Jenny blinked, and her head shook slightly. She'd been through this with the first officer, but now she had to do it again. She had to respond to his "recounting of events" as if she'd had a minor fender-bender. This was her missing child, not a dented vehicle. Maybe his clinical manner made it easier to act as if this was nothing more than a child late from school because he dawdled on the way home.

But school hadn't started yet. Clayton wasn't late from school—he was missing from his own backyard. Jenny's head continued to shake as if the movement might vanquish recent events.

The detectives watched, scrutinizing her while she formed her thoughts into words and chronicled her morning—playing in the backyard, building a sand-castle, going to make lunch, searching—

"What time was that?" Jarvis interrupted.

"Eleven-fifty. I looked at the clock on the microwave when I put the bread away."

She reached for the dishtowel lying beside her and dabbed her eyes with a corner of the material.

"How long were you inside?"

"About ten minutes." Her hand trembled as she dabbed at her right eye, catching a tear before it reached her cheek.

"Are you sure it wasn't longer?" Mahoney asked.

His face tilted slightly, making her think of a Siamese cat ready to pounce on a baby robin. "It was only ten minutes. I just made peanut butter sandwiches."

Jarvis regained control of the questioning, his voice a soft, soothing baritone. Jenny turned back to him.

"Are you sure you didn't need to use the bathroom or make a quick phone call?"

"No. I only made sandwiches, then went to call Clay. I waited at the door for a minute, but he didn't come..."

Her voice took on a hesitant quality, pausing and quavering. She looked at the hands wringing the towel, then back to face Jarvis. "Maybe I should have gone right to the street then. I thought he was hiding from me. I waited. I called. He didn't come. I searched the backyard."

"Now, Mrs. Kingsley, children disappear all the time. They wander off. They walk down the street, turn the wrong way, and then they're lost. Someone will find him and call the police. You wait and see." Jarvis assumed the tone of one trained in the art of maintaining order.

Her eyes stared blankly at her lap. Would they think she was a bad mother? Would they think she shouldn't have left him alone? She'd gone to make sandwiches for them, that was all. Clay was a good boy. He wouldn't have left the backyard without permission. He couldn't even manage the latch on the front gate.

Suddenly, the realization hit her. Clay hadn't wandered out of the backyard; someone had taken him. Her head jerked up, and she looked directly at Detective Jarvis. Her voice gained strength with each word she blurted out. "The gate was locked."

The detective returned her gaze, unmoved.

"Clay can't open that gate. Someone opened it. Someone took him!"

Her voice rose to a hysterical pitch as her mind raged with horrors someone might inflict on her son. "You have to find him. He's not lost."

Tears streamed down her face. She felt the blood drain out of her cheeks, out of her body, and she had an overwhelming urge to throw up. She pressed the tea towel to her lips and willed the foul-tasting bile back down her throat.

"Would his father have taken him?" Jarvis asked.

She shook her head. "He lives in Dresden. We're separated. He doesn't care about Clayton."

"What about a babysitter."

"I don't have one. I work from home. I'm with Clay all the time."

She leaned forward to plead with the detective. "You have to find him before ...He doesn't have his puffer."

"He has asthma?"

"Yes."

"How bad?"

"Sometimes...with the weather, or if he gets a cold. I always carry it." Her voice escalated. "He doesn't have it. What if he needs it?"

Steve shifted on the sofa. His arm slid around her shoulder as her body racked with spasmodic sobs. His gaze caught the detective's, adding his silent plea for action. Save for her uncontrolled sobs, the room was suddenly devoid of noise.

Steve rocked Jenny until she settled. Gradually, the shaking subsided, and Jenny leaned against him like a limp rag doll. Gathering her strength, she stiffened, pulled away, then wiped at her tears.

"I'm sorry," she whispered. Her eyes glazed over, and she slipped behind a frozen mask, hiding from reality.

"Mrs. Kingsley," Jarvis said. "We're doing everything we can. We will find your son."

She turned toward the detective, the lifeline to her son, her only hope for his safe return.

"We've put out an all-points bulletin with his description relayed to all units. Do you have a recent picture?"

Jenny staggered to the dining room. Opening the top drawer of the buffet, she pulled out a white package. It contained pictures she'd developed the week before, yet hadn't had time to add to the photo album. She'd planned to do that tonight. They were going to celebrate Clayton's enrollment in grade one, make a pizza, and put the pictures in the new album. A tear slid down her cheek.

Sitting on the edge of the sofa, Jenny sorted through the pictures. A vein twitched at her throat. Seeing Clayton's face smiling up at her from the glossy paper brought the sting of more tears. Her hands shook as she offered several photos to Jarvis.

"Is this the shirt he has on? The picture showed Clayton wearing a white T-shirt embossed with three brown puppies sitting in a wicker basket.

"It's his favorite shirt. He loves dogs, but he had blue shorts on today."

"Charlton." Jarvis barked.

The young officer, the first to respond to the missing child call, came forward. He nodded solemnly. "Yes, sir?"

"Take this picture downtown. Get copies made. Get them on the streets. Bring back target maps of the immediate area."

Jenny watched Charlton climb into one of the patrol cars, watching as if it was the most normal thing in the world to have a policeman drive away with her child's picture. She sat outside her body, watching the woman perched on the sofa. That woman couldn't be the one who'd lost a child. She was too calm. Tears no longer raged down her face. No heart-wrenching sobs racked her body. No, the woman who handed over her son's picture, with her frozen face showing no emotion, that woman wasn't in enough pain.

Stepping back inside herself, Jenny felt a pain so immense it plunged her into a fathomless black cavern. A thousand tentacles wrapped around her chest, twisting tighter when she tried to break free. Through her pain and darkness, she saw Detective Jarvis stand and speak to the other officers. Their words trickled through the fog to her consciousness.

"Nothing there?"

"Nothing in the basement, the bedrooms, or the backyard."

Excruciating pain, she couldn't breathe, she couldn't scream.

"Go door to door," Jarvis told them. "Cover a twelve-block radius for now, then get back to me. Mahoney, go with them."

Jenny watched the policemen leave, their departure creating an even larger void in the tiny house. She glanced around the room, noting the disruption of her possessions, and her life, but she didn't care. She had no emotion left.

"Mrs. Kingsley?"

Jenny forced herself to turn away from the window and look at the detective. Unable to speak, she nodded.

"Have you ever had your son's fingerprints taken?"

With a shake of her head, Jenny brought herself back to reality. She had to be strong. She had to think. She had to do whatever it took to get her son back. The words seemed to come from someone else's mouth. "They had a Child Find at the mall last year. They took Clayton's fingerprints there.

He wrote something in his notebook. Without looking up, he asked. "Was that here in Scottsville?"

"No, Dresden."

His head jerked up, his eyebrows arched, and his pencil twirled between his fingertips. "Dresden?"

"I grew up there. Married and lived there."

"Where's your husband now?"

"I told you, he's still in Dresden. We're separated. I moved here three months ago."

"Are you sure he mightn't have your son?"

Ray never had much time for Clay—too busy going out with the boys. He wanted to get married, told Jenny how happy he would make her. There had been fighting in both their families, but he assured her they would be different. He wanted the baby—that was until the reality of an infant's demands imposed on his lifestyle. Jenny had put up with years of his fits of anger and drinking away their money. She hadn't fought back when he took his temper out on her, but when it spread to Clayton...

She shook her head. "No, he wouldn't take him."

"Are you sure?"

"Yes. He never had much time for Clayton or me. He was glad to be rid of the burden."

"Would he take him to get back at you?"

Jarvis watched for her response. Jenny saw the thoughts running through his mind—just another family squabble, a child taken after a bitter break-up. But the truth was Ray didn't care. He'd never even tried to contact them.

"No." She met his gaze. "No, I'm sure he wouldn't."

"Have you called him?"

"I didn't think of it."

"I want you to call him. Do you know where he is?"

"At work in Dresden."

With halting steps, Jenny made her way to the kitchen. Unconsciously, she glanced at the table. Several flies nibbled on the discarded sandwiches. She wrenched her eyes away and crossed to the phone. Her hand resisted picking it up. What would she say? How could she tell Ray his son was missing? Maybe he has him. Maybe Clay is safe with Ray. The faint possibility quickened her heart rate. She picked up the phone.

It took all her strength to lift the receiver and punch in the numbers. Closing her eyes, she listened to the shrill scream of the dial tone. She didn't have the energy to move the handset away. Instead, she leaned into it as if it might support her until the call was done.

She counted the rings until a female voice answered, "Sifton's." Jenny forced her lips to move. "Is Ray there?"

The raspy voice of Theresa Gonzales, the receptionist at Sifton's Sign Shop, demanded. "Who's this?"

"Theresa, it's Jenny Kingsley."

"Oh, hi Jenny. Long time no see. How you doing?"

"I need to talk to Ray, now."

"Sure, honey. I'll get him. Nice talking to you."

The vague silence on hold was almost worse than the screaming. Jenny closed her eyes and slumped against the wall. The receiver became a lifeline as seconds turned into minutes. She desperately needed Ray's support. Finally, the connection resumed, and Ray's voice came on the line.

"What do you want?" he snarled. "I told you I'll send support when I can."

A familiar coldness ran down her spine, and she remembered why she'd left him. Visions of their life together flashed in front of her. Not now. Don't think of that now. Tell him about Clayton. "I'm not calling about support."

"What do you want?" he demanded.

"Ray," she paused. "You don't have Clayton, do you?"

"Course not. I'm at work. What's going on?"

His anger radiated through the phone line. She had dared to hope Ray took Clayton, dared to hope that he'd say he had their son and this terrible nightmare would end. She should have known. If Ray was at work, he couldn't have Clayton.

Her reasoning powers distorted, Jenny shook her head, but the headache hammering inside her brain made it impossible to think.

"Tell me what the hell's going on."

The ice in his voice acted like a slap in the face, and Jenny sagged down the kitchen wall. Several seconds passed before she could make her lips move. "Clayton was playing outside…and now…now he's gone…"

"What do you mean he's gone?"

"When I called him—he wasn't there—"

"Did you check under his bed—the basement—the closets?"

For each location, she gave a response. The anger in his voice dissipated, replaced with a hard edge of anxiety. She relaxed slightly. At least he sounded as if he cared. When she'd left Dresden three months before, Jenny hadn't been sure if he ever wanted to see either of them again. There had been no contact with him since they had moved.

"Did you check the street?"

"Yes."

"What about the neighbors?"

"The police are here now. They've checked the house, and now they're checking the neighborhood."

"Why are they checking the house? You've already done that, haven't you?"

"I looked everywhere—the house, the yard, the street. He's not here."

"What are the police doing in the house?"

"Ray, they're looking through everything, even in the basement. Clay wouldn't be down there. It's dark down there. He's afraid of the dark."

"Give me directions. I'll be there as soon as I can."

She rhymed them off and then replaced the receiver. It comforted her to know he was coming. Maybe this time he'd be there for her.

With heavy steps, Jenny returned to the living room. From his expression, she knew Jarvis had heard every word. She saw the surprise mirrored in his pale, cool eyes. He'd decided this would be simple—another domestic squabble over parental rights.

The detective's eyes blinked, closing like a camera's shutter. When they opened again, there was a distinct remoteness. Her voice, responding to his unspoken question, was flat and devoid of emotion. "He doesn't have him."

Both detectives and Steve averted their eyes as if unable to bear watching the life drain out of her. She made her way back to the sofa.

"Mrs. Kingsley?"

"Yes?" Her voice was barely audible.

"I'm going to the station. While I'm gone, think of anyone who might have a reason to take your son, whether to get back at you or your husband. Think of anyone unusual hanging around the house—fixing your plumbing, cutting your grass, taking away the garbage—anything that might give us a clue to who might have taken him. Can you do that?"

Jenny tried to assimilate his questions, tried to remember, but her brain, like her body, was numb.

"Will you be all right?"

Like a puppet on a string, Jenny's head bobbed up and down, up and down. Words no longer came out of her mouth. The bobbing continued as if some cruel puppeteer took pleasure in watching her pain.

"Mrs. Kingsley?" Detective Jarvis's voice slashed through the strings, and her head could finally rest. "I'll be back in a couple of hours."

Jenny sat, unable to speak, unable to respond. Afraid that if she moved her body would be snatched out of her control. She watched Steve go to the door with Jarvis, speak briefly, then return to sit beside her. She wanted everyone to leave, to go, and let her pretend this was only a bad dream.

Reaching out to touch her hand, Steve asked if she wanted something to eat, or a cup of coffee or tea. Nothing appealed; the thought of food brought on waves of nausea.

Jarvis spoke from the open doorway. "Maybe you should rest for a while?"

She didn't want to rest. She wanted to wait right here for Clayton. If she slept, maybe when she woke, Clayton might be back in her arms. The voice answering sounded like a tightly drawn bow, handled harshly and ready to snap. "Yes. Maybe I will."

Jenny watched Jarvis close the door behind him. She curled up in a fetal position on the sofa and closed her eyes. She felt her shoes being removed and a blanket settling over her frozen body.

"Please, I want to be alone for a while."

"Are you sure? I don't mind staying. I'll just sit in the chair over there." Steve pointed to the armchair by the window. He crossed to it and settled his lanky form into the cushions. Smiling gently, he encouraged her to close her eyes and rest. Too exhausted to argue, she obediently closed her eyes, but the sanctuary of sleep evaded her.

After an hour of counting whatever animal might bring her some relief from consciousness, Jenny got up. Steve rose from the armchair and followed her. In the kitchen, she mechanically cleaned away traces of their lunch. Swatting at flies perched on the discarded food, she threw the hardened peanut butter sandwiches into the garbage.

Waves of nausea came and went. Several times, she thought she'd throw up, but somehow the contents of her stomach remained in place. Steve followed her like a faithful puppy, trying to help in any way he could. She convinced him to leave only by promising she would call him or his mother if she needed anything.

She finally had the house to herself. The police would be back soon, and Ray might arrive any moment. She didn't have much time. There was a phone call she had to make, and she didn't want anyone around when she made it.

CHAPTER 6

Jenny gathered her courage. She couldn't avoid the call any longer. Mother was never one to air family business like yesterday's dirty underwear. No, everything must appear to be a beautiful bouquet without one wilting petal. She already considered Jenny a weed in her perfect garden.

No mention of thorns hiding under the bedcovers. Discussions stayed in the privacy of one's home, not aired on the six o'clock news. Jenny glanced at the clock—three-forty-one. She needed to warn her mother in case Clayton's picture appeared on the television. Would her mother blame her? Of course she would. How deep would she press the thorns into Jenny's psyche this time?

The control Gladys Hamilton exerted over her family kept them in constant fear of provoking one of her moods. Surely her mother would consider this dirty laundry. How would she word her barbs? If she had only taken better care of Clayton, he wouldn't have wandered away. Only a bad mother left her child alone. Mother would be sure to tell her that. To her, any time the police were involved, the person had to be guilty of something.

Jenny needed to call before the police came back. She didn't need an audience. It hadn't been so bad when she called Ray—but for God's sake, this was her mother.

She picked up the phone, praying for one of her mother's good moods. Her hand shook as she keyed in the numbers. She kept hitting the wrong buttons.

Depressing the receiver for the third time, Jenny forced her trembling fingers to punch in the numbers she'd known all her life. White knuckles held the receiver to her ear while she listened to the phone's persistent ring. Please, Mom, be home. I may not have the courage to call again.

Could she leave a message on the answering machine? Mom, I lost your grandson, but it's okay, the police are searching for him. I'm sure he'll be home soon. Her grip on the phone tightened.

Jenny glanced at the calendar. Tuesday. Mother should be home from the Dresden Ladies' Euchre Group by now. She counted the rings while she watched the clock's second hand cross the bold-faced numbers. Mom, answer the phone.

Eight rings, then her mother's voice. Jenny closed her eyes. Her knees buckled, and the nausea returned. She leaned against the kitchen wall.

"Hello? Hello?"

Jenny heard her mother's voice, but couldn't make the words come. If she told her mother, it would make it real.

"Who's there?"

The irritated tone jolted Jenny out of the trance she'd been hiding in. Afraid her mother might hang up and sever the cord connecting them, Jenny took a sharp intake of air and forced herself to speak. "Mom—"

"Is that you, Jenny?"

"Mom," she whispered. "Clayton's missing."

Jenny waited for the words to sink in. Would they impact the same terror in her mother as they had in her?

"What are you saying?"

"Clayton's missing. He was playing in the backyard. I went inside to make us some lunch." Jenny paused and wiped at the tears streaming down her face. "When I went to call him...he wasn't there."

"Are you sure he's not hiding somewhere?"

"I've checked everywhere."

"What about in his bedroom? Maybe he's hiding there."

"No. He's not there."

"What about the basement?"

The same frantic tone in her voice sounded in her mother's.

"I've checked there too." Reaching for a tea towel, she wiped at her eyes. The towel became stained with a mixture of dirt, sweat, and tears.

"What about the neighbors?" The pitch in her mother's voice screeched across the miles.

Jenny's response was slow and quiet. "I've searched everywhere—the house, the yard, the street...everywhere. So have Steve and the police."

"You've called the police already?"

"Of course, I called them."

Jenny heard the defensiveness creep into her voice and wondered if her mother even noticed. Right now, it was the last thing she cared about.

"Well, yes. I guess you did need to call them. What about Ray? Maybe he came and took the boy. I know he hasn't bothered with him since you left, but.... Did you call him?" her mother demanded.

A wave of nausea swept over her, and everything in the kitchen blurred. She slid to the floor; the phone cord stretched taut. "Yes. I called him. He doesn't have him."

"Who's Steve?"

What did she tell her mother? Knowing her, she'd construe some story, turning his friendship into something improper. She couldn't take that now. She couldn't explain how kind he and his mother, people she barely knew, had been. She remembered his parting words. "I'll come back after I close the shop. By then, Clayton will be back, and I'll treat the both of you to an ice cream sundae at Shaw's." He had left with a bright smile and a banging screen door.

Jenny thought how odd it was that her world stopped the moment Clayton disappeared, but the rest of the universe kept turning. Everyday functions, like Steve finishing his normal business day, went on as usual.

Her mother continued with a barrage of questions. The nausea increased, and the room spun around her. Her mother's words stuck together like flies to honey, and she couldn't pick them apart. Sweat coated her palm. She gripped the phone, afraid it would slide out of her fingers. "Mom...I have to go."

Dropping the phone, Jenny ran to the bathroom. After her stomach emptied, she clung to the porcelain bowl.

CHAPTER 7

Tyrell shoved the bag of groceries under the crook of his left arm and inserted the key into the lock, the chain rattling loudly against the heavy wooden door. Heat and moisture had expanded the wood. He thrust his body against it. The door groaned on rusty hinges, then swung inward. It was like a pressure cooker inside, steam bursting through the cracks in the walls. A rush of hot air slapped him in the face.

"Blasted heat."

Stepping back a pace, he allowed the hot air to escape before entering the cabin. He slammed the door behind him, then picked up the two-by-four standing nearby and drove it down into the metal brackets on the door's frame. It thudded into place, securing the entry.

He tested the homemade lock. The metal hinge resisted any effort from his muscular arms. It was one of the few improvements he'd made to the cabin—that and the cellar.

He wanted to leave the door open. Too damn hot. Late afternoon and the July sun beat down relentlessly on the black tarpaper roof. It baked the rafters and roasted the still air trapped inside the cabin. Dank, steamy vapors hovered over the spartan furniture. Combined with the scent of neglect, it formed a volatile mix.

Tyrell crossed to the middle of the room, passing the wood stove with its black pipe rising through the center of the cabin. An open shelf stood against one wall, its contents clearly visible—two boxes of cereal, a bag of sugar, one jar of peanut butter, one of honey, a few faded tin cans, and a mixed setting of chipped dishes. He dropped the bag of groceries onto the counter below, shoving aside unwashed dishes to make room. He didn't bother removing the assortment of crumbs and dead flies littering the area.

He surveyed the room. In one corner, an unmade cot and a five-drawer maple dresser sat on a blue-green woven mat. The mat furnished the only spark of color in an otherwise drab setting. Off-center of the room sat a round wooden table. Its multi-stained top showing the degree of care afforded it. Even now, the remains of toast scattered across its width. A kerosene lamp sat on the table beside a worn red plastic fly swatter. A swarm of flies descended on the crumbs; others rested on the inactive swatter.

More flies, also affected by the elevated temperatures, took shelter in the dark recesses of the room. Occasionally, they changed position and flitted to another shadowy surface. Their buzzing in the oppressive heat created an intolerable hum.

His gaze circled the room. Good. A smile formed on one side of his mouth. It didn't reach the steel blue of his eyes. *Nobody's been here. They aren't going to catch me this time, either.*

A fly landed on his arm. He swiped at it, missing it by a hair. There's more of the damn things inside than out. Can't even leave the fucking door open. Should've bought some fly spray. That'd kill the buggers. Tyrell crossed to the table, his gait uneven as his right leg dragged behind him. He picked up the fly swatter and made an unsuccessful effort to reduce their numbers.

As a scattering of dead flies accumulated on the wooden floor, he glanced at the dust-covered top of the dresser then to the wooden floor below. *Better check on the kid. Don't want nothing to happen to this one.*

Tyrell shuffled across to the dresser. Putting his back against it, he slid the cabinet aside. The loud scrape of wood against wood screeched through the cabin.

He kicked at the woven mat. It landed in a pile two feet away, revealing the four-by-four-foot trap door roughly cut into the existing floor.

He grasped the leather strap wound around one board and pulled upward. Gleaming silver hinges made no protesting squeak. He peered into the darkness. At first, the murky blackness obscured the cavity. Then, as his eyes adjusted, he saw him.

A small form, curled in a fetal position, lay quivering on a blue-green woven mat. The mat, a twin to the one under the dresser—both bought at Stockley's General Store. The same store where he'd first seen the boy and his mother.

He'd noticed the similarities right away, the ash-blond hair, the gesture of pushing her hair behind her ears, the same pale complexion. The height was about the same, too. Her smile was shy and sweet like Patty's before he went to war. Not like when he came back.

He didn't know what changed her. Patty said she was the same. It wasn't true. The old Patty would never have ridiculed him. She would have shown some compassion. Maybe he hadn't known her at all.

When he'd returned from the war, Patty was angry and discontent. She'd met him at the train station with her hair long, scraggly, and so blonde it looked like skim milk, or like people you hear about getting a good scare and turning white overnight. "Platinum," she called it.

"I don't care what you call it, it's ugly. You look forty years old."

She flipped her long hair over her shoulder, ignoring him. No matter what he said, Patty kept dyeing it. They argued about it all the time. That and money. Never enough money for her. He told her she looked better before she started messing with her hair. She wouldn't listen.

"It's none of your business," Patty screamed at him.

"You're my wife. It is my business."

Patty had stomped out of the house, slamming the door behind her. She wanted to look like the models in her fashion magazines. Wasting his money on her damn magazines. Didn't make her look like a model, more like a slut; that's what he'd told her.

"How would you know?" She taunted. "You, only half a man now with your gimpy leg. What do you know about sluts?"

He tried to keep his temper, but this Patty was different from the one he'd known before he went to Iraq. This one took pleasure in tormenting him.

"I want a whole man. Not a man shot full of holes." She laughed hysterically at her joke.

He had raised his fist and come close to her, close enough to smell the imitation Opium perfume she doused herself with.

She laughed at him. "Let's see you do it, Tyrell. Can you be a man for once?"

His slap left a crimson mark on her cheek. He was in mid-swing for a second hit when something stopped him. Maybe visions of his mother being beaten by his drunken father. He couldn't do it. He couldn't be like him. He ran out of the cabin, followed by her cackling laugh.

By the time his anger died down hours later, she'd left, taking Tyson with her. That was seven years ago. He hadn't seen Patty or his son since.

Till that day in the store, the hair like Patty's before she started dyeing it. He'd thought it was her. He even thought the boy was his. But Tyson would be twelve now—seven long years since he'd seen him. His hands clenched and unclenched as he watched the tow-headed child sleep, one small hand gripping the edge of the blue-green rug.

CHAPTER 8

Jenny heard a car pull into the driveway and rushed expectantly to the door. Detectives Jarvis and Mahoney were easing out of a dark sedan. Her hopes soared as she waited—hopes dashed as soon as she took one look at them. Their solemn faces told her all she needed to know. They had not found Clayton.

A tremendous heaviness settled on her as she thought of her son, out on the streets, alone, maybe hurt, possibly dead. She had trouble breathing. Her hands flew to her throat. They clawed at the skin, trying to let air in through her constricted windpipe. Her world was turning dark. Then a vortex of brilliant colors flashed in front of her. She had to close her eyes to protect them from the glare.

"No. No!"

Her body swayed. Supporting arms enveloped her, and she leaned into them. She allowed them to lead her into the house. She felt herself being pushed gently down, and feeling the firmness of the sofa behind her, Jenny let her knees buckle and slumped onto the cushions.

"Are you okay?"

Detective Jarvis bent over her. His voice was a soothing mix of baritone and gruffness. Jenny felt the fog encompassing her slowly lift. Her voice was barely more than a whisper. "Yes...I'm okay."

She heard herself repeating the word, "Okay. Okay. Okay." One word to cover a multitude of meanings. How the hell could she be okay when her only child was missing? How could anything ever be right until she could hold his small body in her arms again? Her voice rose in anger. "Yes, I'm alive. I'm breathing. Does okay cover that?"

She saw Jarvis glance at her and then quickly look away. Her body screamed so loudly on the inside she couldn't stand the noise. But outside, she was silent as a tomb. Her anger deflated, she nodded, assuring him she wasn't going to faint again, or go into hysterics. Jarvis sat on the edge of the chair opposite her.

She pleaded, "Is there any news?"

"No, not yet. But we expect some soon. Children his age don't just disappear. He's out there and someone has to have seen him. We simply need time to find him."

His voice was strong and sure and the set of his chin suggested a stubborn streak which Jenny hoped he would apply to finding Clayton. As she watched, the sharp angular face seemed to soften. A gentle smile reached his steel-gray eyes. He patted her hand. "We will find him."

Mahoney came out of the kitchen carrying a tray with three cups of coffee. He handed one to Jarvis and placed the others on the coffee table. "Here, drink this." He pushed a mug into her hand.

Jenny wrapped the fingers of both hands around the cup. The heat of the brimming fluid penetrated the frost that had invaded her. The drink, laced with sugar, warmed the rest of her body. She hadn't eaten since breakfast and the coffee slipped easily over her lips.

They drank in silence. When they had finished, Jenny told them about her and Clayton's move from Dresden to Scottsville.

Jarvis was filling her in on the search when raised voices at the front door interrupted her. Mahoney stood there, blocking her view. Then Ray burst past him.

"Let me through. It's my son."

After a nod from Detective Jarvis, Mahoney let him pass. At five foot seven, Ray's linebacker chest seemed out of proportion with the relatively short legs he'd been allotted. He stopped in front of Jarvis. "What's being done to find my son?"

The detective stood and faced the newcomer. He had a full five-inch advantage. They took measure of each other. When Jarvis spoke, his tone clipped, commanding. "Mr. Kingsley, please have a seat."

Ray looked defiantly at the detective. Jenny held her breath, dreading her ex's response. He was not one to take lightly to being ordered to do anything, especially from someone with a badge. Jarvis tipped his head, his lips tightening he glared at him. Ray was the first to look away. Abruptly, he sat near Jenny on the sofa, his posture stiff, his fists clenched but remaining stationary on his thick blue-jeans-covered thighs. She cringed away slightly as his weight on the cushions shifted her position. Inches apart; neither made any attempt at bodily contact.

Taking the armchair opposite them, Jarvis looked from the one to the other before settling his gaze on Ray. "As your wife told you, Mr. Kingsley, your son has been missing since around noon. We have police officers all across town looking for him. His picture is being circulated to every unit. There are a couple of other things we would like to do if it's all right with both of you."

He paused briefly. "We've put out an Amber Alert. We'd also like to put a bulletin on the six o'clock news."

Jenny looked blankly at him. Six o'clock. That was two hours from now. They had to find him before then. He would miss his supper. He had already missed lunch. He'd be so hungry by six.

"Will that be okay?" Jarvis asked.

"That's fine," Ray answered. "What else?"

"We'd like to get the canine unit out here to see if they can give us any leads. Mrs. Kingsley, you haven't touched any of his clothes have you?"

"No. I looked under the bed and in the closet, that's all."

"Good. Does he have an article of clothing he wore recently, like pajamas or underwear? Something to give the dog a scent."

"His pajamas are under his pillow. He folded them there this morning."

Jenny's spirits rose. She had heard stories of the ability of dogs to find people. They would find Clayton. She got up. "I'll get them for you."

"Mrs. Kingsley, I don't want you to touch them. They'll want the dog to get a scent off them. If you handle them it would interfere with that. One of the deputies will get them."

"Mahoney." Jarvis addressed his partner. "Call for the canine unit."

Within twenty minutes, an officer arrived with a black German Shepherd. The handler introduced himself as Officer Matt Denison and the dog as Jesse.

"Do you want his pajamas?" Jarvis asked.

"No. Jesse works off the last hot scent. Where was the boy before he disappeared?"

"He was in his sandbox," Jenny answered.

"Show me."

Jenny led them to the back door. Denison lengthened Jesse's leash. The dog sniffed around the porch, then along the grass, making his way to the sandbox. A hopeful group of humans followed. Checking out the sandbox, Jesse nosed the pail left abandoned in the sand. The shepherd, nose to the ground, trotted to the gate.

Jesse looked up at his handler. Denison opened the gate for him and followed him through it. The dog sniffed his way to the sidewalk and, after several seconds, turned south. His handler kept him on a loose leash. The group followed as Jesse worked his way to the end of the block and turned east on Willow Street. Partway down the block, the dog left the sidewalk and sniffed his way to the curb. He sniffed the area at the curb, sniffed the air, then the curb again. He made small circles sniffing around the curb, but went no further. His tail dropped. He looked up at his handler and then at the road.

Denison brought him back to the sidewalk. Jesse returned to the same spot at the curb and sat there.

"It looks like the child was taken this far by foot and then taken in a vehicle from here," Denison told the group.

At the house, Denison turned to Jenny and Ray. "I'm sorry we couldn't do more."

He put Jesse in the back of a black SUV and climbed in behind the wheel. Jenny watched him drive away, her hopes for Clayton's quick return going with him. With slow steps, she followed Ray back to the house. Detective Jarvis used the radio in his car before joining them in the living room.

"I've told the officers canvassing the area to ask about any suspicious vehicles, especially one parked where the dog indicated. Can we sit down for a few minutes? I need to ask you a few more questions."

He took out his black booklet and glanced at his notes. It seemed to be filled with scribblings. He looked at Ray, his gaze direct, his mouth pulled tight across his face. "How was your relationship with your son?"

"Fine! It was fine!"

"When was the last time you saw him?"

"Three months ago."

Jenny saw the detective's eyebrows raise in an unspoken question and knew Ray had too.

"Well...she took him away." His voice rose in anger. "She just up and moved away. Took him with her."

The detective glanced carefully at Ray, then paused. "Did she have reason to move away?"

"No! She didn't." Ray glared at Jarvis. "She was my wife. She had no cause to up and move away like that."

"So you didn't come to see them or try to talk her into coming home?"

"No." Ray's voice became subdued. He looked at the hands clenched in his lap. "Well, she left. I thought if she was on her own for a while, she'd decide to come back."

"Did you ask her to come back?"

"No. I haven't talked to her since."

"Did you take your son to get back at her?"

Ray's head jerked up, the defiance back in his eyes. He leaned forward. His hands had formed into claws and dug into his thighs. The detective returned his glare, seeming to weigh just how far he could push Ray.

"You pig! No, I didn't take my son."

A tense silence filled the room as the two men locked gazes. Jarvis was the first to look away this time. After glancing at his notebook, he looked back at Ray, his tone calm and controlled. "Do you have anything to add, Mr. Kingsley?"

"No!" Ray's face reflected his anger. "Should I?" he demanded. "Like I already told you, the first I heard about my boy being missing was when Jenny called me this afternoon. I was at work when she called. I was there all day."

"Do you have anyone who can verify that?" Detective Mahoney asked.

"Yeah! The whole fucking shop!"

As the men stared at each other, the tension in the room became explosive, as if it could be lit with a match, their contempt for each other barely veiled. Jenny felt Ray's anger span the space separating them. She sank further into her seat and wished she were far away. Her son was missing and these men were playing childish games. Did they really think Ray might have something to do with Clayton's disappearance? He may not have been the best father, but there was no way he would take Clayton to get back at her.

But an inkling of doubt had been born in the back of her mind and refused to leave. It sat there germinating as she recalled the times Ray had been irritated with her and how often his temper erupted. Was he angry she had left him? Could he have taken Clayton to get back at her? She watched the interaction between the two men and noted the controlled violence in Ray. The reasons for leaving flashed in front of her eyes. Other than her wonderful son, Jenny wished she'd never met this man.

"Mrs. Kingsley?"

The detective's questioning tone broke into her thoughts. She turned slowly toward him.

"I'm leaving now. I have to make sure a bulletin is ready for the six o'clock news. We need to have the public aware and on the lookout. The more people involved in the search, the greater our chances are of getting your son back quickly." He paused. "If he's not back later this evening, which I'm sure he will be—but just in case—we plan to do a media interview for the ten o'clock news. I'll check with you later. We'll keep you both informed as to exactly what is happening."

Jenny listened to the words as calmly as if he was telling her about a traffic violation. She couldn't fathom the thought of Clayton not being back soon. He had never spent an evening away from her in his life.

Watching the detectives leave, she sat silently, her mind filled with images of missing children she had seen on the news—her son's face now superimposed on their images. She had a vague awareness of Ray pacing the living room and muttering. Gradually, she could distinguish words out of the garble of sounds.

"Damn them. Who do they think they are? Pigs! Asking if I took my son. I should sue them for slander. Damn bastards. Why aren't they out there looking for Clay instead of harassing me?"

Jenny saw the clenched fists, the agitated pacing, the tightened skin over his cheekbones, and the coldness in his eyes. It was no surprise to her when his foot shot out and knocked over the armchair the detective had been sitting in.

"Ray. Please."

He turned toward her. He must have seen her pain, for he dropped his head, shaking it slowly. His fists clenched and unclenched, then fell to hang limply at his sides. Anger seeped out of his blazing eyes; replaced by a helpless sadness that matched her own. He righted the chair and came toward her. "Oh, Jenny. What are we going to do?"

He sat beside her on the sofa and pulled her into his arms. She didn't resist. The close contact eased the pain in her chest. His head pressed against hers and she felt his tears trickle down her face and mingle with her own. Together they gave each other more comfort than either had been capable of for a long time.

It was Jenny who pulled away first. She tried to smile, but her lips only moved a fraction. Instead, she patted his forearm. "Thanks for coming, Ray. And for being here."

"What did you expect?"

Her shoulders shrugged slightly.

"He is my son. Even if I haven't been the best father."

She nodded. It wasn't the time to delve into the past now. They both had to concentrate on dealing with the present. Jenny patted his arm again then felt suddenly restless. She needed to be moving, needed to be doing something, needed to keep her mind from imagining the worst. Unfortunately, what she needed most, to be taking care of her son, had been torn away from her as if someone had ripped out a piece of her heart.

"I'll make us some tea...no, coffee for you. Do you want something to eat?"

"If you wouldn't mind. I haven't eaten since lunch. Can't eat much though. Stomach's a bit upset."

'*Stomach's a bit upset.*' Jenny repeated the words in her mind. She thought of the tight knots in her stomach and the frequent waves of nausea that sent bile up to the back of her throat. Only a supreme effort on her part kept the contents of her stomach inside her body. And his stomach was "a bit upset"! Her fists clenched and unclenched as she made her way to the kitchen. She knew she couldn't eat, but making food always seemed to be the right thing to do in times of crisis.

Going into the kitchen, she took out a loaf of bread and some cold cuts. Sandwiches would have to do. She had no energy for anything more. It took all she had to put the kettle on for a pot of tea for herself and coffee for Ray. Making up a tray, she took it into the living room and set it on the coffee table.

Waves of nausea ran through her as she watched Ray devour the sandwiches. A hand flew to her abdomen, attempting to quell its rumblings. Unable to watch Ray eat, Jenny wondered if Clayton was hungry. Was anybody making him a sandwich? Was he still alive to eat it?

Ray got up from the sofa, half a sandwich in his hand. "Do you mind?" He pointed to the TV.

Jenny shook her head. Maybe the sound of the TV would block out the voices in her head, block out the continuing string of unanswered questions. Where was her son? Who had taken him? Why? What have they done to him? Maybe the

TV would drown out the screeching voices assaulting her with their horrifying answers. Maybe it would distract her from the visions filling her brain—visions with vivid details of what might happen to her son.

She watched Ray walk, sandwich in hand, to the television, dropping bread-crumbs on the carpet. Part of her wanted to tell him to keep his food on his plate, that this was her house, and that she didn't allow food in the living room, but somehow that seemed so trivial now. Her eyes followed his movements as he turned the set on, adjusted the volume to a low level, then returned to the sofa.

A talk show was in progress, something about husbands, affairs, and forgive-ness. The voices wove together, indistinguishable sounds. Suddenly the six o'clock news was on and Clayton's picture flashed on the screen. Jenny's heart almost stopped. She stared, unable to look away, unable to breathe. Icy tentacles stabbed at her heart, then spread throughout her body. She sat frozen in her chair. The announcer's voice penetrated her mindless state.

"The Scottsville police are asking for everyone to be on the lookout for Clayton Kingsley, missing from his Elm St home since early this afternoon. If anyone has any information about his whereabouts, please call the police at 1-800-541-2222. Clayton is five years old and was last seen wearing a pair of blue shorts and a white T-shirt with puppy dogs on it."

A phone number flashed on the screen below Clayton's picture. Jenny sat frozen on the sofa while the announcer's voice went out over the airways, unable to move or breathe until her son's picture disappeared. The acid taste of bile rose in her throat. It was all she could do to make it to the bathroom before she emptied the contents of her stomach in a violent purge.

Ray bent over her. He wiped her face with a wet washcloth, gently dabbing at her mouth and eyes. When she finished retching, he led her slowly back to the living room. He sat her on the sofa and laid a fresh towel beside her. "Are you okay?"

She couldn't remember when she'd last heard him speak in such a gentle tone. She'd forgotten the shy teenager who first attracted her attention. Back then, they'd found refuge from the world in each other. An escape from the hurts their families inflicted on them. That was before they found their own arrows to sling at each other.

She nodded mechanically. Ray sat beside her on the sofa and held her hand. One arm slipped around her shoulder and pulled her close. She leaned gratefully against him. He held her there for a long time, past hurts forgotten, for now. After a while, he shifted away and reached for the teapot. "It's cold. I'll make you some more. Something hot would be good for you."

Like a marionette, she found herself nodding at Ray as he rose and picked up the tray. Shortly, he was back with a fresh pot of tea. He poured the steaming liquid into a cup and settled it in the curve of her hands. At first, its heat stung her fingers, but gradually some of its warmth penetrated her body. Ray hovered over her as if she were incapable of maneuvering the cup.

She felt stronger after the cup of tea and forced herself to drink a second one.

She leaned back on the sofa and let her body relax. She needed to think. Was there something she should remember? Anything she could do to help get Clayton back? Could anyone she knew have taken him? She thought of the few people she'd met since moving to Scottsville. There was Myrtle, Steve, the Sawyers, and Mr. and Mrs. Stockley, who owned the combination grocery store and restaurant. She'd met women at the park, but she barely knew their names. None of them would have taken Clayton. Would they? Her brain spun with possibilities.

In the background, Jenny heard the television. Occasionally, she glanced at the screen. The faces merged in a psychedelic show. Shadowy visions of Clayton lying face down in a pool of water, still and flaccid, partially covered by old leaves or buried in a shallow grave kept flashing across the television screen. She turned away from the set and clamped her eyes shut, but the images continued. She couldn't focus, but the television provided an excuse not to talk. Jenny sat beside Ray, inches and worlds apart, as stiff and uncomfortable as two total strangers.

CHAPTER 9

At eight o'clock, there was a knock at the front door. Ray bolted from the sofa and was there before the second knock sounded. Detective Jarvis strode into the room.

Jenny demanded. "Have you found him?"

From the look on his face, Jenny knew there was still no news. She slumped back onto the sofa and waited for him to speak.

"We've had some calls since the six o'clock news, but nothing has panned out yet."

Jarvis sat in the armchair, leaning forward. He looked expectantly at them. "Have you thought of anything that might be helpful? Anyone who has been hanging around?" He paused and looked directly at Ray. "Anyone who might want to get back at you for something?"

She shook her head, but saw a spark of anger flare in Ray's eyes. Her own eyes pleaded with him to not react. Then he, too, was shaking his head.

"Okay, then. Just to update you, we've been in touch with the National Center for Missing and Exploited Children and we're also checking for any suspected child predators or molesters within a hundred-mile radius of Scottsville. Mrs. Kingsley, we would like you to come to the station tomorrow morning and look at our mug shots of suspected criminals. Could you do that?"

"Yes. What time?"

"I'll have one of the deputies come and get you. It will probably be in the morning, sometime after nine."

"I'll be ready."

Ray sat at the end of the sofa wringing his hands. A nervous twitch attacked his left eye. His voice shook with emotion. "What can I do? This waiting around is killing me."

"We've got police officers still looking, and they'll be out all night if necessary. We've organized an extended search party for the morning. You can help us with that. We've arranged for extra officers, and a lot of folks in town have offered their assistance. We're setting up a command post in the community hall. During the night we'll have maps and fliers with your son's picture made up to distribute. We will assign teams to search different areas. We set up a hotline, and the number was on the news tonight. If you come to the station at six, we'll let you know what you can do to help."

"What about now?"

Jarvis shrugged his thin shoulders. "We have helicopters out now. They're going over the area outside of town, the woods, and the farms. They're equipped with infrared sensors to pick up body heat." Detective Jarvis paused. "Would you let the media come and interview you tonight? The personal touch might help to draw people into the search. The more volunteers, the better."

Jenny's first instinct was to refuse. She didn't think she could talk to reporters. She didn't want them in her home, asking questions, flashing their lives to the world. "Are you sure it will help?"

She looked at Ray. His earlier anger dissipated, he looked to Jarvis, as she did—a lifeline to Clayton.

"At this point...we want everyone helping," Jarvis said.

"When will they be here?" she asked.

"I can have them here within the hour. The interview should only take a few minutes. I'll stay and make sure they don't harass you."

They arrived at eight forty-five, technicians swarming through the front door, dragging tripods, bright lights, video cameras. Electrical cords stretched like spider webs across her carpet. The living room resembled a disaster zone. Then the door swung open again and a stunning woman strode into the room. Her raven hair swept into a French braid framing her flawlessly made-up oval face. Effortlessly, she maneuvered her stiletto heels over the multitude of cords.

Pausing by the sofa, she nodded at Detective Jarvis. Rhonda's black eyebrows tweezed into an artful line, rose in a silent question. Her claret-tinted lips formed a practiced smile as she stretched out a matching manicured hand toward Jenny. Her handshake was fleeting, and Jenny bet her periwinkle silk suit cost more than Jenny's rent for a year.

Detective Jarvis made the introductions. "This is Rhonda Fleming of WSTO."

Rhonda stretched her hand toward Ray. "I'm very sorry about your son's disappearance. I'm sure the television exposure will help find him."

"I hope so." Jenny agreed.

"What do you want to know about Clayton?" Ray asked.

"Let's sit down. You can tell me something about him."

Scrutinizing the couch and chairs before sitting, Rhonda settled herself on the edge of an armchair and waved the rest of the group where they should sit. Jenny and Ray sat on the sofa, with Detective Jarvis opposite them. Rhonda took the microphone from the technician and pinned it to the lapel of her suit.

"I know Clayton is six..."

"Five. He's almost six. He'll be six, October nineteenth—"

"Yes," Rhonda interrupted. "He has blond hair, blue eyes, and is about four feet tall?"

Jenny nodded. It sounded like Rhonda had memorized the police report.

"He was wearing blue shorts and a T-shirt with animals on it?"

"Yes. A white shirt with three puppy dogs in a basket."

"Three puppy dogs. Right." Rhonda's eyes narrowed. She nodded to the cameraman. Untwining her long shapely legs, she crossed to the sofa. Motioning Jenny to move over, she squeezed in beside her, careful not to wrinkle her designer suit. Forcing Jenny to slide along the sofa until her body rested against Ray's hipbone, Rhonda took a moment to adjust her skirt and jacket. Satisfied that everything was in order, she again nodded to the cameraman.

Suddenly, incandescent lights illuminated the room. Rhonda faced the camera, her flashing smile laced with just the precise touch of sympathy for the occasion.

"This is Rhonda Fleming reporting to you live from Scottsville, the site of a terrible tragedy today. Five-year-old Clayton Kingsley is missing from his home. He was last seen at noon, playing in his backyard. These are his parents, Jennifer and Raymond Kingsley."

A manicured hand waved toward her. Jenny felt the heat of the lights blazing down on her as the camera zoomed close. Thankfully, Rhonda's voice quickly pulled the camera's focus back to her.

"Clayton has blond hair and blue eyes. He was wearing a white T-shirt with puppy dogs, and blue shorts. He is about four feet tall and weighs forty pounds."

Tears stung Jenny's eyes. She tried to blot them away before the camera picked them up, but a lens bore down on her, exploiting her pain. She tried to sit calmly and ignore the tears trickling down her cheeks. Jenny heard her mother's voice. Don't be making an exhibition of yourself. And don't be letting everybody know your business. An invisible mask slid over her face. She hid her trembling hands in her lap and prayed the interview would soon be over.

"Detective Jarvis?" Rhonda turned to Jarvis and the camera's focus shifted to the detective. "Can you tell us anything about the investigation?"

Jarvis faced the newswoman. His face retained the cloak of professionalism, his voice controlled and sure. "We are doing everything possible to find Clayton. But we would like to ask for help from the public in finding him. If anyone has seen the child or knows anything that might help us, please call the hotline number: 1-800-541-2222."

"Do you think he has wandered off—or do you suspect foul play?"

"It's too early to say."

"Do you think it was an abduction?" Rhonda persisted.

"As I said, at this point, we have no reason to think that."

"Is there a possibility?"

"Miss Fleming—" Detective Jarvis' lips constricted and his voice lowered almost to a snarl. "—abduction is always a possibility with a missing child—but we have no suspects and no witnesses. We need your help in alerting the public and requesting their help. If anyone saw anything that might be relevant, please come forward. If we don't find Clayton Kingsley by tomorrow morning, we're organizing an extended search and would appreciate volunteers. Anyone wishing to help, come to the community center at six-thirty tomorrow morning."

"Thank you Detective Jarvis and Mr. and Mrs. Kingsley. This is Rhonda Fleming reporting live from the home of Clayton Kingsley, missing today from his Scottsville home. Please call 1-800-541-2222 with any information."

The camera zoomed back to the sofa and centered on the group there. Suddenly the lights switched off, casting the room into semidarkness. Jenny felt as if she'd awakened from a bad dream, but one look at the activity in the room assured her this was no dream.

Retreating into herself, she watched as, miraculously, her living room returned to its previous state. Spotlights rolled away, electrical hardware coiled up, bodies vacated, disappearing as magically as they had appeared, and suddenly the house seemed too quiet. Oddly, she felt as if the walls were closing in on her. Jenny sat passive, unable to act. She hated herself for her inactivity. She should do something to find Clayton, but what? Surely the police would find him. They had to. How could she go on if they didn't?

Everyone was gone, except for Ray. He sat at the other end of the sofa, his body catatonically facing the muted television. From the glazed look in his eyes, she knew he too couldn't focus on the images flashing across the screen.

"I'll get some sheets and make up a bed for you in the family room," Jenny said

He didn't acknowledge her. She doubted if he had even heard her.

She forced herself to get up and stumble to the stairs. Leaning heavily on the railing, she made her way to the landing. Yesterday, she would have run up these stairs two at a time, but tonight it was an effort to force one foot to follow the other. It seemed an eternity before she reached the second story.

Unsure if she could bear any more pain, Jenny planned to avoid Clayton's room, but when she tried to pass his doorway, her feet refused to go any farther. She found herself tip-toeing into his room. Her gaze moved slowly from one familiar object to the next.

The closet, partially open, exposed clothes hung neatly on small hangers. At the open window, the clown curtains Clayton had picked out waved in the breeze. Below the window sat his toy box—cars, trucks, Legos scattered inside. Her gaze stopped at his empty bed.

The only occupants now were an assortment of stuffed animals along the back of the bed. Suddenly she was beside the bed holding Frazer, Clayton's favorite toy, a fuzzy brown bear. He pretended he was too old for Frazer, but every night the bear ended up sleeping beside his pillow. Weak-kneed, she sank to the floor and laid her head on the clown-covered quilt. Clutching the worn bear to her heart, she let its fur absorb her tears.

She had no idea how long she lay there, hugging the stuffed animal tightly to her breast, letting her tears flow unchecked. Then, Ray was there, pulling her to her feet and taking her in his arms, Clayton's bear crushed between them. They stood, wrapped together in their pain.

Eventually, she remembered why she had come upstairs; she had been getting sheets for Ray. "I'm sorry. I forgot the sheets."

Ray dropped his arms and turned away. She suspected it was so she couldn't see the tears that stained his sun-baked skin.

"It's okay," he mumbled. "I don't need them."

"It might get cool in the night."

Once the words were out of her mouth, her thoughts flew back to Clayton. Was he warm? Had someone given him a blanket? Did he need one? She had to stop letting her imagination run rampant. The police would find him anytime now. She had to keep thinking that. Thinking anything else would drive her insane. Ray needed sheets and a pillow.

One arm stretched out to take Clayton's pillow, then recoiled. No! Don't touch anything of Clayton's. He'll need it soon. Jenny's fingers shook as she placed Frazer back in his spot of honor by Clayton's pillow. She crossed the hall and took one of her pillows from the hall closet. She added sheets and a light blanket.

Ray came out of Clayton's room. Jenny saw the fresh stain on his T-shirt where he had wiped his tears. She handed him the bundle of linen.

"You can make up a bed in the family room. It's off the kitchen."

The hands that reached out for the bedding grasped hers. He drew them upward, forcing her to look at him. His eyes were soft and pleading.

"Jenny...leaving was a mistake. Won't you come back? We can try again. We can make it work. I'll change. I promise."

His voice sounded so sincere and confident. Could he so easily forget everything that had gone on before? Jenny kept her eyes focused on his, but gently withdrew her hands.

"Ray, this isn't the good time. I can't think straight. When Clayton is home—then we can talk."

She saw the sincerity in his eyes and felt sorry for him. He was trying hard, but it was too late. All the injustices of the past couldn't be wiped away by tonight's promises.

Right now, she didn't have the energy to tell him how she felt. She needed his support as a friend, but she would never feel the same love for him she had six years ago. He'd done too good a job of whittling that slowly away. No, she couldn't take the wimpy way out and leave him with false hope. She was done with being pushed around by people.

She turned back to him. "I appreciate your support now, but—Ray, there is nothing to talk about. I left, and I am not coming back."

"Please, Jenny, I need you. I'll change. I promise."

"No, Ray."

She left him standing in the hall and hurried into the bathroom. Passing the sink, she had a glimpse of her reflection. Her usually pale face had taken on a grayish tinge. Mascara stained the dark circles under her eyes. The green in her hazel eyes now glowed like emeralds from the multitude of tears she had shed.

Hair that hadn't seen a comb since morning hung limp and lifeless around her face. Jenny hardly recognized the wild-eyed woman staring back at her. She closed her eyes and stumbled to the toilet.

Her body convulsed as it retched up the meager contents of her stomach. Could her stomach hold nothing in it today? Clammy hands clung to the toilet. When her body finally quieted, Jenny lay her head against the cold whiteness. It was the same temperature as her heart.

It was a long time before she could move. She knew she should shower. She could smell her fear mixed with the stale scent of vomit. Using the wall to pull herself upright, she reached for the water taps in the tub. She tried to turn them, but there was no strength left in her hands. Did it matter if she stank? Right now, nothing mattered. She staggered out of the bathroom and across to her bedroom. She collapsed on the bed, frozen, her eyes open, staring at the blank ceiling.

Clayton was alone for the first time in his life. He had no one to put him to bed, no one to tuck his covers around him, no one to kiss him goodnight.

Please, God, whoever has my child, let them be kind to him. Let them keep him warm. Let them keep him safe. She rolled on her side and, curling her legs to her chest, hugged the pillow to her. Soon, her tears saturated the pillow.

CHAPTER 10

A damp chill invaded the small space. Darkness so black his eyes couldn't penetrate it. Clayton shivered. The worn blanket covering him was moth eaten and gave little warmth. He pulled it closer to his body.

He wanted to be home. He wanted to be back in the house he and his mother just moved to. He wanted to sleep in his own bed with Frazer, his teddy bear beside him. He couldn't remember ever going to sleep without Frazer. He couldn't remember a night without his mother coming to kiss him goodnight. Even when she had gone to school or work, she still came home before he went to bed. She always gave him a kiss goodnight.

Where is she now? Why hasn't she come to get me?

When he closed his eyes, he could see his toys piled up in the toy box—Tonka trucks, Dinky toys, Lego pieces, transformers. He saw his stuffed animals lined up on his bed with Frazer closest to his pillow. He should be in his bed, sleeping under his new quilt with the bright red and blue clowns on it. His mother should be tucking his covers around him, reading him a story. Here, he had nothing, not even Frazer.

With his eyes closed, Clayton could almost feel her tucking him in. He could see her dark blonde hair slipping past her shoulders and falling to cover her face. He liked to watch her push it away from her eyes. It would fall right back and she would push it away again. If he listened hard, he knew he could hear her laugh.

It reminded him of Gram's crystal. When he would reach up and push her hair away, uncovering her face, she would make a game of peek-a-boo with the long strands of her hair.

They would play the game for a long time before she would pretend to be serious and tell him. "Enough games. Bedtime, my prince." She'd try to hide her grin behind her hands, but he could see the light dancing in her hazel eyes and knew she wasn't really angry. She'd lower her voice, tip her head to one side, and speak firmly. "It is bedtime, Clayton. Now close your eyes and go to sleep." Her lips would brush his cheek. Then she would tuck the covers tightly around him and place another kiss on his forehead. "Sleep well, Prince Clayton." She'd check the night light before turning off his bedroom light. "Sweet dreams, my love," she'd whisper.

There was no night light here. There were no whispered goodnights. There were no mother's kisses. Clayton reached up into the darkness, wanting to feel one silken strand of her hair, one stroke of her soft cheek, one butterfly kiss.

A draft of cold air blasted against his arm. Quickly, he pulled his hand back under the blanket. A slow trickle of wetness started at the corners of his eyes, bubbled over, and ran down his dirt-stained cheeks.

Clayton squeezed his eyes shut. *Maybe if I keep my eyes closed tight, I will hear her.* He curled up on the thin mat and listened to scampering noises somewhere in the black spaces.

CHAPTER 11

The morning sun blazed through the bedroom window, foreshadowing another sizzling day. Jenny felt hot and tired, too tired to open her eyes yet. She rolled over, her efforts impeded. She wiggled, trying to get comfortable. Her pajamas bottoms constricted her legs. Pulling at them, she tried to loosen them. They were snug around her legs and the material felt coarse, not like the thinness of her cotton pajamas. It was heavy and tightly woven.

Slowly, she opened eyes still groggy with sleep. Jenny wiped the fine crusting away from her lashes, and peeled away the top sheet. She had a cotton shirt and jeans on instead of her pajamas. These were the clothes she'd put on yesterday. Why had she gone to bed with her clothes on? She never took a nap in the afternoon. The sun poured through the window. She looked at the digital clock on her night table, eight-oh-five.

She blinked several times. It couldn't be eight in the morning. Where was Clayton? He never slept past seven. If she overslept, he would jump on her bed, pull off the covers, and tickle her until she got up. Where was he?

Jenny lifted her head and listened. A spasm of pain shot through her as a heavy weight pressed on her forehead and a pounding squeezed the sides of her head. She put her hand to her forehead to stop the pounding. Slowly, the terrible realization came. Clayton didn't come to wake her up because he was gone! How could she have slept while he was missing?

She leaped out of bed. She had to call the police! Then the nightmarish memories of yesterday's events came back, one by one, hitting her like a tidal wave, and she fell back on the bed. She lay there for several minutes before she could gather the strength to move. Every time she tried to lift her head, the pain increased. Finally, she struggled upright and sat at the side of the bed. She reached for the phone on the night table and dialed the police station. Maybe they'd found him and she hadn't heard the phone when they called.

"Detective Jarvis, please."

"He's out right now. Can I take a message?"

"This is Jenny Kingsley. Have you found Clayton?"

"Sorry, Mrs. Kingsley, not yet. But we have half the town out looking. I'll have Detective Jarvis call you."

"Thank you." Her hand shook so violently it took several attempts before she could settle the phone back on its cradle.

Somehow, she made her way to the bathroom. Avoiding her bedraggled reflection in the mirror, she opened the medicine cabinet. She leaned against the vanity and struggled with the childproof cap on the Tylenol bottle. She downed four of the tablets. Using the wall for support, she edged her way to the shower. Stripping off yesterday's clothes, she stepped under the tepid water. The spray felt good, cleansing away the scents of yesterday's fear and the faint tinge of vomit. She still felt nauseated and wanted to vomit again, but there was nothing left.

Lathering the washcloth, she scrubbed her body. She wanted to remain under the cleansing spray, letting it wash away her tension, and letting herself pretend it was only a nightmare. Suddenly, it hit her. She wouldn't be able to hear the phone with the water running. If the police called, she wouldn't know. She dressed quickly and ran downstairs.

It was only then that she remembered Ray had stayed the night. Where was he? Jenny hurried into the family room. The room was empty; the blankets piled neatly at the end of the sofa. She saw the note on the coffee table.

Have gone to the community center. Will be
back later to drive you to the bus station to
get your Mom. Ray

She had slept through Ray's departure. What kind of mother was she? How could she have slept at all? She had even forgotten about her mother coming this afternoon. Oh, Mom, I need you now. I need your support. Maybe by the time you get here, Clayton will be home. Then we can have a party.

Something nagged at her. What should she be doing? There was something she had to do. She wished she could remember. The pounding in her head made it hard to think.

Leaving the family room, she crossed the hall to the living room. There was a commotion on the street. Jenny pulled back the curtains and looked out the window. Vehicles lined the street. A television news van from WKJB sat across the road and a car with Scottsville Daily News scrolled in red letters was behind it. The occupants of both vehicles stood on the sidewalk with high-power cameras trained on the house. The rest of the street, as far as she could see, was crammed with cars and trucks, their drivers standing about in small groups, chatting and holding their coffees in paper cups, all of them focusing their attention on her house.

What did they want? She wasn't a specimen in a bottle. Did they want to expose her pain to the universe? She dropped the curtain as if flames fingered up the fibers. Putting a hand to her head, she tried to quell the pounding.

She heard a tapping on the back door. She didn't have the energy to answer it, but the knocking continued. It made the pounding in her head unbearable. Reluctantly, she crossed to the door. The Tylenol wasn't working. *If it's one of those damn people from the street, I'll* scream. *I really will.*

Easing back the curtain on the back door, Jenny peeked through the glass. She sighed with relief when she recognized Myrtle's face. Sliding back the deadbolt, she opened the door and let the woman slide past her into the kitchen. Myrtle carried two large plastic containers.

"I just came to see how you were managing, dear. I brought you a little something."

Myrtle placed the containers on the kitchen counter and then turned back to Jenny. Before she knew what had happened, Jenny found herself wrapped in Myrtle's arms. The scent of baby powder and lavender made Jenny think of her grandmother and Clayton all at the same time.

She remembered being held on her grandmother's lap. Her gnarled fingers stroking Jenny's hair, she would sing lullabies in her lilting Irish voice. Gram's old wooden rocker would sway in rhythm with the song, the scent of lavender floating in a cloud around her. It was to her gramma that Jenny had run for comfort. It was in her arms where she found safety.

Shortly after her ninth birthday, she found her Gram asleep in her chair. But it was a sleep the elderly lady never woke from. For weeks, Jenny had been inconsolable. Gram's tender side had never passed on to her daughter, Gladys. Jenny's mother told her to stop her sniveling; Gram was an old woman, and it was her time, but Jenny never forgot the love her grandmother had shown. She had vowed Clayton would always feel loved.

Emotions mixed, steeped, and bubbled over. The tears she had been trying to hold back burst forth. Her body racked with sobs and tears coursed down her cheek. She buried her face in the curve of Myrtle's neck. Inhaling deeply, she let the aroma of lavender fill her, and for a few moments, she allowed herself to feel safe.

She tried to stop the tears, tried to apologize. She wanted to be strong, but all that came out of her mouth were broken words, words chopped into syllables by her sobs.

"It's okay, dear. Let it come, let it all out."

Myrtle held her, continuing the age-old-custom of mothers since time began as she rocked the weeping girl in the circle of her arms, whispering words of solace. "It will be okay. Everything will be fine. You just wait and see. They'll have the lad home soon."

The rocking continued. The soothing words continued. Jenny's tears flowed unchecked. Years of hurts and injustices intermingled with the pain of Clayton's loss, finally able to find a home. When the tide finally ebbed, Myrtle led her to the kitchen table, and with a gentle push, sat her in a chair.

"You just sit there. I'll make us a spot of tea."

Myrtle made herself at home, opening cupboards until she found what she needed. Soon the tea was steeping in a pot and the cups sat ready on the table. Myrtle opened the plastic container of homemade cookies and rolls she had brought with her and placed a plate of them on the table.

Jenny, her energy spent, sat silently. She smiled gratefully at her neighbor. She wished she could tell Myrtle how much she appreciated her presence. But the words wouldn't come. She could only smile dumbly.

Somehow, Myrtle knew. She squeezed her shoulder and spoke gently. "I'll do all I can for you, dear. You just ask. I'll be there for you."

The tears threatened again. Jenny pulled a handkerchief out of her pocket and dabbed at her eyes with a corner of the cotton. Jenny noticed Myrtle's glance at the embroidered handkerchief.

"This was my grandmother's." Jenny held up the square of fine cotton with the border of delicate violets. "I remember her sitting in her rocking chair. She was always doing some needlework project."

"She did a lovely job. Violets are my favorite flowers."

Jenny didn't know if she should tell Myrtle how much she reminded her of Gram. Would she take offense? She didn't want to hurt her feelings. She needed someone to help share her pain. "They were Gram's favorite too."

They sat drinking their tea. Automatically, Jenny reached for one of Myrtle's oatmeal cookies. Maybe some food would make her headache go away. She realized she hadn't eaten nothing since yesterday morning, other than a couple of bites of the sandwiches she'd made the night before for Ray. She nibbled at the cookie. Then took another one. Before she knew it, the plate was empty. Then she thought of Clayton and guilt washed over her. How could she stuff her face with her son still missing? Jenny put the half-eaten cookie down and pushed the plate away. Her mind screamed, Where are you, Clayton?

Yesterday seemed an eternity away. The kitchen clock ticked loudly, each tick like a hammer pounding in her head. As the seconds passed, she felt each beat of her heart. Each beat another in a heart so full of sadness she didn't know how it had the energy for the next one. But beat on it did. And Jenny was aware of every beat, as it was one more without her son. Was his heart still beating?

She thought of the first time she had felt him move and how amazed she had been that a living being was growing inside her. She remembered her first ultrasound and watching his heart beating when he was only inches long. Jenny prayed his heart was still beating.

She looked at the clock. Was Clayton counting each second, as she was, until he was home with her again? She remembered teaching him to tell time. The little hand was at the nine, the big one at the five. He had been a fast learner; quickly able to distinguish the numbers on the face of the clock, understanding that the little hand pointed to the hour. They had made a game of telling time. He had helped make a schedule of their daily routine on construction paper with the numbers blocked out in big print. Even now it was taped to the refrigerator along with several of his drawings.

Myrtle's voice interrupted her thoughts. "Is anyone going to be with you today?"

"Ray, he was...is...my husband...we're separated. He's out helping the police look for Clay. And my mother, she's coming later."

"That's good. I'm glad someone will be with you. Steve is out looking, too." She paused. "Do you want me to stay until they come?"

"Oh, please. I don't want to be alone." Another tear tracked down her cheek. She wiped it away with the back of her hand and smiled gratefully at Myrtle.

Then she remembered what she had to do. "I have to go to the police station whenever the deputy arrives...but if you could stay till then?"

"Of course I can."

Silver curls surrounded Myrtle's peaches and cream complexion. The beauty of her plump oval face marred only with tiny furrows by the upturned corners of her lips and tunneling out from soft gray eyes. A depth of kindness lay there. Eyes full of life's joys and sorrows.

"Thanks, I would appreciate it," Jenny said.

They sipped their tea, and the minutes passed. Jenny thought about her mother coming. She would be on the five o'clock bus. She longed to have her mother's arms around her and feel safe in the circle of those arms. She needed her support. She needed someone to lean on, someone to reassure her that everything would be okay, someone to tell her they would find Clayton safe and unharmed. That's what a mother would do at a time like this, wouldn't she?

She thought of her mother. Maybe this time she would be different. A knocking at the front door broke the silence. Both women jumped at the sudden intrusion.

"Would you like me to get it?"

"I'll get it. But will you come with me?"

Jenny's mind was a mix of emotions—fear of who was there, and what news they would bring. Maybe it was the police, and they had found Clayton. She rushed to the door. She could see the uniformed officer through the window in the door.

Maybe he was bringing Clayton back! Holding her breath, she pulled the door inward.

CHAPTER 12

Steve watched from his kitchen window as the police car pulled up to the house next door. He'd been with the search party since six-thirty but had come home to change into boots as the search was being extended to the woods beyond town. He'd grabbed a quick coffee and was just taking a sip when he saw the police car. Joe Roberts got out of the cruiser.

The coffee mug stopped midway to Steve's mouth. Suddenly, he lost all desire to finish the drink. What was Roberts doing here? Have they found Clayton? Was it going to be bad news?

He froze, unable to move. Steve felt bile edging up from his stomach, burning as it crept higher, singeing the delicate tissues of his throat. He tasted the bile on the back of his tongue and swallowed, forcing the foul fluid back.

Have they found the boy yet? Are they going to find him? It can't be like the last time!

He loosened his death grip on the coffee mug and placed it back on the kitchen table before it shattered. Roberts walked up the driveway. Steve felt the bile fill his mouth. He hated him.

Roberts was an arrogant ass who hid his perverted nature behind the guise of propriety and a gold badge. Yeah, I'm bitter. But don't I have every right to be? I've seen him in action. Steve snorted. No, rephrase that, I've felt him in action.

Feeling his throat constrict, Steve forced himself to turn away from the window. He knew there were good cops out there, but there were those few that spoiled it for the rest. The ones who thought that when not watched that they could get away with anything, even murder.

Damn Joe Roberts! Damn him and his old partner.

It was years ago now, but he still couldn't forget. Kelly had been his best friend and the two cops, Joe Roberts and his partner, had beaten him and left him to die. The police officers never charged; probably never even reprimanded. Lied through their teeth, telling everyone they found him like that. They didn't know Cheryl had seen them, didn't know she was watching from behind Kelly's bedroom curtains.

Cheryl watched as they clubbed him with their fists and kicked him with their shiny black boots, striking and punching until Kelly was unconscious. But she had been too afraid to come forward; scared her daddy would find out she had been with Kelly again. So while they beat him, she climbed out the bathroom window and high-tailed it for home, a nice safe suburb on the right side of town where mansions sat on an acre of manicured gardens and sprawling velvet lawns. She hadn't even called 911.

Steve knew from the first time he saw Cheryl she was nothing but trouble. He and Kelly were at Casey's Bar and Grill and there was Cheryl, leaning over the jukebox, hips squeezed into a glitzy scarlet mini-skirt, swaying to some melancholy tune. Her long, bare legs, tanned to the edges of her mini-skirt, tempted any male who saw her to discover where the tan lines ended. Brightly painted fingernails tapped out a rhythm on the jukebox's glass top. She flashed an inviting smile at any male who looked her way. Too bad Kelly looked.

Cheryl, taken by Kelly's Brad Pitt appeal, made a play for him. Kelly was bashful and easily flattered by her attention. The flaunting of her voluptuous body, the winking of her painted eyes, and the flashing of her randy grin were all the aphrodisiac his latent virility needed.

When she sauntered over to their table and pulled him up to dance, he hadn't resisted. Snuggling so close he didn't have room to breathe and touching him in places no decent girl should. Kelly was defenseless. To top it off, she let him drive her gleaming fire-engine-red Mazda Miata. That was the only thing about Cheryl that had impressed Steve.

She came to Casey's almost every night after that to meet Kelly, but never let him drive her home or meet her family. They were snobs, and she hated them. At least that's the story she gave.

Steve remembered the night Kelly found out she was pregnant. He'd floated on a cloud the whole evening. He wanted them to get married right away, planned for them to live in his bachelor apartment until the baby was born and he could find something bigger. Cheryl just sobbed that it was all his fault. She screamed at him for not using condoms. Kelly couldn't understand. Getting married to her and having a baby was the best thing that had ever happened to him. He was so infatuated with Cheryl that he didn't see the side Steve saw.

It devastated Kelly when he realized Cheryl didn't want him, or the baby. She was going to have an abortion. He was livid. If she didn't want their child, he would raise the baby himself. But she wouldn't let him do that either. Cheryl was too highfalutin to be associated with a grease monkey. Not too good, though, to sneak around with him and get herself pregnant.

In the end, she didn't get the abortion. She hid away and secretly made adoption arrangements. She continued to sneak out and meet Kelly, keeping him on a string, promising they'd get married once the baby was born. He wanted to get married right then, but she kept putting him off. She would flutter those false eyelashes and tell him she wanted to fit into her wedding dress. There was no wedding in her plans, at least not with Kelly.

Steve went to the hospital with Kelly after the baby was born. Kelly's eyes brimmed with tears, and he wore a smile that split his face in two. He was bursting with hopes and dreams for his new baby girl. Then Cheryl dropped the bomb that shattered his life.

She wouldn't marry him and was giving the baby up for adoption. In a week, her father was sending her to Europe. She would be gone for six months. Kelly couldn't believe what he was hearing. He argued with her. Cheryl cried, her voice screeching as tears flowed down her reddened cheeks. "It's the chance of a lifetime, I'm too young to be tied down with a Goddamn baby. I deserve more out of life."

Someone called security. They dragged Kelly out of the hospital and dumped him outside the building with warnings not to return. Steve left to follow in his wake. At Casey's, Kelly proceeded to drink his way to oblivion. In the early morning hours, Steve drove him home and deposited him like a rag doll on his bed. When Kelly awoke from his stupor, he formulated a plan—he would take the baby and raise her by himself.

Cheryl laughed in his face. "There's no way I'm letting a grease monkey raise my child."

So Kelly borrowed Steve's car when the baby was discharged from the hospital, followed the social worker to her office, and then to the baby's foster home. When Kelly picked him up at his shop, Steve had no idea how he had gotten the baby. Steve only knew they needed a ride home. He agreed to drop him off. They were almost at Kelly's apartment when the lights and sirens forced them off the road.

Joe Roberts was a rookie cop then, and Cheryl's friend. She'd told him Kelly was in Steve's car, and about his plans. Roberts and his partner hunted them down. Steve had just been giving them a ride home and Cheryl got them both arrested.

The baby went to a social worker. After hours of sitting in a holding cell, Steve and Kelly were fingerprinted, photographed, and interrogated.

Steve became angry every time he remembered the humiliation of facing the police camera and holding that black-lettered number sign in front of his chest while the camera flashed in his face. All Kelly wanted was his baby. A little girl he never got to see again.

Finally, at three in the morning, they'd been released with warnings and fingers stained with indelible black ink. Kelly went ballistic. He demanded Cheryl let him raise their daughter. Maybe she didn't want him, but how could she give up their baby? Steve dropped Kelly home with his promise to do nothing until he consulted a lawyer. That was the last time he ever saw Kelly alive.

Steve heard about Kelly's death at work the next day. He didn't hear the entire story until the night before Cheryl left for Europe. She came slinking to his door at one in the morning.Cheryl thought if she told him the truth, she would get absolution. She blubbered about how devastated she was. Kelly would still be alive if she hadn't gone to reason with him. If he hadn't gotten so angry, if he hadn't scared her, she wouldn't have called Joe Roberts. She never thought it would go so far.

Roberts told her to go home, but she hid in Kelly's bedroom. They didn't know she was still there when the beating began. Maybe if she'd gone to help him, or called 911? Steve begged her to go to the authorities and tell them. She refused.

Yeah, she made a big production with all her tears, but she still took her plane to Europe the next day. She never came back. She married a banker in Switzerland. Cheryl got what she wanted. She didn't get her name in the paper, and Daddy didn't find out she had been back to see Kelly. She kept her mouth shut, and nobody paid for Kelly's death.

CHAPTER 13

He must be bringing Clayton back! Jenny's heart raced. Holding her breath, she yanked the door open. Deputy Dave Charlton stood in front of her. Another officer, Joe Roberts, was behind him.

Charlton closed the door against the media rush. "No, Ma'am, there's still no news."

The deputy's gaze connected with hers, then slid away. His short time on the force had not given him the hard edge he would need, the edge that came with time and would allow him to divorce his own emotions. This man wasn't there yet. Jenny saw her pain reflected in his eyes and the discomfort with his inadequacy.

"We've canvassed the neighborhood. Some people, like the Sawyers down the street, weren't home, but we'll get back to them. We expanded the search. It was on the news last night, but I guess you know that."

She nodded. How well she knew. Instead of bringing her son home, it had lined her quiet street with media and onlookers. Over the deputy's broad shoulders, she saw the people still camped out on the street.

"Detective Jarvis wanted me to bring you downtown to look at mug shots."

While she grabbed her purse, she missed Myrtle's gasp. When Jenny turned to thank her for her support, the concern she saw in the woman's eyes seemed totally for her.

Jenny followed Charlton to the car. Roberts hustled her into the backseat and slammed the car door against the media. She sat, silent and withdrawn. From behind the bullet-proof glass, she watched as spectators rushed at the vehicle, clamoring for any tidbit of news.

Through the tinted windows, their faces took on monstrous proportions. Eyes glowed a piercing yellow. Nostrils pressed flat and became wide cavernous tunnels. And the mouths, they were the worst. They flapped open and closed, open and closed, exposing sharp white teeth with each movement. Jenny felt as if dropped into a scene from a Stephen King movie and the car was being attacked by a swarm of savages. She shrank back in the seat and closed her eyes while the car backed out of the driveway.

She kept her eyes closed most of the way to the police station. The pain in her head heightened and the effort of opening her eyes was too much. Charlton continued to chatter, not seeming to expect a response. He told her how the search was proceeding—the bulletins on police radios, the flyers, the computer links extending throughout the US and extending into Canada. He assured her they would find Clayton soon, he couldn't have just vanished. It was only a matter of time and they would have him home safe and sound. His voice, filled with such optimism and hope that Jenny almost believed him.

The police station was an old gray brick building on Main St. recently renovated to allow for wheelchair access. Jenny took that entrance. Her feet felt too heavy to navigate the flight of stairs that led to the main entrance. Charlton walked beside her, finally silent. Roberts followed.

Inside, they led her past the main reception desk to a caged elevator that rattled up to the second floor. Uniformed policemen loitered in the offices. She wanted to ask why they weren't out looking for her son, but she knew that was unreasonable. Clayton's disappearance was not the only problem they had to deal with. Life went on as usual. They did their jobs, took their breaks, finished their shifts, and went home. It was only for her that life had stopped.

They passed by several offices before Charlton led her into one near the end of the hallways where Jarvis waited for her. He was on the phone and motioned her to a chair across the desk from him. She was vaguely aware of Charlton leaving the room.

Glancing around the office, she saw the bulletin board on one wall crammed with notices and wanted posters. Clayton's picture was there, tacked by one corner on top of previous bulletins. His face smiling brought on a new wave of tears which she wiped quickly away. She had shed enough tears. It was time to do something constructive to find her son. While she waited for Jarvis to finish his conversation, Jenny concentrated on her surroundings.

A wooden file cabinet stood against one wall, the top drawer partially open, exposing overflowing files. Jarvis had one picture on the wall, a pastoral scene, like the ones you bought from distressed artists on street corners. On the opposite wall, various diplomas in wooden frames adorned the beige paint. Loose papers and file folders covered his mahogany desk. One personal picture occupied a corner of his desk, a framed photo of the detective, his arm around a plump middle-aged woman. Three dark-haired children between the ages of ten and fifteen sat in front of them.

So he has children too. He must understand what I am going through.

Jarvis placed the phone back on the receiver and looked across at her. His smooth olive skin stretched over high cheekbones and he met her gaze with serious gray eyes.

"We don't have any news yet. The hotline is up and running. We've had a few calls. We're checking them out. The number will continue to be on the news. And we've set up an Amber Alert bulletin to flash on the television every hour. There will be more about your son on the local radio stations. We should hear something today."

He paused, letting her digest his report. His voice was confident and sure. Jenny wished she felt the same.

"I want you to look through our photos of known suspects. Deputy Evans will take you to the interview room. While you're doing that, I'm going back to the search. I'll check in on you later and give you an update."

As if on cue, a deputy entered the office. Jarvis introduced him. Chad Evans was in his thirties, a big muscular man with a mane of brown curls. The softness in his brown eyes gave Jenny the impression of a big bear, a kind big bear. Even the hand he extended reminded her of an enormous paw. His powerful grip transmitted an aura of trust.

Wordlessly, she followed him into a room with several desks arranged as mini workstations. Each desk had a phone and various paper paraphernalia. Uniformed deputies sat behind the desks. He led her into a side room. Three large black photo albums were already waiting for her.

"See if there is anyone there you recognize. Maybe the person who took him has been hanging around your home, or places you frequent."

She glanced at the standard circular clock that hung on the station wall. It was just after nine and the phones in the room beyond rang continuously. The books were full of glossy black-and-white photos, one profile, and one full-face view per screen. The thickness of the books shocked Jenny. Would she see a familiar face amongst them?

Her fingers shook as she pulled the first book toward her and opened the sturdy black cover. The starkness of the photos, with their common white background and numbered signs, jarred her thoughts. But after the first hour of turning pages, her eyes swam from seeing faces that blurred one into another. Eyes, noses, and mouths that at first looked distinct and different now took on a vague similarity. Faces she had never seen before began to look eerily familiar. Jenny shivered despite the heat of the day.

Jenny had come to the station just after nine, and now it was almost eleven. She still had one book to go through. She was stunned by the number of people who'd come in front of the police cameras. Rubbing her temple, but the headache refused to leave. Had it been the recommended four hours? Not caring, she took three Tylenol out of her purse and swallowed them. She glanced at the clock again, opened the last book, and began turning the pages.

Halfway through the book, she noticed something familiar about one of the black and white mug shots. Was it the shape of the jaw, the width of the nose, or the serious eyes? Suddenly, she realized she was looking at a younger version of her next-door neighbor, Steve Townsend. She stared at the stubble-covered face. Was it? Her eyes flew to the bottom of the page. Steven David Townsend. It was him. What was his picture doing here among common criminals?

"Have you seen someone who looks familiar?"

Jenny heard the officer's voice beside her. She looked up at Chad Evans. What did she tell him? Did she say that her next-door neighbor's picture was here? She liked Steve. She thought of the day he had helped her take out the trash and the friendship that was developing between them. He'd helped look for Clayton yesterday and stayed to comfort her later. No. She could not believe he could have taken her son. What should she do? Before she knew it, her index finger slid to his picture.

"This." Her finger pointed toward Steve's picture. "This looks like my neighbor."

Chad Evans gazed at the picture. Squinting, he seemed deep in thought, as if debating whether to speak. His lips opened and closed again before he spoke.

"Yes, it is your neighbor, Steve Townsend. That—" He waved at the picture. "—happened long ago—a situation blown out of proportion. I don't think you have anything to be concerned about. But, let me assure you, we're checking every lead until your son is home."

Her finger slid off the page. Slowly, she shut the book and looked up at the deputy.

"I want to go home."

CHAPTER 14

J enny dreaded the thought of returning to the silent, empty house. She needed to be doing something. She couldn't just sit and wait until they found her son. There must be something she could do. Troops of men were searching the streets of Scottsville, and more were in the countryside. She wanted to be with them, but Jarvis had refused. Ray was there; that was enough. So here she was, twiddling her thumbs while strangers looked for her child. At least at the community center, she could keep busy.

"Could you take me to the community center?" she asked Evans.

"Yes, ma'am. I'll drop you there."

Evans stopped at a red light. He focused kind eyes on her. Years on the force had taught him the empathy Charlton had yet to learn.

"Now, Mrs. Kinsley, if you decide you want to go home, just ask someone to take you. It might be hard for you to be there. We have a lot of volunteers, so don't be shy about asking them for anything you need."

"Thank you, I will."

The light turned green and Evans drove on. Within minutes, he stopped in front of the Scottsville Community Center. Cars filled the parking lot and spilled out onto the street. There were several small groups of people outside the building. They turned to stare at her as she got out of the car, then looked discretely away. Evans walked with her into the building. She smiled thankfully up at him. He knew instinctively that she lacked the courage to go in alone.

Bright lights illuminated a main hall that buzzed with activity. Several long tables stretched along two of the walls. People milled around the large room like worker ants. A copy machine hummed. Phones rang. People answered the phones, listening intently and taking notes. Large maps covered one wall. Areas of the town, and its surrounding countryside, marked off with different colored markers. Pushpins held an assortment of flags scattered across the surface.

She looked around the room in amazement. Dozens of volunteers scurried about, yet she only recognized a few: Mrs. Stockley from the grocery store, Dolores, a waitress at the coffee shop, and Mr. Lee, the realtor who had arranged for her to rent the McLaren property. The rest were strangers to. But they were all here, lending a hand in times of trouble. Jenny silently thanked them for their help. The tears threatened to start again.

Evans led her toward one of the long tables. Jarvis was talking on the phone. While she waited for him, she glanced at the long tables. There were stacks of posters with Clayton's face smiling up at her. Bold letters demanded:

HAVE YOU SEEN THIS CHILD?

Call 1-800-541-2222

A tear slid down her face. Someone handed her a Kleenex. Jenny turned to thank the person and recognized Mrs. Stockley, the owner of the combined grocery and restaurant.

"I'm so sorry, Mrs. Kingsley."

"Thanks. Please...call me Jenny."

"Sure I will, dear. Now, you just let me know if you need anything."

Jenny nodded to the woman and wiped her eyes. She wished she had some control of the tears that kept coming. She saw Jarvis talking on the phone. He waved her over. Thanking Mrs. Stockley again, she approached the detective.

He hung up the phone. "How are you holding up?"

She nodded her reply. Couldn't he see his answer in the dark circles under her tear-reddened eyes? He must have seen something. Instead of making further inquiries, he left his chair and came to stand beside her.

"Most of the men in town are out searching. We made up teams this morning. Each one has a different area to search. I'm going out shortly to see how they're doing."

He led her over to the wall map and pointed out grid areas on the wall map. "The helicopter with infrared sensors was out all night. The pilot covered the area within a fifty-mile radius of town. We should find your boy today. If not, he'll go up again tonight when it gets dark. Now, do you want to go home, or do you want to do something here?"

"Stay here, please. I need to be busy."

He nodded his understanding. "I'll take you over to Mrs. Chalmers. She runs the community center and is organizing the volunteers."

Jenny followed him to a large office off the main hall. Through the doorway, she saw the back of an auburn-haired woman working on a computer. At Jarvis's voice, the chair swiveled to face them. A tiny woman occupied only a portion of the large chair, her feet inches from the floor. Dark-rimmed glasses covered a pair of myopic green eyes. With a smile of recognition, the tiny feet hit the floor and bounded toward them. Jenny found her hand grasped forcibly between the woman's small, soft ones.

"Mrs. Kingsley, we're doing everything we can to find your son. As you can see," she said, waving one hand toward the main hall, "we have a super group of volunteers. Would you like some coffee or maybe a nice cup of herbal tea?"

"Tea would be nice. Thank you."

"Can I leave you in Mrs. Chalmers' care? Jarvis asked.

Before Jenny could respond, Mrs. Chalmers answered for her. "Yes. You just leave her here. I'll look after her."

Jarvis looked inquiringly at Jenny. Overwhelmed by the bustling woman, she could only nod in agreement. It was a relief to be taken under Mrs. Chalmers' wings. Tiny as those wings might be, Jenny could see her using them to beat off tigers one moment and tenderly stroking a gosling the next. Mrs. Chalmers looked capable of organizing her home and career by just rustling a few of her fine feathers. Jenny felt grateful to be in her nest.

After making the promised tea, Mrs. Chalmers pressured Jenny to eat a cream-filled donut from a box sent over from a local coffee shop. Their tea consumed, Mrs. Chalmers, or Grace as she insisted she be called, put Jenny to work printing flyers. Volunteers had been posting them all morning and were coming back for more.

At four-thirty, Ray arrived to take her to the bus station to pick up her mother. He looked drained and defeated. So far, the hundreds of volunteers had found no sign of Clayton. During the afternoon, with the support and activity of the workers in the hall, she become hopeful that Clayton would be found. Surely, with all those people helping, someone would find her son.

But when she looked at Ray, it was as if someone had taken a pin to her balloon.

CHAPTER 15

The muscles at the back of Jenny's neck tightened, and the pounding in her head returned. For several hours, it had been only a vague pressure somewhere at the back of her consciousness. Now, it felt as if it was pushing through the top of her skull.

She rummaged through her purse for the Tylenol bottle. After struggling with the cap, Jenny dropped three of the white tablets into her mouth and swallowed. The pill residue left a foul aftertaste on her tongue.

In the distance, she heard the rumble of the bus's engine. Within a minute, the bus pulled around the corner of the building and screeched to a stop beside the curb. Jenny rubbed harder at her neck, her fingers extending their circular motion to her shoulders. She rotated her neck in a circle, hoping the movement would relieve the tension.

Out of the corner of her eye, she saw Ray watching her. He smiled and came closer. His hand took over massaging her neck. Jenny let her arms drop to her sides. She closed her eyes; letting the pressure of his hands ease some of the tension out of her strained muscles.

With a loud wheeze, the bus door opened and people poured out. She started away from Ray's touch. Before letting his hand drop, he gave her neck a gentle squeeze. She turned to him. His usual rough demeanor softened by the gentleness in his eyes. He shook his head slightly and spoke quietly. "Don't let her get to you."

"What are you talking about?"

"You know how she affects you."

"That was before. She won't be like that. Not now!"

Ray shrugged his shoulders. "Just don't let her get to you."

"I won't." Her voice was sharp. Of course, her mother wouldn't chastise her now. She was a grown woman, raising her son on her own. A cramp assaulted a muscle at the back of her neck. Instinctively, she reached up and massaged it. Yes, she had a child of her own now—a child taken from her backyard. Her mother never lost her children. Jenny rubbed harder.

She was aware of Ray's gaze on her and turned away, concentrating on the bus's open door. A cap of tight red curls peeked out from behind the disembarking passengers. Her mother caught sight of them and pushed her way through. Jenny rushed toward her, flinging her arms around the older woman's wiry shoulders.

Jenny clung to her mother. She felt the stiff, thin arms wrap automatically around her, and the pat of her mother's hand against her back. Then her mother's body tensed and Jenny was pushed away. She tried to hold on, but her arms were gently removed. Jenny felt a familiar loneliness ebb into her body. She took a self-conscious step backward.

Her mother's sharp green eyes examined her. "You look pale. And thin too."

"Mom—Clayton's missing." Jenny shook her head in disbelief. What did it matter if she was as thin as a matchstick, or the same color? How could her mother even think of how she looked when her only grandchild was missing?

Her mother looked past her. "Hello, Ray."

"Hi, Mom."

Gladys nodded at his greeting. The tightly wound curls of her recent perm barely moved. Not a gray hair was discernible. That had been one of her pleasures of having her children grown and gone from the house. Raising the four of them on her husband's wages had left her little money to fritter away on what he called her vanities. Now, with his progressing emphysema, and confined to the house, she had taken over the banking.

She ensured there was enough money for her euchre outings with her girl-friends and getting her hair done weekly. Jenny knew the thought of exhibiting a single gray hair brought on one of her mother's black moods.

Jenny had learned early not to provoke one of those moods. Taking cues from her father, she'd learned to measure her words and actions. Even now she never knew what might provoke a tempestuous fit of temper from this tiny woman. The loosening of the pocketbook had at least decreased their frequency and intensity.

"How is Dad?"

"Same as usual—tied to his damn television and that oxygen tubing. He want-ed to come. I told him he'd just be in the way with that damn tubing stretching all over. People would be tripping over it all the time. Besides, he's too weak to lug that oxygen tank around. You can call him later."

Jenny's face tightened, but she didn't comment. She noticed her mother watching her and turned away. Unable to show affection to them as children, her mother resented Jenny's closeness with her father, despite his familiarity with the brown bottle.

She understood her father's escape. She'd found her own in the girl's track team. When she ran, she could pretend life was going to be different. She'd dreamed of racing in the Olympics, hoping her feet would be her ticket away from Dresden and the reality of her life there. But the dreams had been only that because at some point she had to stop running and return home.

"Jenny." Ray interrupted her thoughts. "We should head back to the house."

He led the way to his baby blue Mustang. Gladys and Jenny followed. Gladys reached for the passenger door, then stepped back, leaving Jenny to slide into the back seat.

"Nice car, Ray. You always did like your cars."

Jenny saw the quick look Ray shot her mother and knew from the twitch in his cheek that he was holding back a retort. Ray could never tell if Gladys meant to sound sarcastic, or whether he was reading more than he should into her words and tone. But then, Jenny'd had a lifetime with her mother, and she couldn't tell either.

"So, Jenny, what are the police doing to find my grandson?"

Before she could respond, Ray spoke up and briefed his mother-in-law on what was happening.

Her voice was harsh. "So, have they found any clues?"

"No. Not yet."

Ray turned his attention to maneuvering the car out of the parking lot. He clenched the steering wheel with hands blanched white.

CHAPTER 16

Martha Hawthorne slumped in her burgundy velvet recliner. Looking out the living room window, she watched the children playing in the Taylor's front yard next door. There were three of them there today. Two belonged to the Taylors—Amanda, nine, and Jason, eleven. The third was Terry Sawyer. He was the same age as Jason and lived a few houses down on the opposite side of the street. His parents had gone to his aunt's funeral and Terry was staying with the Taylors while they were away.

The children played tag. The boys were getting the better of tiny Amanda. Her freckled face was as red as the mass of unruly curls that covered her head.

Looks like Orphan Annie, that one. Was the child from McLaren's old place with them this morning?

She thought about Steve asking about the child. She hadn't meant to be so rude, but she had never made friends with the neighbors. They thought she was a nasty old woman, and it was too late to change that. All because she didn't want kids ruining her gardens. It was all she had left.

Martha tried to remember, but the children's voices rose to such high-pitched squeals distracted her thoughts. She didn't want to hear them or watch them, but today she couldn't look away.

Every morning, after weeding her garden, she tried to find something else to do. She scrubbed her already spotless house or watched one of the perpetual soaps that littered the airways. But always she this chair drew her. Strategically placed just to the right of the burgundy velvet curtains, she could look out with no one seeing her. She could look at the street beyond her door. She could sit in her worn armchair and look at other people's children and other people's grandchildren, and lie to herself that it didn't matter.

She tried to tell herself they had done the proper thing. She had to believe Joe had been right. It was her duty to go along with his decision. He was her husband. Yet, a small, nagging voice at the back of her head kept talking. A voice saying they had been too harsh. Maybe Joe had been wrong. Maybe it was time to end the exile. She looked at the table beside her, and the shoebox with the red ribbon tied around it. Her hand reached out to draw it close.

Then she heard Joe's voice, and her hand dropped back into her lap. But lately, the other voice was getting louder, more persistent. Now, not a day went by that the voice didn't come.

Martha had always prided herself on being strong. She wasn't one of those wimpy women with their handkerchiefs at the ready to dab at their tears. Tears that, to her way of thinking, came pretty conveniently sometimes. She thought of her sister Alice. The Shirley Temple look-alike who got her way with their parents all through childhood, with her big blue eyes and the dimple she could display at will. If the put-on smile hadn't gotten what she wanted, the pouts and the tears that she could make flow at a drop of a hat, and usually did. Even their teachers had been under Alice's spell. Martha hated her.

The dislike had been mutual. Alice knew Martha was the only one she couldn't fool. Martha learned early who was the apple of their parent's eye. And Alice basked in all their attention. She'd been quite content to watch Martha, plain and ungainly, sit in her shadow. Martha vowed she would never be like her.

And she wasn't. She kept her emotions in check. Nobody could call her weak. She didn't cry at the drop of a hat and she didn't waste time on make-up or fancy clothes. Joe had been proud of her too, said he didn't want a woman who wore her heart on her sleeve. No, to him things were kept private—especially family disgraces.

Like that day eighteen years ago...

Eighteen years, Martha. That's a long time. Time it was over and done with. Nobody's going to care now. Times have changed. You have to, too.

No! Joe would be mad.

Joe's dead. You're not. It's time. It's way pastime. *Do it.*

No. She couldn't. Cecily had been wrong to marry that man. Joe had been right to send their daughter away. They couldn't let her disgrace the family like that. Yes, she and Joe had been right about their decision. He'd made her promise never to contact her and she hadn't.

But he's dead now.

He'll know.

No, he won't. He's dead.

Martha thought about how many times her hand had reached out, almost picked up the phone, almost let her fingers dial the number. She had the number. Memorized. Even when Cecily had moved, and she had, frequently, Martha memorized each new number. She wrote and rewrote it until it was as familiar as her own. Then she'd put it away in the shoebox. The one she kept hidden in the bottom of her nightie drawer. Kept it hidden in case Joe found it, just like all the letters she had kept. She'd found a pretty red ribbon to tie around the box. Now, the time had faded and frayed the ribbon.

She looked at the box. It sat on the table where she'd put it the week after Joe died. The letters inside were yellowed and fragile from frequent readings. At first, Cecily had pleaded with Martha to relent and let her bring her grandson to see them. Now, she just sent a school picture every year, and a card on her birthday and Christmas.

Pick up the phone. Call her.

She's probably moved again. Her number won't be the same. It's been five years since she sent me her number.

You won't know till you try.

Martha looked at the silent phone. Joe had been gone for over a year now, and she still couldn't make herself do it. What would she say? She never could say she was sorry. All those years... Cecily shouldn't have married him.

Martha looked out the window and saw the eager faces, smiling and laughing as the children chased each other around the yard.

"No wonder the neighbors don't plant a garden. Those kids would have it trampled in a heartbeat."

She thought of her own heart and the irregular beating she tried to ignore. It was happening more often lately, not just coming when she'd been working too hard. Now it even woke her in the night.

Should go to the doctor.

What's he gonna do? The old ticker is just wearing out.

Might be some medicine to calm it down. Make it stop feeling like a locomotive running out of control.

He didn't help Joe any.

He told you there was nothing anybody could do for Joe. Massive heart attack. Nothing to do about that. Too much damage to the old pumper.

Well, there's probably nothing he's gonna do for me. He'll just tell me the same thing.

Now, Doc Crawford was good to you. Remember when Cecily had meningitis?

I remember.

We would have lost her if it hadn't been for him.

Martha thought of her daughter lying curled up in a fetal position, pale as the bleached sheets at St Joseph's Hospital. The unruly curls that Martha brushed for half an hour every morning lay like a damp dishrag around her tiny face. The dark mat of hair was a sharp contrast to the lifeless color of her skin. An intravenous line inserted in a tiny vein in her arm gave her the fluid she couldn't drink. She would whimper every time the nurses ran in the antibiotics. Martha would hold her in her arms and pray for her to get better. Doc Crawford had stayed with her the first night as her lethargy deteriorated into a coma, checking her every thirty minutes until the next morning when she finally roused. He was at her bedside frequently over the next few days until Cecily was well again.

Yes. Doc Crawford had been good to them.

Martha remembered Cecily as a child, smiling up at her, following her everywhere. It warmed her heart. She wanted to feel that warmth again. She reached for the phone, felt the unyielding plastic, and tried to pick up the handset. Fear of the consequences prevented her from doing it.

Would Cecily hate her? Her hand returned to her lap. She stared unseeing out the window. The boisterous activity of the children next door went unnoticed. Her gnarled hands worked the folds of her dress into a damp, wrinkled mass.

CHAPTER 17

When Ray's Mustang turned onto Elm Street, Jenny sighed with relief. Only a few cars continued their vigil. Maybe they had gone home for supper, or maybe they had gone to join the search for Clayton. She hoped it was the latter.

Ray maneuvered around a media van partially blocking the driveway. Jenny saw her mother's pursed lips as she looked up and down the tree-lined street with its moderate-sized homes and well cared for lawns.

Was she deciding if the neighborhood was good enough for her daughter or if her daughter was good enough for it? Immediately, Jenny reprimanded herself. People change. Her mother was here for her now, and that was all that mattered. Jenny undid her seatbelt and took the house keys out of her purse.

"So, this is where you're living now. How can you afford this big house?"

"Mom, the house isn't expensive. Mr. McLaren, the owner, is in a nursing home right now, and his son just wanted it rented to someone who wasn't going to destroy it. I've promised to do some fixing up for a reduced rent."

"Are you sure there aren't other catches?"

"No, Mom. There are no other catches."

"Well, it just seems like a bigger house than you need or can afford. You always did think you deserved better. Wanting to go to that fancy college. What did you need to go there for anyway? And now you're married and got a child. That's your job. See, you wasted your time thinking about going off to college. Your son and your husband, that's your job."

Jenny wanted to remind her mother that she and Ray had separated and she had no intention of going back to him. The sooner her mother realized it the better. Not something to get into now, though. Her mother's view on marriage was rigid. Once you tied the knot, you lived with it no matter what. How many times had her mother reminded her how she had stayed in her marriage because divorce was not an option? Jenny remembered her father's tight-lipped silence and wondered which of her parents had *really* sacrificed themselves to those ideals. Gladys liked control. She had the knack for finding the only rain cloud in an otherwise sunny sky.

A muscle in Jenny's neck twitched. Jumping out of the back seat, she slammed the door behind her. She saw her mother's sharp look and waited for the reprimand. Gladys must have thought better of it. Her pursed lips remained closed as she followed her daughter into the house.

The phone was ringing. Jenny raced to the kitchen. By the time she reached the phone, she was out of breath and panted a hello into the receiver. A flush crept up her cheeks as she gripped the phone. "Hello. Hello. Is someone there?"

Her tone was bright with hope and anticipation. Ray followed her into the kitchen and stood waiting for news. Jenny felt the blood drain from her cheeks, and her face distorted in horror. Closing her eyes, she screamed into the phone. "No. No. I didn't hurt him! I didn't kill my son! How can you say something like that?"

Ray was beside her in two steps. He wrenched the phone from Jenny's white-knuckled hand and barked into the receiver. "Who is this?'

A loud click, then the whine of the dial tone.

Jenny screamed, "Oh, Ray! They said I killed Clayton."

"Damn perverts. Got nothing better to do. Just never mind. They're crazy." He pulled her into his arms and held her against him. He gently massaged the back of her neck, his anger dissipated by her greater need. Over his head, he saw his mother-in-law watching from the doorway. He saw the realization suddenly hit her that the situation was more serious than a child being lost after wandering away from home.

Always a practical woman, Gladys came into the kitchen and began opening cupboards. She filled the coffeepot, then rummaged through the refrigerator to find something to eat. Ray led Jenny back into the living room, leaving Gladys to prepare supper.

They ate quietly. After supper, they moved to the living room. Ray flipped on the television. At least it gave them something to focus on besides each other's faces and covered the gaps in their stilted conversation. There was only so much they had to say to each other, and that accomplished within their first half-hour together.

Occasionally, the ringing of the telephone broke the silence. Each time, Jenny jumped with a hope intertwined with fear. Ray answered the calls. He kept them brief, once coming to tell her that Myrtle and Steve had asked how she was doing, and once for Detective Jarvis to give them a progress report. There was no progress.

She watched the television with unseeing eyes. When her mother rummaged through her purse and brought out a package of cigarettes, Jenny roused from her fog enough to protest.

"Mom, we don't smoke in the house."

"You don't, I do. And I've been dying for one for two hours now!"

"Clayton's allergic to smoke."

"Well, Clayton's not here now. And I need a smoke!"

Her mother defiantly took out a cigarette and put it to her lips. The lighter poised and ready to flick into action. Jenny opened her mouth, but before she could speak, Ray interrupted.

"I need a smoke too, and some air. Gladys, why don't we have a look at the backyard? You and I can have a smoke at the same time. Jenny's got a really nice garden planted out there—tomatoes and sweet corn and green beans. Let's go check it out."

His tone was conversational but held an edge of authority. He had never stood up to her mother before. He had noticed the garden. That was a surprise. Jenny. Maybe he *was* changing.

A loud gush of air came from between Gladys' pursed lips. Taking the cigarette out of her mouth, she rose and stomped out of the living room. Jenny heard the slam of the backdoor. A muscle in the back of her neck twitched. She reached up and massaged it. The pain eased only slightly. Maybe she needed to stand up o her mother more often. She was a grown woman now. An unconscious grin teased the corner of her mouth. Her daughter, and ex-son-in-law's defiance definitely shocked her mother.

Her simple, "Thanks Mom," on their return caused a surprised look to flicker across Gladys' face. She only nodded, but was there some degree of respect for her daughter in that nod?

After hours of trying to pass the evening with stumbling attempts at conversation, it was a relief when, at ten o'clock, Ray announced he was tired and going to bed.

"I want to be at the community center first thing. Detective Jarvis will be there to organize the day's search."

Jenny sighed, glad for an excuse to be alone. Unable to face seeing Clayton's face flashing across the eleven o'clock news, she turned the TV off. Bringing sheets and a blanket downstairs, she made up a bed for herself on the living room sofa. Her mother had made a feeble protest at staying in Jenny's room. Without comment, Ray retreated to the family room.

After tossing and turning on the makeshift bed for what seemed like hours, Jenny got up and wandered into the kitchen. The family room door was closed, and no light filtered through the cracks. At least he's getting some sleep. Jenny cursed Ray's ability to sleep no matter what was going on. She poured herself a glass of milk and put it into the microwave. Maybe the warm liquid would help her get some sleep.

How many times had she given Clayton warm milk when he couldn't sleep? Where was he now? Was he sleeping peacefully somewhere? Had someone tucked him into a nice bed? What were they doing to her son? She tried to force the ugly thoughts away.

Visions of his short life passed through her mind. The first flutter of him inside her, her swelling body as he grew, the shock and pain of the contractions that had brought him screaming into the world, the first time he smiled, his first steps... Her fist hit the kitchen counter. They had to find him! There were still too many firsts she and Clayton had to experience. She had to be there for his first day at his new school, his first baseball game, his first girlfriend... Yes, Clayton needed her to be there. He needed her praise and support for each new stepping stone.

She drained the glass of milk and walked back to the living room. Still too restless to sleep, she went to the picture window. Clayton was out there somewhere. She pulled back a corner of the living room curtain and looked out. Street lamps gave soft illumination to the starless sky.

It was late, but people continued to watch the house. She glanced at the clock on the mantle, eleven-twenty. Her gaze caught the picture farther along the mantle, the photo of Clayton taken on his fourth birthday. She'd had it blown up to an eight-by-ten and bought a fancy frame for it. Now, that was all she had—pictures and memories. She had to believe that the police would find him soon. She looked back at the window.

Through a sliver in the curtains, she watched the cars and vans lining both sides of the Street—reporters and spectators watching, waiting. Some had binoculars trained on her house. Television cameras, video recorders, and telephoto lenses protruded from vehicle windows.

Why were they here? What were they expecting her to do? Why weren't they out looking for Clayton? She watched, unable to move away. She wanted to yell at them. Stop watching me! Go find my child. Frozen, she stood and looked out the window, careful to stay hidden behind the folds of the heavy damask drapes.

They started coming yesterday, right after the six-o'clock news broadcast; parking in front of her house, knocking on her door. Vultures searching for any scrap of excitement—they fed off her misery. Last night she had wanted to go out and ask if they knew where he was, if anyone had seen him. Detective Jarvis stopped her, reminding her if they had any news, they would tell the police stationed outside.

Tonight, there was no one to stop her. Jenny pulled open the front door and went out to speak to them. They rushed at her.

"Do you know anything about my son?" she cried.

They didn't listen. They came closer, cameras flashing, microphones shoved in her face, hurling questions at her. Pushing and shoving, they demanded answers. "Did your ex-husband take your son? Did you do something to him? Was it an accident? Where did you put the body?"

Jenny realized her mistake. Their only interest was the sensational. They didn't care about finding Clayton. She ran back to the house. They surrounded her, continuing to barrage her with questions. She tried to cover her ears to drown them out, she tried to get to the house. Bodies blocked her way, hands reached out to grab her. Her head pounded. She had trouble catching her breath. She tried to fight them off.

Suddenly Steve was there. He pushed through the crowd, pulled her into the protection of his arms. She sank against the soft cotton of his T-shirt. "Leave her alone. Go home, or go help find her son."

The crowd pressed closer, almost knocking the two of them over. Steve's fist struck out. The crowd backed off enough that he could get her back to the house. Yanking the front door open, he shoved her inside and slammed the door as the spectators mobbed the house. Steve secured the lock, then led her to the sofa. He pulled her into his arms. With one hand, he called the police to disperse the mob outside.

A police car arrived within minutes. Its flashing red lights dissuaded most of the onlookers and they hurried away. A few paid more attention to the two burly officers and the billy clubs they waved at them. The officers threatened the spectators with charges of trespassing, harassment, or anything else to force them to leave Mrs. Kingsley alone if they didn't keep a fifty-foot distance.

With the crowd controlled, the officers came to speak to Jenny. Going back to the door was an effort, her steps robotic, her body a jumbled mass of unconnected nerve endings that had difficulty following her commands. She saw the glances of pity pass between the officers, but didn't care. The hopeful question in her eyes dashed by the regretful shake of their heads. There was still no news.

They told her not to hesitate to call them again if the crowd continued to harass her. Steve bolted the door after them. He checked the living room drapes, ensuring no curious eyes could find a crack to peer through. Jenny huddled on the sofa, letting the shroud-like darkness of the room surround her. It was the same blackness surrounding her heart. Steve sat beside her, silent, but there, holding her in the safety of his arms. One part of her wanted to ask him about his picture at the police station, another part needed the security of his body against her.

Could he have anything to do with Clayton's disappearance? She had to know. Backing out of his hold, she took a big breath and started. "Steve...I was at the police station today—"

"Yes. You saw my picture, didn't you?" His eyes met hers. He shifted so he could face her, continuing to keep eye contact. "It's a long story."

"Please, Steve, I need to know. I can't sleep anyway. "

Steve told her the story of his best friend Kelly, his relationship with Cheryl, and the baby. He told her how Kelly had died and of Joe Roberts's involvement. He told her about the hate that festered between them and how Roberts still harassed him whenever he could. He left out nothing. His voice was low and edged with bitterness. "A couple of years ago, there was a child who went missing from a campsite just out of town. He was six years old. Roberts pulled me into the station and questioned me, even though I'd been out of town visiting my sister at the time."

Afraid of what his answer might be, Jenny turned her face slightly away. "What happened to the child?"

Steve put his hand gently on her chin and turned her face to meet his gaze. "They found the child in the woods where he'd wandered away from his parents. They said he died of pneumonia. Jenny..." His fingers would not let her turn away again. "I promise you I had nothing to do with it."

She nodded her head slightly. The deep pools of his eyes seemed so clear and sincere. She wanted to believe him. He pulled her back into the shelter of his arms and they found a refuge together.

CHAPTER 18

At some point, Jenny fell asleep. When she woke, it was morning, and she lay fully dressed on the sofa, a light blanket covering her. Steve was gone. Ray and her mother had somehow slept through all the commotion of the previous evening. She was thankful for that. She found a note on the coffee table.

Mom will be over in the morning. Hope you got some sleep. See you tomorrow.

Steve

Her head felt as if a ten-pound weight sat on top of it. She rose slowly from the couch. Her body ached, and she had no idea what time it was. With the curtains drawn, the room remained in darkness. The oppressive lack of sunlight added more pressure to the weight on her head. Unable to stand it anymore, she made her way to the window. She drew the curtains back, letting the early morning sun burst into the room and erase the shadows. Some of the pressure in her head lessened. She hoped Tylenol would clear the rest.

The street was quiet. The vigilantes and media had finally gone home. Jenny went to the kitchen. The family room door was open, the room empty. Ray must have already gone to join the day's search party. Putting on the kettle, she made a pot of tea. Soon, her mother would wake, and Jenny wanted to get rid of her headache before facing her. She never knew what her mother's mood would be. Jenny kept herself busy tidying the kitchen and family room. Letting her sleep as long as possible was the best idea.

Yet part of her wanted to go wake her, tell her Clayton was still missing, tell her they needed to go join the search. But she hesitated—surely she would be up soon.

Jenny needed to be doing something. She went to the living room and, hiding behind the heavy living-room curtains, watched those watching her. When she had awakened at seven-thirty, the street had been empty. Now, at ten to nine, the vultures lined the street again.

Suddenly, there was a flurry of activity. Reporters were getting out of their vans; cameramen were right behind them, popping lens caps. They were focusing on something beyond her line of vision. Spectators lobbied for a front-row seat on whatever was happening. The camera flashes and microphones stuck in her face last night had been more of an intrusion than Jenny could bear, yet despite her fear of being seen, she had to know what was happening.

She inched back the curtains and watched as the media rushed, scrambling past onlookers, one trying to get ahead of the next. They were making a beeline towards the sidewalk directly in front of her house. A black sedan pulled into the driveway, but tinted windows hid the occupants. Jenny's heart raced as the car stopped close to the house and two dark-suited men exited. The first one was over six feet, his lean frame disguising the muscles beneath the cloth fibers of his suit. His companion stood half a head shorter, his linebacker shape distending the dark linen material with each step. Pushing away the microphones stuck in their faces, they strode toward the house. With each step, Jenny's heart rate increased.

She was halfway to the door before the sharp rap of knuckles hit the wood. By the second knock, she was turning the handle and pulling the heavy door inward. Jenny felt as if her heart had suddenly stopped beating. Who were these men? Then she saw the flash of their badges. Why were they here? Did they have news of Clayton? She looked at them expectantly. But instead of hope, she noted the startled look in their eyes, quickly masked by professionalism. What had caused it? Was she younger than they had envisioned, or were their expectations of someone quite different? Whatever their reaction had been, it was gone, leaving only blank, courteous respect.

"Mrs. Kingsley?"

"Have you found Clayton?"

The two men watched her, their gazes intent on her face. Their eyes examined her. Eyes trained to seek for any revelation of character, or a hint of something concealed.

Jenny's heart pounded in her chest. So loud they must be able to hear it, but they made no sign. Jenny glared at them. "Do you know something?" Neither officer answered.

Leaning against the doorframe for support, Jenny stared anxiously at them, waiting for some sign of hope, some sign that would wipe her fears away. Their eyes, devoid of expression, refused to respond to her. Their voices, when they spoke, were flat and quiet.

"Mrs. Kingsley, I'm Detective Sanders and this is Detective Hansen."

Jenny's voice rose insistently. "Have you news about my son?"

"Detective Jarvis asked us to come and talk to you. May we come in? We're from Sutton County Police Department."

Jenny stepped aside, allowing them to enter. She closed the door behind them. Why were police from Sutton County coming to see her? They covered the area west of Scottsville.

She crossed the living room, her shoeless feet making soft padding sounds on the carpet. Seating herself on the sofa, she waited while the two detectives sat across from her. Her voice was stronger than she felt. "Do you know something?"

"As we said, we're from Sutton County." Detective Sanders paused. "There is...There has been a child found in our area..."

Jenny felt her heart stop. A strangled cry came out of her mouth. "Is it Clayton?"

"We're not sure."

"But Clayton knows his name—"

Then, like a tidal wave of frigid water smashing her in the face, the awful realization hit her. The child they had found could not give his name. That meant he was either severely injured or dead. Her mouth went dry, and a knife stabbed through her heart. Her body suddenly flushed with so much heat she felt as if she had walked into a furnace. Then, just as suddenly, the heat disappeared and a chilling frost filled every cell of her body. She went numb. She couldn't feel the lips that opened like a crack in an icy lake nor the frozen tongue as it tried to form the question she didn't want the answer to.

"Is he hurt? What? Tell me!"

The two detectives exchanged glances, the younger of the two finding something of interest on the wall above her head. Sanders turned his guarded eyes back to her.

The keening moan of an animal in pain rose from somewhere deep inside her.

"Now—we're not sure it's your son. A body found this morning—it's a child of about five or six—he has blonde hair—we need you to come with us—to let us know..."

Her heart had stopped pounding. In fact, it didn't seem to be beat at all. Jenny struggled into her shoes, grabbed her purse, then trudged behind the detectives, following them to the sedan. The media surged—camera bulbs flashed, questions hurled. Hansen used a long black billy to warn them back. Sanders opened the rear door and strapped her seat belt around her. He slid behind the wheel and started the engine. Hansen climbed in beside him. The sun shone through the car windows, but Jenny didn't see it. Her frozen state allowed neither light nor warmth to penetrate.

Sanders backed out of the driveway, scattering the crowd as he went. Somewhere in the distance, Jenny heard the babble of voices raised and mingling together as the people on the street lunged toward the car. Faces pressed against the windows—faces distorted by the curved glass, noses wide and flat, eyes huge and glowing yellow from the glare of the sun. Jenny closed her eyes and willed the car to speed away, to get far away from those monstrous faces.

She felt the car turn out of the driveway and head down the road, but she was afraid to open her eyes, afraid that the distorted faces remained plastered on the windows. Leaning her head back against the car's seat, she tried to make her mind go blank.

But then words came to replace the faces. Only two words, but they filled the empty spaces of her brain. Clayton. Dead. Two words that kept repeating over and over. Clayton. Dead. Clayton dead. Like some child's cruel rhyme, they chanted on and on. She pushed the words away from each other. Like wrestlers in a ring, before the bell has rung, they face each other, ready to lunge at each other and intermingle forever. She had to keep them apart. To let them come together and intertwine themselves would be more than she could bear. So she sat immobile in the back seat of the vehicle, warding off the demons in her head.

The car stopped abruptly. Jenny had no idea how long the drive had lasted, or where she was. She looked through the tinted glass. They were parked in front of a multi-story yellow brick building. The two detectives got out. Jenny wanted to stay where she was. Maybe if she stayed here, refused to move, maybe this would all go away. Maybe someone else would come to identify his or her child. But there was Detective Sanders, opening the door for her, waiting patiently for her to get out.

Jenny wanted to scream in protest, but she slid obediently out of the car and followed the two men up the stone stairs and through the double glass doors of the building. They crossed the hall to an elevator and Hansen pressed the down button. As the elevator descended, Jenny put a hand on her abdomen to control waves of nausea. The lurching stop created another wave. She swallowed hard. Anxious to exit the elevator, she followed the detectives down a corridor with institutional pale green, unadorned walls.

Sanders stopped at a set of double metal fire doors. He held one open, and the group entered a small, nondescript beige office. They passed by a long scarred wooden desk covered with files and books and a woman filing papers into a gray metal file cabinet. They crossed to a door at the far end of the room.

Jenny saw indistinct forms moving beyond the panes of frosted glass. The odors of disinfectant and formaldehyde permeated through the cracks. She put a hand to her nose in a vain attempt to avoid inhaling the fumes.

She waited while sanders slipped through the door. A moment later, he returned with a distinguished, older man with a silver-gray beard. The man grabbed a white lab coat off a hook by the door and slipped it over his operating room greens. The knee-length coat, stained with coffee and pen marks, at least it hid the stains of blood and other bodily fluids.

"Mrs. Kingsley, this is Dr. Murray," said Sanders.

Automatically, Jenny accepted the large, callused hand he extended, her gaze drawn to his serious blue eyes. They seemed to hold a wealth of wisdom and kindness as if he had been through hell and back again. With his warm handshake and gentle smile, Jenny felt some of his strength radiate into her, almost enough to carry her through this ordeal. Stooped shoulders leaned toward her and his eyes searched hers. His voice was at once soft and firm. "Can you do this?"

"I have to know."

"Yes." He nodded slowly. "Is no one with you?"

"His father is out with the search party." Jenny didn't tell him she could have wakened her mother to be with her. She wasn't sure if she had the strength to deal with both this and her mother's unpredictable reaction. If her son was beyond these frosted doors, nothing would ever matter again.

Nodding his head, Dr. Murray's voice took on a clinical tone as he related the information. "This morning, someone found a child in the Tomac River just north of the city. He drowned...we think...yesterday or the day before. We don't have the exact time yet. His body is bloated..."

Jenny searched his face, her eyes pleading. She didn't want to see the child, didn't want to know, but she also didn't want to wonder any longer. She had to know. He must have understood, for he turned and led her through the frosted glass doors into a large sterile room.

The sudden drop in temperature caused her to shiver. She took a breath and inhaled a lung full of frosty air. She almost expected to see the shimmer of frost clinging to some of the metal surfaces. Glaring fluorescent lights reflected off shiny steel cupboards. In the center of the room, a large operating room light shone on a gray metal table. Her eyes caught the glint of stainless steel instruments neatly arranged on one of the gleaming countertops.

The metallic clang of a drawer opening startled her. Turning toward the sound, she saw a steel slab table sliding out of a cabinet in the wall. Taking up only a portion of the table was a small form covered by a thin white plastic sheet. Jenny heard a gasp echo in the silent room and realized it had come from her. Sanders moved to her side. Taking her elbow, he led her toward the table. She tried to focus on the gleaming silver end of the table, avoiding the end with the stark white material and the small body it covered.

After a quick glance at her, Dr. Murray took an edge of the sheet and slowly peeled it back. Her breath caught in her throat, forming a large obstruction. She tried to inhale, but all she managed was a shrill wheeze. Short blonde hairs became visible, then a pale, swollen white face. Eyes bulged out of bony sockets, partially open, staring blankly at nothing. The body and extremities bloated with fluid absorbed from its final resting place in the river.

Her breath on hold, she stared at the boy lying rigid and cold, with only a thin plastic sheet to protect him from the hard steel table. His skin tinged a bluish-white, large purple bruises spread across his left hip. Several bloodless scrapes decorated the outer surface of his leg below the bruise.

She stared at the lifeless form, unable to shift her gaze away. The breath she had been holding finally let go in an audible wheeze. Gathering her strength, she twisted away from the table, away from the still form, away from the form that would never move again. She looked up at Detective Sanders and shook her head. This tiny, bloated body was not her son.

Doctor Murray drew the sheet back over the body and slid the drawer back into the wall. Jenny hurried toward the frosted doors. The clang of metal hitting metal echoed across the sterile room as the drawer snapped closed.

She pushed through the doors, not waiting for the others. Crossing her arms, she tried to rub some warmth back into her body.

CHAPTER 19

Myrtle turned up the radio. Would there be any news about Clayton? Crossing to the kitchen table, she took her cup of tea and sat perched on the edge of the seat. The aroma of fresh apples and cinnamon filled the room. She had just taken pies out of the oven. Steve was going to take her to the community center. A casserole for Jenny was still baking.

The song ended and the announcer's voice came on. Myrtle felt a sudden nervousness, and then the palpitations started. She wrung her hands on the tea towel she had forgotten to put down, wiping away the flour that stuck to her fingers.

Would they say anything about Clayton? Had they found him? Would they report what the police were doing to find the child? Please, God, let them find him soon. Let him be safe.

She and Steve had talked superficially about the child's disappearance, both afraid to delve into the past. The police hadn't come to question Steve yet. Myrtle knew it would only be a matter of time. Then Joe Roberts would come calling. Just like before.

"Pop diva Loretta Leone died today. Narcotic overdose suspected...Governor Taylor has announced he will run in this fall's election..." the radio announcer droned on.

What about Clayton? Is there going to be anything on about him?

"Police are still searching for five-year-old Clayton Kingsley who disappeared from his home in Scottsville two days ago...Clayton is blond-haired, with blue eyes, and was last seen wearing a white T-shirt and blue shorts...If you have any information or were witness to anything that may be of assistance call the police or this station at 1-800-541-2222... Last night, someone broke into Buckley's Variety store.

Myrtle shook her head. That was all. The poor child gone three days now and all they could give was thirty seconds of airtime.

CHAPTER 20

C layton heard the slam of the cabin door above him, a thud as the board pushed into the metal latch. A shudder ran down his spine.

He's back!

The throbbing began over his eyes. It spread to fill his head. Clayton closed his eyes and curled his body into a tight ball. He rubbed at his forehead. The pain wouldn't stop.

He waited. He knew the man would come soon. He knew he would open the trapdoor and check on him. Clayton tried to press himself into the blue-green mat that he lay on. Pulling the blanket over his body, he pretended to be asleep. Involuntarily, he shuddered. Above him, he heard the shuffling of heavy feet across the wooden floor, scraping as the chest of drawer moved away from the wall—the dresser that hid the trap door.

He couldn't stop shaking. The man would open the trapdoor soon. Then he would reach down and pull him out of the hole. Clayton wanted to fight. He wanted to kick the man or bite him.

Mommy didn't like him biting.

He remembered when his cousin Jamie had taken his dump truck and hit him with it and Clayton bit his cousin on the arm. He'd spent a long time sitting on a chair in the corner. But when Jamie called him "a flea-biting cur," Mommy made Jamie sit in another chair until they could both behave.

I don't think she'd be mad at me for biting the man, though. It would be worth sitting on a chair all day if I could bite him and run away. I don't know how to get home, but I'd find a way. If I bite him, he might hit me again. He might not let me go to the outhouse, or give me any food.

His stomach rumbled.

Maybe Mommy's mad at me for talking to him. But I have to. If I don't answer him, or if he sees me cry, he gets angry and hits me. Mommy would be mad at him for hitting me.

Clayton waited for the door to open. If he climbed the wooden ladder, he could just reach to push on the wooden planks, but they were too heavy for him to move. Once, when he was sure the man was out, he had tried to open it, but the boards hadn't budged, even with all his weight pushing against them.

He heard a creak, and the door opened. Light filled the space. Clayton shuddered. He tried to stay quiet, but his body betrayed him. His stomach growled loudly. Was it lunchtime? It seemed like hours since he had eaten. And he needed to pee.

If he were good, maybe the man would take him back to his mother. He prayed every night. Maybe his mother had come for him. He looked up at the opening door. The light blinded him. All he could see was the man's dark form peering into the hole.

The man could lift the trap door easily. He could lift it any time he wanted and check on Clayton. And he checked often. It was as if Clayton was a specimen in a bottle to be taken out and observed, examined from all directions, and then put back in its container until the next time.

I'm like one of those bugs that look bigger when you see them with the magic glass Mommy gave me for my birthday.

He lay still, just like one of the dead bugs on his slides.

A routine was in place. Every morning, the man brought him out of the hole and gave him toast and cereal. When Clayton finished eating, the man put the rope on his arm and made him walk ahead of him to the outhouse. After he was done, the man took him back to the house, removed the rope, and shoved him back into the hole. The same would happen at lunch and supper. After he was back in the hole, Clayton would escape to sleep. He was tired. He slept a lot. There was nothing else to do. Nothing to do but sleep and wait.

Sunshine filled the small space as the trapdoor lifted. This time, instead of wasting time cowering in fear, Clayton looked around him. When the door was closed, very little light filtered through to the dugout. Now he could see most of the area. It was about three times his length one way and twice his length the other way. There were some wooden crates piled on the floor by one wall. That was all there was down here, except for the woven mat and one worn blanket.

I wonder what is in the crates.

He saw the man's jean-covered legs coming down the ladder. Suddenly, a long arm reached out toward him. A gruff voice commanded: "Get over here, boy."

Clayton went slowly toward the man.

A large, hairy hand grasped his right wrist and pulled as Clayton hurried up the ladder. It felt like his arm was being pulled out of the socket. He made his feet go faster to lessen the pressure. Then he was in the cabin. The man nudged him to the table. At least this time, he had put the peanut butter sandwich on a plate. Clayton ate slowly—the longer he took, the longer he was out of his cave. He swatted at the flies that tried to share his food.

"Hurry up, boy. I don't have all day."

Clayton kept his eyes on his plate. He munched on his food. He didn't care if the man hit him again. It was worth it to be out of the dark space. He felt a nudge on his back.

"I said hurry up." The man looped the rope in his hands.

When the last crumb was gone, Clayton looked up at his captor. A rope looped around his wrist. He rose and followed the man out of the cabin. Once outside, the man shoved him ahead and Clayton made his way to the outhouse. He looked from side to side, checking for a way to escape. But he was careful, careful not to move his head and draw the man's attention.

He did the same on the way back from the outhouse. He saw more, the old gray truck parked in the ramshackle shed and the woods surrounding the cabin, and the single car-width track that led away from the cabin. There was a break in the tree line behind the cabin. Broken branches revealed a footpath leading into the woods.

"Get moving, boy."

A hand shoved his shoulder, and Clayton stumbled. He landed hard on the ground. Pain stabbed his left knee as it grazed a small rock in the long grass. Blood poured from the slash and streamed down his leg.

"Now look at what you've done, stupid kid."

Clayton wiped at the blood, but the rope yanked him upright. He staggered behind the man to the cabin. Inside, the man washed the blood off with a stained tea towel and slapped a bandage over the inch-long gaping cut. At least the bleeding had settled.

"Here, clean your leg up." He handed Clayton the still-damp tea towel.

Clayton wiped at the blood that had trickled down his leg.

"Do you want a cookie?"

Clayton nodded and devoured the oatmeal cookie. The taste of the cookie still fresh on his tongue made his mouth water for more. The plate of cookies sat inches away from him. His stomach growled. His voice trembled. "May I have another one?"

"Just one."

This one, he ate slowly, enjoying each bite. Maybe he would bite the man another day.

"It's time."

Clayton rose and followed the man to the trapdoor. He went down the ladder and curled up on the mat. His tummy full, he slept.

CHAPTER 21

"**M**ommy. Mommy, come and get me."

The words drifted through to Jenny's semiconscious state. She floated somewhere between sleep and wakefulness, somewhere where not all senses roused with the same speed. Her ears heard the voice, Clayton's voice, but her mind jumbled the thought process. She tried to open her eyes. Her lids felt heavy and resisted movement as if someone glued them shut while she slept. She tried to wipe away the sleep holding her eyes closed, but her arms refused to move.

"Mommy. Please...come get me. I don't like the dark."

She fought through the layers of cotton batting shrouding her thinking. Layer by layer, she peeled them away, each one bringing her closer to full consciousness. Her eyelids fought past the grainy, sand-like substance. Finally, her eyes opened, and she peered into the darkness. Not even a sliver of moonlight came through the bedroom window.

Vision was no help to her now. Jenny focused on the only sense that was her hearing. She closed her eyes and lay listening for the faint voice in the darkness, a voice that might lead her to her son. But now the room was silent. An oppressive stillness surrounded her, like a weight pressing her deeper and deeper into the bed.

She fought the urge to drift back into a safe unconscious state, where her world was normal again and Clayton lay sleeping peacefully in his bed. Her mind was groggy from the sleeping pill Myrtle had insisted she take last evening. Why had she taken it? She had a vague recollection of Myrtle coming over to check on her just as she had every night since Clayton had been missing.

"You look terrible, dear. You need sleep. Just take one of these."

Myrtle handed her a bottle of red capsules. Without comment, Jenny had taken them from her. She hadn't planned on taking any, but she didn't have the energy to protest. She slipped them into the pocket of her sundress and thanked Myrtle for her kindness.

Jenny didn't know how she would have gotten through the last few days if Myrtle hadn't been there for her. She had her mother, but sometimes that was less comfort than being alone. She was relieved when her mother went back home. Despite her protests that she could not leave her daughter at a time like this, she had business to attend to and Jenny's invalid father to look after. She didn't say that she might miss her weekly hair appointment or euchre with her friends. Her mother was careful about that. She made a vague promise to return after dealing with her business.

Jenny hoped her business would keep her away longer than a few days. Immediately, she felt guilty. She knew her mother meant well. It wasn't her fault that she got on Jenny's nerves. If only she wasn't so controlling and opinionated. And why did she always worry more about appearances than her own family? She couldn't think about her mother now. There were too many old hurts, too much pain. She couldn't waste energy or emotion on the past, she needed to concentrate on finding Clayton.

She recalled last night when Myrtle insisted Jenny take one of the pills to help her sleep. She'd even gone into the kitchen and brought Jenny back a glass of water. She stood over her until she'd swallowed the small red capsule. Then she made them a pot of herbal tea and insisted Jenny eat some of her freshly baked oatmeal cookies. Myrtle's compassionate ways were such a contrast to her mother's.

Jenny let her eyes slide closed, remaining conscious of any sound. There was none. No tiny voice penetrated the stillness. Opening her eyes again, she stared up at the ceiling. She couldn't see through the darkness. The words came back to her.

'*Mommy, please come and get me. I don't like the dark.*' She thought of Clayton somewhere in the dark and tears flowed down her pale face. The pillow became soaked, but she couldn't move, her body frozen as if she'd taken a paralyzing drug instead of a sleeping pill.

A chill ran down her spine. Visions danced in her head. Not of sugar plum fairies, but of tiny bodies torn and bleeding, limbs hanging by tender threads as they danced around freshly dug four-foot graves, their shoeless feet sinking in the soft earth. Tiny blue bodies with bloated faces. Clayton's face, bloated and blue, dancing above a shallow grave.

No! No! Please God, no. She shook her head, trying desperately to erase the images.

She had to believe he was alive. She had heard his voice. He must be alive. Jenny couldn't, wouldn't, think of him being dead. She saw the still form lying under the stark white sheet in the morgue. She shivered, remembering the chill of that sterile room. Couldn't someone have found a decent blanket to wrap him in, something to keep him warm from the frost that permeated the room, protection from the stone coldness of the stainless steel table he lay on?

Ridiculous thoughts, she knew. That body was past feeling cold or hot, or anything. His dead fish eyes would never see again. He would never feel a mother's arms around him, never have another goodnight kiss, never…From a deep recess of her mind came an unbidden vision of Clayton's face on the lifeless form. No, no!

Mentally, she pulled back the white sheet and saw the face of the child in the morgue. She stopped herself. She couldn't dwell on that child. His life was over. She said a silent prayer for his mother, then one for herself that it had not been Clayton.

CHAPTER 22

Unable to exorcise the visions that haunted her sleep, Jenny got up and made coffee. She hoped it would take away the fuzzy state of pill-induced sleep. It didn't work. Finally, she gave in and lay on the sofa.

Until last night, she had barely slept more than a few hours. And now, with the drug still affecting her body, she felt exhausted. She dozed, troubled by frequent visions of children floating face down in a stagnant pond or decomposing under a carpet of brush. Loud knocking on the front door broke into Jenny's restless sleep. It was a welcome release from the images.

The lethargy that had invaded her body since Clayton's disappearance seemed so normal that she couldn't remember feeling different. She uncurled from the sofa and made her way to the front door. Instinctively, she drew back the curtains and checked the driveway. This had become a necessary habit. So many neighbors, media, and strangers gawked from the street. Some had the gall to knock on her door and harass her with questions or give her their jaded opinions. It stunned Jenny that people could believe she might have harmed her child.

At first, police cars had patrolled the street and kept the bloodhounds at bay, but with the passing days, the frequency of their patrols decreased. Though the number of spectators shrank, there were still unknown people staring as they walked by, some trying to peer through the curtains.

A police cruiser parked in her driveway made her heart leap into her throat and she rushed to the door. Chad Evans stood waiting, his hands working the stiff fabric of his uniform cap.

"Did you find him?" She blurted before the door was fully open.

"No ma'am. Sorry, nothing new." He paused. "I need to ask you some questions."

Jenny stepped back and let the deputy cross the threshold. "Come in."

He followed her into the living room. She took him to be in his early thirties, about the same age as Steve. Were they friends? Or had they gone to the same school? She'd noticed the nod that passed between them the first time Evans came to the house. Maybe Steve fixed his car? Whatever their acquaintance, it had nothing to do with the problem of finding Clayton.

"Would you like some coffee or iced tea?" Jenny asked.

"Iced tea would be nice. Sure is a hot one out there today."

Jenny nodded. She guessed that was the right response. In the past few days, she hadn't even noticed the weather. It must be warm though. She'd put on shorts and a T-shirt when she got up this morning. Did she feel hot? No, her body was still too numb to feel anything.

"Come into the kitchen. We can talk there."

Turning, she walked to the kitchen, leaving him to follow. She took two glasses out of the cupboard and filled them with iced tea. She slid one across the table to the seated deputy, then sat across from him. Evans had taken out his notepad and laid it open on the table. Her eyebrows rose in question.

"I just need to check a few facts with you, Mrs. Kingsley."

"Please, call me Jenny."

"Ah yes, Jenny." He paused. "What can you tell me about the split-up with your husband? You not divorced, are you?"

"No. We're separated. Is this necessary?"

"I'm sorry, but it's important to know as much as we can about everyone involved."

"Is Ray a suspect?"

"Anyone who could have access to your son is under investigation. We have to rule out everyone."

"Ray isn't a suspect is he?" Jenny heard her voice becoming shrill as she repeated the question. "He didn't take Clayton. He was at work."

"We check everything. We've talked to his boss and he was there...except for his lunch hour. Now, about your marriage?" Evans twirled the pen as he waited for her answer.

Jenny looked down at the hands in her lap, then back up into the intense gaze of the man seated across from her. "We're separated. I left him a couple of months ago when I moved here. We hadn't seen him since then."

"Was he angry?"

"Well, yes—but not enough to take Clayton—he wasn't a really good father. I mean—he wasn't mean to Clayton or anything like that. He just wasn't very interested in him."

"Did he ever hurt him?"

"No!"

"Are you sure?"

The shrillness returned. "Yes, I'm sure."

"Does Mr. Kingsley have a temper or a problem with anger?"

The blue eyes watched her, intent on any reaction.

"Well, sometimes he would get mad, especially when he was drinking."

"Was that often?"

She looked at her hands holding the frosted glass of iced tea before facing him again.

"It was becoming more frequent in the last year."

"Did he ever hurt you?"

What should she say? It had been more the constant, emotional degrading that made her decide to leave. He'd only started pushing her around in the last few months. She wanted to forget the time he kicked her. How could she tell this stranger about that? How could she tell him how Ray's yelling had scared Clayton? He had never hurt Clayton...yet. "No."

She glanced at the officer and saw the disbelief unspoken in his eyes. Not able to bear his inspection, she looked away. Suddenly, she was aware of a blast of heat that filled the kitchen, making her tongue feel like a piece of coarse-grade sandpaper. Grabbing the glass of iced tea, she put it to her lips and swallowed deeply before putting the glass back on the table. Intent on the swirling patterns made by the dark fluid, his next question startled her.

"What about last February when Clayton went to Dresden Memorial Hospital?"

Her hand jerked, almost spilling the ice tea. The sandpaper thickened. Her mouth felt as parched as if she'd been lost in a desert. She ran her tongue over her lips. She could feel her heart pounding as she turned a startled gaze to face him. "What?"

Evans glanced at his notebook before meeting her gaze again.

"They treated Clayton at the Dresden Hospital on February 11 of this year for a pulled elbow."

She felt anger flushing her face as she raised her voice. "That was an accident!"

"Was it?"

"Yes! Clayton was playing on the monkey bars at the park. He got stuck at the top. He was crying and scared. Ray had to climb up and get him. When he helped him to get loose, Clay's arm dislocated. The doctor told us it happens all the time in young children." Her voice sounded as shrill as a fishwife. "I was there. Ray didn't hurt Clayton!"

"Okay, Mrs. Kingsley. I just had to ask about it."

His face had softened. Empathy, if not total belief, evident in his eyes. He drained his glass of iced tea, watching her over the rim. Jenny took several deep breaths. She had to remember he was only doing his job. And his job was to find out where Clayton was and who had taken him.

"Well, that's all I need for now."

Wordlessly, Jenny led him to the front door.

CHAPTER 23

Tyrell heard the dogs getting closer. Their ferocious yapping shattered the morning air. Sound waves of each bark hit the tree trunks, bounced off, then echoed through the dense woods. It sounded as if there were fifty of them, but he knew there weren't. He knew about sounds. He knew how sounds echoed off trees, canvas tents, vehicles, anything in its way. He especially knew how gunfire sounded.

The sounds of gunfire came back, surrounding him, suffocating him. He remembered the flashes of light when a bullet hit a concrete object, and the absence of light when it hit a living target. He remembered blood spurting out from that target, first on his fellow soldiers and then on himself. He felt the burning pain as the bullet tore through his skin. And, he felt the searing jolt as it struck bone, embedded in his tibia, and shattered it into a thousand fragments.

Today, he couldn't see the blood gushing from the open wound, oozing into his uniform pants, spreading like ripples in a pond, staining the khaki material. No, he couldn't see the blood today—but the pain, it was there, the same as every day since he'd been shot. Some days were worse, especially if rain was coming.

He remembered the doctor's clinical tone, telling him about the arthritis that would doubtless set into the damaged bone. What he didn't tell him about was the constant pain he would have to endure, or that now his injured leg was shorter and he would have a permanent limp. And he remembered Patty's reaction to his injury. The names she'd called him—cripple, hop-a-long, peg leg. They kept repeating over and over. He heard Patty's taunting laugh still echoing in his head. The Bitch.

The dogs' barking was closer now.

They're starting early. Damn hunters. Should be a law against them making that much noise. There are enough damn laws about everything else. Stupid idiots out hunting rabbits or squirrels, too early in the season for deer. Wouldn't be so bad if they were responsible, but no, they shoot some poor animal for the fun of it and leave it wounded.

He remembered his grandfather's words. 'Now, boy, don't you go shooting no animals just for fun. You shoot it; you make sure you kill it, so it don't suffer. I catch you doing that and you'll get your hide tanned so good you'll never sit for a month of Sundays. And boy, you just kill what you gonna eat, and use whatever you can of the rest.'

He heeded his grandfather's principals and only used the old rifle he gave him to shoot food for his table. He even used as much as he could of the innards and hide. He still wore the hat he trimmed himself with one beauty of a raccoon tail. Wore it all the time. Right proud of it he was. His grandfather would have liked the way he was living, out here with nature, living off the land. He wasn't sure what Gramps would say about the boy. He didn't want to think about that now. The boy was here, and that was done.

He glanced at the dresser. It was quiet down there now. Thank God he'd finally learned to stop his whimpering. Just like the other one. He hadn't been able to make that one a man. He would this one. This one had no interfering woman's skirt-tails to hide behind, sniffling and shaking. This one would be different.

Incessant barking broke through his thoughts. The yelping and howling of several dogs echoed across the clearing around the cabin. They were getting closer. Pain shot down his left leg. Must be another fucking storm coming. He rubbed his scarred limb.

He had had only three months left on his stint with the army. He would have been home free. Then, in the middle of the night, the gunfire started. His troop had been taken off guard. Fifteen men had been hit. Three died right away, two more later that day. The rest had been airlifted to the nearest medical station. They told him he was lucky—just his leg. Just his leg! Damn bastards. Wasn't their leg that was fucked up for the rest of their lives. It was his. And he had been so close to getting home without an injury. At least not visible ones. You couldn't be normal and get away from there without any scars. All that senseless killing and violence. Insane. He thought of the nightmares, the visions, the voices, and shook his head.

Tyrell limped across the room. He tried to hurry but only made the pain worse. He reached the window and peered through the grimy pane. Shit. I should clean the window. What for? The damn windows can stay dirty for all I care. Don't want nobody looking in here!

He pulled back one side of the sun-bleached curtain hanging loosely from a rusted rod. They had come with the cabin. Once they'd been brightly patterned, now they were so faded that any pattern was indistinguishable. Washing them might destroy the last threads holding them together.

Dogs, their leashes straining, advanced out of the woods. Tyrell cursed. He had heard the police search parties were out looking for the boy, but so far they hadn't come this close.

He scanned the cabin. Was anything out of place? Would they see anything suspicious? His eye caught the blue-green of the rug, the rug under the dresser. One corner was ruffled, exposing the wood floor beneath it, exposing the freshly sawn cut in the floorboards. Exposing the trap door. He looked back out the window. Men holding straining animals were crossing the clearing. They were coming to the cabin.

He shuffled to the other side of the room where the dresser stood against the wall, the blue striped rug below it. Ignoring the pain stabbing into his thigh, radiating to his calf, he forced his legs to move faster. Fine beads of sweat formed on his brow. Larger beads formed across his chest and under his arms. It mingled with the musty unclean scent of him. He didn't notice. He reached the dresser, and stretching down, yanked the rug flat, smoothing out the edges till the severed line of plank flooring was no longer exposed. He leaned against the dresser waiting for the knife-like pain in his right leg to subside. His heart raced, his hands trembled, but the trap door was covered. A banging on the door shook the wood. The two-by-four in the latch rattled, almost shifting out of place.

"Tyrell. Tyrell Watson. This is the police. We want to talk to you."

Piercing pains continued to shoot down his leg, screaming protests from his hurried movements yet he straightened himself to his full six feet two inches. Taking a deep breath, he tried to quell the emotions waging a war inside him. He knew he couldn't look anxious when he opened the door. He needed to get rid of them as soon as possible. *Don't want those pigs snooping around. They got no reason to suspect me of anything. The kid better stay quiet if he knows what's good for him.*

Tyrell dragged his leg behind him as he crossed to the door. He was in no hurry to open his door, or his life to them. He heard the insistent banging again. "I'm coming," he growled. "Hold your horses." As he slid the two-by-four out of the homemade lock he cursed his leg, the police outside, and the world in general. He yanked the thick wooden door open and glared at the two policemen, "What do you want?"

"We're looking for a missing child."

"Don't know nothing about a missing child."

"You haven't heard about Clayton Kingsley? He's a seven-year-old who's been missing almost a week now."

"Nope, don't have a television, or a radio."

"Can we have a look around?'

"Sure. I got nothing to hide. Just make it quick." He stepped back to let the policemen into the cabin. He glanced at the group of volunteers, most of them, he recognized from town, none of them he called friends. The ash-blonde woman was there. He turned his back and followed the officers into the cabin.

Jenny had finally persuaded Jarvis to let her join the search. They had covered miles of countryside around town, stopping at every house or farm they came to. So far they had come up with nothing. Now she watched as the police approached the sheltered, log cabin. A tall, muscular man came to the door. Was he familiar? She tried to place him. She watched as he spoke briefly to the police, then stood back and allowed them into the cabin.

She felt a sense of apprehension as she waited. Would this man know anything about Clayton? She had a sudden vision of Clayton, in the ground, calling her, stretching out his hand. Then the vision faded. Her heart sank when moments later the police came out of the cabin. They had taken two minutes to investigate the shed, the outhouse, the cabin, before ordering the search party to continue.

Jenny went with them despite the strange feeling that she should remain.

CHAPTER 24

Clayton awoke to shivers running up and down his body. The blanket had slipped while he slept, and now only partially covered him. The short-sleeved puppy-dog T-shirt he wore left his arms exposed and goose bumps covered the bare area. He reached out a hand and grasped an edge of the blanket. It was threadbare; several small holes scattered across its length. The blanket gave him little warmth in the dampness of the dirt hole. He pulled the blanket up to his chin and curled himself into a tight ball. Shivers traveled along his arms and legs. His body felt like a block of ice, but his head felt hot, so hot.

He wanted to go home. He wanted to be in his own bed with his mother tucking his blankets around him, blankets that were thick and warm and had no holes in them. Clayton wanted his mother to hug him. More shivers. Grabbing the edges of the blanket, he tucked it around his limbs. He shut his eyes, wanting to keep them closed. He tried to go back to sleep. At least then he didn't have to think about anything. He didn't have to think about why he was here.

What did I do? Did I do something bad? Why won't Mommy come and get me? Why is she leaving me here? Why? Mommy, please come. I want to go home.

Clayton fell asleep. Tears left tracks down his pale cheeks. He dreamed of being home in his bed. In his dream, he thought he heard voices. Not the voice of the man in the cabin above him, but other voices mixed with his. And he heard dogs barking.

He dreamed they were coming to find him. They were coming to take him back to his mother. He dreamed his mother was there, reaching out her hand to him. He tried to call out but knew it was only a dream. When he woke, he was still lying on the hard floor and it was still dark.

The shivering returned.

CHAPTER 25

The clang of the bell over the front door alerted Steve to someone entering the garage. He was in the middle of a tune-up on a 'ninety-nine Tempo and hoped to have it done by noon. Mrs. Alfonse was coming at twelve-thirty to pick it up. Maybe she was here early. He was almost finished replacing her oil filter and doing a tune-up. Assuming she would come through to the back shop, he continued working.

Steve heard footsteps on the cement floor, but they were louder than a woman would make. His mechanic, Mike was taking a car back to an owner. He would have come in the back way, and his shoes were soft-soled. This would take a heavier shoe, like a uniform boot. He took a deep breath.

Glancing away from the Tempo's engine, Steve saw the pair of shiny black uniform boots and blue pants beside the car's fender. Setting the oil filter into place, Steve slowly turned to face the owner. He cursed silently. He'd been expecting him. It had only been a matter of time. Would he never stop hounding him? Steve reached for the rag lying on the front of the car and wiped at the grease on his hands.

"So this is your little shop."

Steve saw the smirk on Joe Roberts' face, felt the bitter taste of bile rise in his mouth, and cursed himself for it. Damn him. He'd done nothing, but Roberts continued to harass him using the power of his badge. Steve knew he was helpless.

He couldn't protest. Who would listen to him? Joe Roberts had been trying to get his goat for a long time and used the slightest excuse to do it. Steve was surprised it had taken him this long for him to come and have a little chat.

He hated having to brown-nose to this asshole just because he had a piece of silver tacked to his chest. Steve made himself take several long, controlled breaths before speaking. He kept the tone even and controlled. "Can I help you?"

"Maybe we can make a deal. I need some engine work on my Mustang. What can you do for me, Townsend?"

"My shop rates are listed in the office. I run an honest shop here. I don't make deals. Unless you're a senior, I give fifteen percent off for seniors."

Steve met Roberts' gaze. What was he trying to do, trap him? Did he really think Steve might give him a deal? Roberts was crazier than he thought. He wouldn't do anything for this son of a bitch. Steve glared at him. Roberts was the first to look away.

Altering his stance, Roberts hooked one thumb in the pocket of his uniform pants. "We need to have a little chat."

Steve concentrated on getting grease off his hands, wiping the length of each finger before he replied. Only then did he look back at Roberts. "About what?"

"About things in general. A few things in particular."

"Like what?"

"Your attitude for one thing. You don't give me much respect."

Steve wondered how to answer. Tell the truth and he might get his head kicked in plus a charge for assaulting a policeman. Kowtow to him and he'd walk all over him. He wished Roberts would take off the badge and fight like a man. He'd take him on, no problem. He wasn't a fighter, but this was an issue of honor—his and Kelly's. Voices in his mind warned him. Don't be stupid. You've got no witnesses.

"I've done nothing to you. And no one says I have to like you."

Robert's cheek twitched. Steve watched as the officer weighed his comment. A corner of his thinned lips turned up and his eyes blazed with barely concealed fury. With a sharp intake of air through flared nostrils, Roberts tipped his head back and glared at Steve. "Townsend, I'm taking you downtown for a little talk."

"What for?"

Roberts sneered. "We'll talk about that downtown."

"I have a right to know what this is about."

"It's about the missing boy."

"Have you found him?" Steve turned to the man he despised; praying his presence could consist of something positive, something other than his usual harassment.

"Not yet. I was hoping you would tell us what you know."

"I've told the police everything I know."

Roberts cocked his head to the side. A sly grin tilted one side of his face. He knew he was back in control.

"Maybe there's something you neglected... I'm sorry—" His lips curled in a sarcastic smile. "—forgot to mention."

Steve fought to stay where he was, fought to resist the overwhelming urge to wipe the smirk off Roberts' face. He felt every muscle in his face contract. He ground his teeth and fought to keep control. His hands clenched and unclenched the grease-stained rag. "I was looking for him before the police were called."

"That's what you told us."

Steve glared at Roberts. He's suggesting I had something to do with the boy's disappearance. I knew this would happen. It was just a matter of time.

He wished the bastard would leave him alone. Would he never get tired of harassing him? Steve wished there was some way to end it, but he knew he could never forgive Roberts for Kelly's death and Roberts knew Steve couldn't prove anything, so he took great pleasure in tormenting him.

"Maybe you know more than you told us. Maybe you even know where he is. Do you Steve?"

"I told you everything the other day."

"Like you did with the other kid, Steve. You've got a history of taking kids. We've got your prints downtown. You know about taking kids, don't you?

"You son of a—" Steve's face twitched convulsively. He took a step forward. The grease-stained rag dropped to the floor.

"Come on, Steve. What do you want to call me? Come on, I'm ready for you." His voice a taunting chant, Roberts raised his fists in front of his chest. His eyes issued an unspoken challenge.

Steve looked directly at him. Their eyes locked. Old animosities burned like a torch between them. His breath came in quick, searing intakes. The room felt unbearably hot. Sweat beaded his forehead, and dampness soaked his armpits.

Across the room, a clunk of heavy metal hitting something solid drew both men's attention.

"Sorry boss. Clumsy. Tripped over the jack."

Mike Thompson picked up the three-foot-long jack and walked toward the two men.

"I got that car delivered. Now I'll start work on that old Chevy, if that's okay with you."

"Sure Mike, the clutch is over by the welder."

Mike waited, watching the two men. The tension in the shop was like sparking wires as the men glared at each other. Without looking away, Steve spoke to Mike, his voice low with controlled anger. "I'm okay."

"If you say so, boss."

Steve heard Mike shuffle away to the other side of the garage. He wondered how long he had been back and how much he had heard. "Am I under arrest?" He demanded.

"Did you do anything we should arrest you for, Townsend?"

Roberts managed to draw his name out to sound like a curse. Steve ground his teeth but kept his clenched fist in check. He kept repeating to himself, *Easy, easy, he's not worth it. Keep control. That's what he wants, wants you to lose control. Wants to have some excuse to beat the shit out of you, too. Don't give it to him. Easy now.*

"Let's just go downtown, Townsend. And, do it quietly."

The calm words belied the unspoken challenge that glistened in the officer's eyes. One arm went out to grasp Steve's forearm. Steve pushed past him and walked quickly toward the squad car.

"Look after things, Mike."

"Sure, Steve. Don't worry. I'll manage." Mike paused before he added. "You take care."

Mike's words rang in Steve's ear. Yes, he would have to take care, real good care.

At the station, Roberts led Steve past the desk sergeant, shoving him onto a bench in a busy hallway. Steve flinched away every time Roberts attempted to control his direction, but never obviously enough to be construed as resisting. He sat on the hard bench and waited.

He glanced at the occupants on the other end of the bench. Two teenagers, old beyond their years, sat gossiping and examining their painted nails. They were dressed in spiked heels, mini-skirts, and knit tops that stretched taut across their breasts. The lace of their push-up bras exposed an expanse of tanned, nubile flesh. The provocative swinging of their bare crossed legs made Steve even more uncomfortable. He shifted his body closer to the far end of the bench, withdrawing into his own reflections.

It seemed as if a couple of hours passed while he waited. His body protested the pew's hardness, but he knew better than to make a fuss. The two girls had been led away ages ago while Steve was left to cool his heels. Roberts has probably gone for an extended lunch, leaving me here to stew. Steve tried to remain calm. Roberts would love to know he had got to him. He would play on it and push Steve to say something he would regret later. Steve tried to avoid watching the clock ticking away his day.

Every time a door opened or someone passed, Steve looked up expectantly. Finally, Roberts and a young uniformed cop came down the hall. This young officer was at least six foot four with the build of a quarterback. His barrel chest was almost twice the width of Steve's broad chest. Walking with surprising grace for someone his size, the policeman's feet trod lightly on the wooden floor. Steve wondered how much time he had spent wearing a football jersey. The slight left shift of his nasal bones suggested some past contact injury. What had the other guy looked like? Not many would want to tangle with this guy, Steve knew he wouldn't.

Silently, the big cop followed Roberts to where Steve sat. They motioned him to follow. The quarterback led, leaving Steve to follow with Roberts close on his heels. They walked along the hall, through a glass-topped door, and down a flight of stairs to the basement, passing several rooms before entering one.

Steve looked around the nine-by-twelve area with its large scarred desk and four straight-backed chairs. The air was heavy with the scent of stale coffee and rancid perspiration. A small table stood in one corner, a container of sugar packets and an open jar of coffee creamer sat on top. Spilled grains of sugar and coffee had been left to form tiny mounds. Three empty coffee cups lined the edge of the table. Nobody had bothered to add them to the already overflowing garbage can. Three flies vied for position on the mounds. The rest of the room was bare except for the large table and the video camera in one corner of the ceiling. Was the film running?

Roberts shoved him into a chair. Steve didn't look at the window in front of him. He already knew it was a one-way mirror. He shifted uncomfortably, wondering if anyone was on the other side.

"This is Officer Ramanski," Roberts nodded to the other policeman. "He'll be here while I ask you a few questions." Roberts straddled a chair across from Steve. Ramanski tipped his head to Steve, then took a chair.

"Where were you the morning of July twenty-third?" Roberts started.

"I was at the shop working."

"And what shop is that?"

"My garage."

"The one on Main Street?"

"Yes." What sort of game is he playing? He knows damn well where my shop is. Steve took a deep breath and answered coolly. "The same one you picked me up at this morning."

"So you were there the whole day?"

"No. I came home for lunch."

"And what time would that be?"

"Same as most days. Twelve o'clock."

"So you were home having lunch at that time?"

"Yes."

"Can anybody confirm that you were at the shop that morning?"

Steve thought for a moment as to who was in the garage that morning. His mechanics, Mike and Dez, had been working. James Taylor had come in to pick up his car at eleven and Mrs. Jenkins had been by just before twelve to get her Saturn. He gave them the names. Ramanski wrote in his notebook.

"Tell me what happened when you came home for lunch?"

"Like I told the other officers, I was eating lunch when I heard my neighbor screaming. I went outside. Jenny Kingsley was crying. Said her son was missing."

"Did you see the boy?"

"No. Jenny said the boy was missing. I went to look for him."

"Had you seen the boy that day?"

"No, I left for work at seven-thirty."

"You didn't leave the shop that morning?"

"No. I mean, yes. I left for about half an hour to pick up a part for a car I was working on."

"Do you usually do pickups yourself? Don't you pay employees for that?" Roberts's voice took on a mocking tone. He tilted his head at Steve, tempting his anger.

Steve paused. He looked levelly at Roberts. Mike's words come back to him. Take care. "Dez and Mike were in the middle of replacing a transmission, so I went myself."

"How long were you gone?"

"Like I said, half an hour."

Steve saw Roberts staring at him, like a lion tamer, his black whip poised, ever watchful. His eyes were like shards of gray metal. Then suddenly, his voice like a crack of the whip, he snapped, "So you had time to come by and snatch the kid?"

Steve's fuse was lit. He bolted out of the chair, shoving the table into Roberts's chest. Fury glinted from his eyes. He glared at the man across the wooden obstacle. "I didn't touch him, and you know that, Roberts."

His opponent's eyes showed surprise and a glimmer of something that looked like fear. He had pushed too far. His whip had unleashed a buried wound.

Steve faced his enemy. His heart hammered, dilating the veins in his neck, and sweat spread like a cape across his back. He tasted the acrid bile that rose in his mouth. Mike's voice whispered in his ear. 'Take care.' Don't let him rile you.

Steve glared at Roberts but forced himself to slow his breathing, calm the flame of his anger. He stood still, noting the hint of fear in Roberts' cold gray eyes. He knows he's pushing me too far. Forcing himself to relax, Steve felt the pounding of his heart soften as his anger dwindled to a controllable level.

From the corner of his eye, Steve saw Ramanski watching their interaction with interest. The heavy atmosphere in the room was explosive and he looked ready to disperse sparks before the fireworks started. Ramanski coughed. His tone was low. "Settle down. We're just here to get the events of that day, right, Roberts?"

"Right." Roberts lowered his head. "That's right."

"Would you like a lawyer present?" Asked Ramanski.

"Do I need one? I haven't done anything wrong."

Ramanski's gaze was direct and Steve met it full-on. Without speaking, he nodded at Steve to be seated again. Steve surveyed the quarterback. His light blue eyes showed no hate, no concealed anger—kind blue-gray eyes. Steve was willing to give this man a chance. He eased back into the chair.

Roberts remained standing, his right cheek twitching as he tried to control his emotions. He pulled a chair back several feet, the legs scraping like nails on the tiled floor. He sat stiffly, his arms folded across a chest that heaved with his attempt to regain control.

Ramanski continued the questioning. "So, Mr. Townsend, am I right in saying that the first knowledge you had of Clayton Kingsley's disappearance was when you heard your neighbor outside at about twelve-twenty on July third?"

"Yes. I was eating lunch. Our neighbor, Jenny Kingsley, was crying. She said her son was missing."

"Did you know the boy?"

"I've met him a few times. They moved into the house next door a couple of months ago. I went over to help Mrs. Kingsley get rid of garbage the previous tenants had left, and my mother has sent me over with baked goods for them. I've seen them both a few times."

"You didn't see him earlier that morning?"

"No, sir."

Steve noticed Roberts shift in his chair. He kept his attention focused on Ramanski.

"Have you seen him any time since?"

"No, I haven't."

"Would you be willing to take a lie detector test?"

Steve sat up in his chair, taking a quick glance at Roberts. He turned back to Ramanski His voice was firm when he finally spoke. "Yes, sir. I would."

"When would you like to do that?"

"As soon as you're ready."

Ramanski nodded his approval. He shot a warning glance at Roberts and left the room.

The silence was charged with emotion. Steve kept his gaze on the door, awaiting Ramanski's return. He heard Robert's heavy breathing across the table, but refused to look at him. Within minutes Ramanski poked his head into the room. "They can do you now."

Steve rose without a backward glance and followed him down the hall. The room was small. A worn vinyl armchair sat in the middle of the brown tiled floor. The pale green walls and stainless steel cupboards reminded Steve of a dentist's office. Beside the chair, a technician untangled a series of wires connected to a black box-like apparatus. He indicated the armchair to Steve.

The technician, introduced as Sam, gave a brief description of the process, then attached wires to Steve's pulse points. To Steve, his command to relax was a joke. How the hell can you relax with all these wires connected to you? As someone recorded every heartbeat, every breath, even how much you perspired. Relax. No problem.

Sam examined the sheet of paper Deputy Ramanski handed him. He turned on the black box and began his questions.

"Is your name Steve Townsend?"

"Yes."

"Is your address one-twenty-five Elm Street?"

"Yes."

"How old are you?"

"Thirty-three."

"Do you know Clayton Kingsley?"

"Yes."

"Did you see him July third?"

"No."

"Did you take him?"

"No, I didn't."

"Did you know Kelly Taylor?"

Steve felt his heart rate increasing. Was this one of the trick questions? "Yes."

"Were you an accomplice in the abduction of Cheryl Hubert's baby?"

"It wasn't abduction!" Steve could see the needle on the graph moving frantically. He tried to remain calm but the old feelings of anger surged back.

"I was helping him get his baby back before she gave it up for adoption. He was the father."

"Just yes or no, please," Sam instructed.

"Do you own your own business?"

"Yes."

"Where is it?"

"Ten-sixty Main Street."

The change in questioning gave Steve a chance to calm down. Was this how they worked it; give you something they know will upset you, then change venues? It had worked. Thankfully he'd been able to get his anger under control. Now his pulse and breathing were almost back to normal.

"Did you take Jimmy Waters?"

"No!"

His pulse rate soared. That was five years ago. Would they never let it go?

The child had been found dead, lost in the woods five miles out of town. The coroner said he died of pneumonia due to exposure to the elements. The police had concluded there was no foul play. The child was camping with his parents and wandered off. Police, family, and volunteers had scoured the woods for two weeks and hadn't found him. Then, in the fall, a hunter found his body lying under a bush. There was no sign of abuse, sexual or otherwise. Steve had been cleared of suspicion. He hadn't even known the child, but Roberts had pulled him in and questioned him.

"Did you take Clayton Kingsley?"

"No, I didn't."

Steve watched the needle soar again, making more erratic tracings on the thermal paper. He waited for the next question, watching the needle return to the baseline. Suddenly, the wires were being removed and the black box turned off.

"That's all." The technician's tone was flat and clinical. "You can leave now."

Steve sat stunned for several seconds. That was all! They tear at your emotions, rip open old wounds, then blandly say, "That's all."

Shaking his head, Steve got up and left the room without a backward glance. He strode out of the station. If Roberts wanted to harass him anymore, he knew where to find him.

Once outside, he exhaled deeply, forcing the stale air of the police station out of his lungs.

CHAPTER 26

Watching out Clayton's window, Jenny heard the wind whistling through the poplars surrounding the house. Their silver underbellies faced upward. The evening was suddenly cold and the approaching storm tangible in the darkening sky. Clouds covered the full moon, casting a ghostly hue. She leaned against the wooden frame.

Ray had gone to bed earlier, worn out from the continuing search. She was grateful for his presence, yet relieved he was spending more and more time out of the house. During the day, he worked with her at the community center or walked the streets questioning anyone if they had seen Clayton. But the last couple of evenings he had brought her home and then found somewhere beer was served. Jenny smelled it on his breath and on the clothes he left lying around the family room. His initial neatness and consideration had waned.

At least he had made no further attempts at reconciliation. He even ignored her mother's pointed remarks about them "working things out." Eventually, her mother had dropped the subject. Maybe she finally realized Jenny was an adult and no longer under her thumb.

A sudden flash illuminated the charcoal sky, followed closely by a boom of thunder that shattered the still night. Jenny shuddered in response. Torrents of rain beat against the house in a staccato rhythm. Reluctantly, Jenny closed the window.

Clayton hated storms. Was he afraid now? Jenny prayed he was somewhere safe.

She wrapped her arms around her chest. She ached to hold her son and comfort him. When it stormed, he would run to her arms and she would hold him, distracting him with stories and rocking him until he calmed. Often she told him the story of God's angels having a birthday party at Heaven's Bowling Alley and how the lightning was the bowling balls speeding so fast they lit up the sky and the thunder was the balls knocking down the pins. Eventually, he would fall asleep in her arms and she would hold him until the storm was over.

Is it storming where you are, Clay? Think of me holding you wherever you are.

While the rain smashed against the window, the tears inside flowed silently. Jenny leaned against the window frame until the storm had exhausted itself. Before turning away from the window, she made a silent prayer for Clayton's safety. Shoulders stooped, she made her way to her room, and mechanically went through the preparations for bed. She needed to at least try to sleep. It would be another busy day looking for Clayton.

But maybe tomorrow would be the day. Maybe they would find Clayton tomorrow.

Startled from his sleep by a tremendous crack, Clayton jerked awake. He listened to the storm raging above and pulled the worn blanket snugly against his body, but its thinness gave no protection from the damp, and he shivered uncontrollably. Clayton, cold and frightened, he tugged the blanket over his head, trying to block out the noise above. He hid there. The sounds of thunder boomed through the darkness. His body trembled. I hate storms. Where's Mommy? She shouldn't leave me alone the storm.

He closed his eyes and counted as high as he could until the next boom of thunder shattered the darkness. At least down here he couldn't see the flashes of lightning he knew were coming with the thunder. The sudden change in the temperature chilled his small body. Any warmth from the blanket had long since dissipated. Trickling streams of water filtered through the ground and seeped into the mat beneath him. The dampness penetrated through to his bones and he trembled feverishly.

CHAPTER 27

The trill of the phone penetrated her restless sleep. Raising herself on one elbow, Jenny groped in the darkness for the receiver. The ringing was a harsh intrusion in the still night. Every time the phone rang, a shudder ran through her. Was it going to be news of Clayton, or one of the tormenting calls that continued to harass her? She lifted the receiver, silencing its banshee cry.

"Hello."

"Is this Jenny Kingsley?" a gravelly voice asked.

She sat up higher in bed and glanced at the radio clock. The time was one-oh-seven a.m. Why was anyone calling her at this time of the night? Had Clayton been found?

"Who is this?"

"You don't know me..." The deep female voice spoke hesitantly. "But...I...had a dream about your son..."

"About my son?"

"Yes. I had a dream about your son?"

"What...Who are you?" Still only partially awake, Jenny's voice became shrill. Who was this person calling her at this time of night? What was she talking about? What was she saying about dreams?

"My name's Zaphira VanAlton."

"I don't think I know you."

"No—you don't—but I'm psychic. I had a dream, and your son was in it."

A fog of semi-consciousness jumbled her mind. Jenny hadn't been sleeping well and her mind was so tired she couldn't make any sense out of the conversation.

"I want to help. I see things—"

"Have you seen Clayton? Is he alive?" Jenny demanded.

There was silence on the other end of the line. A pause lengthened by the oppressive silence of the house around her. The palm holding the receiver went cold and clammy. Jenny wanted to switch the phone to the other hand so she could wipe the wetness away. She couldn't. She needed to keep it to her ear. She had to be able to hear what the woman was saying.

"Please...tell me he's okay."

Suddenly, the silence was broken and the woman's voice penetrated the line. "Well—I haven't actually seen him—but—I had this dream..."

Jenny squeezed her eyes shut and slumped back into the bed. A tear slid out one corner of her eye. Who was this crazy woman phoning her in the middle of the night telling her she had had a dream about her son? Jenny had dreams about Clayton too, but they would be considered nightmares. She didn't want to hear about anyone else's. Hers were bad enough.

"I saw him in the ground...with dirt around him...there's wood over him...it's very dark...there's lots of trees...he's in a hole...about six foot long."

Jenny couldn't stand hearing anymore, but she had to. The dreams of children dancing around the shallow grave came back. Then the voice was gone, replaced by a dial tone. She let the phone slide through her fingers. It rested in the crook of her neck. She didn't have the energy to hang it up. Now she had only the voices in her head to deal with. Like a shroud, the silence in the house descended around her.

When Jenny woke the next morning there was no confusion, no escape from a semi-conscious state. Even before she opened her eyes, she was aware of a deep pain that spread through her body. She knew immediately what was wrong. Clayton was still missing. Her pain released itself in an audible moan.

The woman's raspy voice came back to haunt her. She needed to call Detective Jarvis. He answered on the third ring.

"No. I don't have any news for you."

"I had a call last night," Jenny paused. "A woman...I don't remember her name...she had a dream..."

"Now, Jenny." His voice was firm. "You can't pay attention to these calls. I'm sure it was a crank—"

"She said he was in the ground...dirt around him ...wood." Jenny tried to remember the woman's name, but couldn't.

"I'm sure it was a crank call. I don't want you to think about it."

"But—"

"Now, Jenny, if she was a reputable psychic, not that I believe in them, she would have contacted us. She wouldn't be calling you in the middle of the night."

"I guess so."

"Don't think about her anymore. I'll be in contact with you." The connection was broken.

Jenny forced herself to get up and dressed. Pulling a short-sleeved top over her head, she settled it over bony hips. She zipped up her blue jeans. They gaped at her waist. Less than a week ago they had been a snug but comfortable fit.

She had to make herself eat. It was important to keep up her strength. When Clayton got home, she had to be ready to take care of him.

She glanced in the mirror and was startled by the image that confronted her. How long since she had paid attention to what she looked like? Lines radiated out from eyes swollen by frequent crying. Her lips were pale and drawn tightly across her face and her dirty blonde hair hung limp around her sunken cheeks. She had to do something. She'd scare Clayton if he saw her looking like this. She rummaged in her makeup bag and found a tube of lipstick. She applied a thin coating, then used cover-up on the dark circles under her eyes. She checked the mirror again. At least now she looked almost human.

Going to the kitchen, She wandered about, straightening cookbooks, rearranging appliances, and wiping the table. She roamed from room to room. There must be something to do. Passing the laundry basket, she lifted the lid. It was full. At least washing the clothes would occupy her for a while. She gathered the laundry and took it to the basement.

Folded laundry filling her arms, she made her way up the stairs but her feet slowed. She thought it would feel good to be busy, to keep her mind off Clayton. And, it had for a short time, but here she was with an armload of his clothes to put away. The fresh scent of his shirts and underwear filled her nostrils. His face flashed into her mind. She saw his wide-mouthed grin that was part angel, part urchin, and a burst of sunshine in her day. A cloud crossed her mind and brought her back to the present, a present without sunshine, without Clayton.

Questions continued to race through her mind. Questions without answers. A tear slid down her cheek. She stopped midway up the stairs and slumped down on a step. Leaning her head against the pile of soft clothing, their fresh scent mingled with her salty tears.

She had to get out. The walls were closing in on her. Yesterday's storm had done nothing to dissipate the heat and the humid air closed around her like a shroud. She tried to take a deep breath but her chest was as tight as if she wore a straightjacket.

The sense of claustrophobia heightened. She couldn't stay in the house another minute. She had promised Grace Chalmers she would rest this morning and come to the community center after lunch. But it was only nine-fifteen and she had been awake since dawn. At least, dawn was when she had finally dragged herself out of the damp and rumpled sheets. She had tossed and turned all night, watching the digital clock, its fluorescent numbers marking each passing minute. She lay staring at the ceiling, her body exhausted, but her mind racing with thoughts of Clayton.

He was constantly with her. Flashes of him as a newborn, then all of his firsts; the first time he called her Ma-ma, his first tooth, his first step. Every waking moment was filled with thoughts of him, as he was, and nightmarish visions of what could be. The sight of the child she had been asked to identify came to her. She shivered. Thank God the lifeless blonde child hadn't been Clayton. But where was her son? Was he lying lifeless somewhere not yet known?

Grabbing her purse, she slipped outside. The street was quiet. She saw Myrtle through her kitchen window but hurried by. Jenny didn't want to talk to her now; she didn't want to talk to anyone right now. She just needed out of the house.

Thankfully, the media had found other fish to harass. They still drove by at odd times of the day hoping to catch a glimpse of her but she spent her days out with the search parties or at the community center. It was seven days since Clayton had disappeared and the search parties had dwindled—the volunteers had jobs to return to, lives to get back to. Now, only one person at a time manned the phones at the community center. With each passing day, the number of calls decreased. Even her home phone had stopped ringing. At first, the constant ringing had driven her crazy, but now, the silence was worse.

Jarvis reassured her they were still working hard to find Clayton. She called him twice a day. She had to keep calling. She had to believe they would find him, otherwise she had no reason to keep going. The thought of his safe return was the only thing that got her out of bed every morning. The police had interviewed her and Ray for what seemed like hours. Then they had interviewed the neighbors, and anyone they thought could have a connection, but still nothing.

Steve loaned her a car, and every day she drove the streets, praying she would magically just find Clayton at the park, or playing with other children. It had been a fruitless effort but at least made her feel that she was doing something.

Starting the old Ford now, Jenny backed out of the driveway. When Clayton came home, she needed to have fresh milk and bread in the house. She headed towards Stockley's grocery store.

The store had been there for over seventy years, passed from father to son. As the town's population and needs grew, so did the store. A recent addition housed extra aisles overflowing with produce, canned goods, hardware, and an assortment of general household supplies. Their motto was "If we don't have it, we'll get it for you." They'd worked long and hard to maintain this business ethic and prided themselves that everyone in town shopped at their store. Their most recent addition was the small café where coffee, sweets, and a light lunch could be bought. It had become Scottsville's unofficial meeting place. Townsfolk learned about the latest births, deaths, weddings, and divorces while they filled their grocery carts and their stomachs.

Jenny had trouble holding back her tears when she saw the poster of Clayton in the store's window. As she pushed through the door, conversation halted, faces turned toward her, some with looks of sympathy, others full of questions. Most looked away quickly, only one couple stared rudely at her. Jenny kept her head down, grabbed a cart, and headed down the first aisle.

As she passed the restaurant area of the store, she felt the burn of someone's gaze on her. It was the man who lived in the cabin in the woods. He nodded at her, smiled, then stroked the fur of his raccoon hat. She thought she read concern in his eyes but was unable to do more than tip her head and move on.

She hurried down the aisles gathering the few groceries she needed—milk, bread, and bananas. She grabbed a jar of peanut butter. *Clayton loves peanut butter.* She knew she had a full jar at home, but she kept it in the cart. She added a box of Frosted Flakes—the sugar-coated ones she rarely bought. *It will be a treat for him.* She added a carton of eggs and headed for the checkout.

The chattering of the two women ahead of her stopped abruptly at her approach. They turned towards her. "You're Mrs. Kingsley, aren't you?"

Jenny nodded, afraid of questions from these unknown women.

"Sorry about your son. Have you heard anything?"

"No." Jenny's voice was barely above a whisper. "Nothing yet."

"I'm Edna Sadler, dear and I'm praying you hear some good news real soon. He can't just have disappeared. Not in a nice, respectable town like Scottsville. We don't have much crime here, do we, Norma?"

"No, nothing like this. Not since..."

Jenny felt the tears threatening and hurried toward the checkout. She was rushing out the door, juggling three grocery bags, and not paying attention. One of the bags grazed the man standing outside the door. The box of cereal flew out of the bag and tumbled to the pavement. Jenny bent to grab it but another hand was there first. She drew back as the man in the raccoon hat held the box out for her. But instead of handing it back to her, he shoved it into one of the bags, then took all of them from her.

"Let me carry them."

His voice was soft, his smile shy. Jenny led the way to her car. He placed the bags in the front passenger seat.

"Sorry to hear about your son."

She nodded quickly then slid behind the wheel. The tears that flowed made it difficult to maneuver the car through the streets. Finally, she pulled into the safety of her driveway. At least she thought she was safe. She hadn't noticed the reporter who pulled in behind her.

The media were supposed to keep a fifty-foot distance, but some were bolder than others. They hoped they could convince Jenny to give them an exclusive. She grabbed the bags of groceries and hurried into the house before the reporter could get close.

Slamming the door, Jenny twisted home the deadbolt. She leaned against the door until she heard the reporter's car pull away. The house was just as she had left it – empty and silent. The overwhelming quiet was like a slap in the face, almost knocking her over. She clenched the grocery bags to her chest and closed her eyes. A vision of a man took shape.

It was that strange man who'd been watching her at Stockley's, the man who helped her with her groceries. Was he the hermit? The one who had the cabin in the woods? She was there when the police questioned him. His cabin was so small there was no way he could have Clayton there without them knowing. But there was something about the way he had looked at her...yet he had been so nice, helpful, concerned. He had even said he was sorry Clayton was missing. Jenny was suddenly freezing and despite the heat of the day, her body shivered uncontrollably.

CHAPTER 28

After lunch, Jenny went to the community center. Posters of Clayton had been put up all over town within twenty-four hours of his disappearance. She wanted to put up more. Steve offered to help her. Jenny approached Mrs. Lindsay, today's hotline volunteer.

"Sorry, Mrs. Kingsley. It's been a quiet day. No calls."

Jenny thanked her and went to find Mrs. Chalmers. As soon as the woman saw her, she wrapped her arms around Jenny and led her to the office.

"I'm just going to have some tea. Will you join me?"

"That would be lovely, Mrs. Chalmers."

"Grace, please. I don't feel old enough to be a Mrs. yet."

Jenny smiled at the woman who was old enough to be her mother. "Yes, Grace, I would love a cup of tea."

Grace kept the conversation to anything but the slow progress of finding Clayton. She told Jenny about how the town had gotten together twelve years ago to build the community center. And just last year, they had expanded. Now they boasted a wide range of programs and activities. Jenny glanced at the brochure Grace handed her. Her attention tried to focus on the long list of classes—horticulture, painting, crafts, languages, dance. They even offered several business courses, from typing and accounting to computers. There were courses for both young and old.

"Quite impressive. Maybe—" Jenny paused. "—when Clay is in school, I could take some courses. I'm taking a correspondence course but it's hard to keep at it."

"That's a wonderful idea."

"I do bookkeeping from home but I'd like to take some computer courses."

"Taking courses here would be a way for you to make friends in town. We have children's activities too. Clayton would enjoy it."

There was a rap at the door, and Steve came into the office. "Hello, Grace. Hi, Jenny."

"Steve, good to see you. Your mother was in today. Brought us some mouth watering butter tarts."

"She loves to cook. I'm surprised I don't weigh three hundred pounds."

There was an easy rapport between the two. It was obvious they shared a mutual respect. Steve turned to Jenny. "Are you ready to get started?"

Jenny picked up a pile of flyers while Steve grabbed a hammer and box of tacks. He greeted other volunteers who were busy sorting flyers, or like him, gathering them to distribute. Scottsville, well covered with posters, they were now expanding to the countryside and nearby towns.

Thanking Grace, she nodded to the hot-line volunteer and followed Steve out of the building. It was difficult dealing with the pity she saw reflected in everyone's eyes, and Jenny blinked away the threatening tears. She smiled at Steve as he handed her a Kleenex. He always seemed to have one ready when she needed it. Jenny didn't know what she would do without his support. No matter how Ray tried, he could never make her feel safe the way Steve did.

The town, divided into sections, volunteers had put up posters wherever they could. Steve and Jenny drove the streets, adding more and replacing damaged ones. Jenny and Steve spent a few hours tacking them up on telephone poles on the country roads and anywhere possible in the nearby towns and hamlets. On the way back to town, Steve stopped in front of Stockley's.

"Would you like to get something to eat?" Steve asked.

"I'm okay."

"When was the last time you ate?"

Jenny saw the concern in his eyes and felt the warmth and strength of his hand as it covered hers. She tried to remember - tea with Grace Chalmers, and part of a donut... before that..a couple spoonfuls of cereal for breakfast. She had no urge to eat and usually ate only when someone reminded her. Even then, she could only eat a few mouthfuls before waves of nausea overtook her. It reminded her of morning sickness, but she was definitely not pregnant. When she tuned into her body, Jenny realized her head was spinning. Maybe it was time to eat. "I guess I am a bit hungry."

He held Stockley's front door open for her and she hurried past the poster of Clayton. She didn't know how much more she could handle. With his picture plastered all over the town, you would think someone would know something.

Steve led her to a booth. She was relieved to be away from people's curious stares. Even if they were out of kindness, Jenny grew tired of having to give the same answer. "No news." When the waitress, Dolores, came over, thankfully, Steve gave her little opportunity to ask questions.

"I'll have a club sandwich. What about you, Jenny?

"I'll have the same."

"Good then. And we'll have a couple of coffees."

Dolores wrote the order on the pad she carried, then paused with her pencil just above the paper and looked expectantly at Jenny. Jenny just shook her head. Dolores shoved the pencil behind her ear and headed toward the kitchen. Within five minutes, she was back with their order. Steve nodded, then picked up his sandwich denying the waitress the desired gossip. Dolores took her dismissal with a slight shrug of her broad shoulders.

Jenny ate half of the sandwich before realizing that she felt better, and that her head had stopped spinning. She needed to remind herself to eat, needed to remind herself to take care of her body and keep up her energy. But most of all, she needed to find Clayton. She trusted the police, but they didn't seem to be getting anywhere. Where could she start? Where could she search they hadn't? Her head hurt thinking about it.

Dolores was back, collecting her tip and clearing the table. Arranging to meet Steve at the magazine rack, Jenny went to the washroom. She was on her way back when she saw Joe Roberts standing close to him.

"What have you got there, Steve? You intending to pay for that, or you just gonna walk out with it under your arm?"

Jenny saw Steve's face tense and how his arm clamped on the Auto Trader in the crook of his arm.

"Never stole a thing in my life, Roberts, and you know it."

"Then why are your fingerprints on file downtown Steve? Pretty boy like you never did a thing wrong."

"You know I didn't."

"Is that right?" leered Roberts.

"One day..."

"Is that a threat? You threatening me, Townsend? Did you hear that, Evans? I think we've got to keep a closer eye on him. That's what I think."

Steve's fist clenched and unclenched, turning white as the blood compressed out of them. Chad Evans walked over to them. His left eyebrow arched. Obviously, he'd overheard part of the conversation. Steve forced his fingers to relax. He read the unspoken words from Chad's wise brown eyes. He's not worth it, Steve, don't respond.

Steve shook his fingers allowing the circulation to return. He needed to shake off the tension that had invaded his body the moment he'd heard Roberts' voice. Turning his head, he acknowledged Chad's subtle nod.

Chad Evans was the fourth officer partnered with Roberts in as many years. Supposedly, Roberts wore thin the patience of his partners as they grew fed up with his power hungry ambitions and demeaning attitude.

He had been suspended several times for undisclosed reasons. Vacations, he called them. But the fact was, nobody on the force had as much time off as he did, except for old Jeremiah Thurley and he'd been on the force as long as anybody could remember. Roberts made a point of working out at the local gym. People saw him there more than they saw him at work. He remained as evasive as a groundhog about all his vacation days.

Roberts and Evans had become partners last May. One of Roberts' previous partners was Dave Charlton. That had lasted about eight months. Charlton would clam up when anyone asked him about Roberts. Maybe Sheriff Douglas teamed him up with Evans to see if some of his compassion and wisdom would rub off on the hotheaded cop. So far, no one had noticed much difference.

Evans faced his partner. Hisis voice soft, but there was no mistaking the command. "Let's go Roberts,"

"Now, I just want to make sure that Steve here doesn't take anything out of the store."

"Steve isn't a thief, and you know it," growled Evans.

As the officers walked away, Jenny heard Steve mumbling. "Will that son of a bitch never change?"

Jenny waited until the policemen left before joining Steve at the checkout. She saw the pursed lips and the vein twitching in his neck as he paid for the AutoTrader. She smiled brightly and made no indication she'd overheard the conversation.

It was a silent drive. Out of the corner of her eye, Jenny watched the tension ebb away as they got closer to home. When he pulled into his driveway, Steve shut the car off and walked her to her door.

Reluctant to be alone, Jenny asked. "Do you have time for a lemonade? I...wouldn't mind some company...if you have time."

He smiled. "Sure. I'd love some lemonade."

Jenny made fresh lemonade. Steve sat at the kitchen table and watched. He made idle conversation about the changes she had made to the house. They took the fresh lemonade into the living room. "Tell me what it was like to grow up in Scottsville."

Steve told her about his childhood, about his sister and brother, both living in Chicago now, and about his father who had operated the garage until his death five years ago. Suddenly, his voice became softer, and he leaned toward her. "Enough about me, how are you holding up?"

"Not very well." Jenny twisted her hands in her lap. Looking down at them, then back up at Steve. "Sometimes, I think it's all my fault. I should have brought him in while I made lunch." Jenny dropped her face in her hands.

"Stop now. Clayton is old enough to play alone for a few minutes. He's going into grade one, not kindergarten."

"But if I hadn't left him alone..."

"He was in an enclosed backyard."

Steve's hand touched her cheek. He took her hands in his, gently turning her face toward his. His hands were rough and tender at the same time. Strong hands, callused from years of manual labor, darkened fingertips tinged from the imprint of everyday contact with grease that grime-eaters refused to erase. When she met his gaze, she saw concern and compassion reflected there. It touched a place in her heart, and for the first time in a very long time, she didn't feel totally alone.

"I keep praying he'll just come walking through the door. Walk in and demand to know what there is to eat" Sobbing silently, she was unable to stop her tears that began to flow.

Steve's response was automatic. His arms stretched out, and he pulled her close. One hand cupped the back of her head, the other spread across the small of her back. He held her securely against his chest and let her cry. Her body molded into a perfect fit with his. He wanted to pull her closer, wanted her to fill the gaping hole in his heart. The hole he knew would be larger once he let her go.

He stroked the back of her head. At first, he had just meant to pull back the ash-blonde strands that clung to her wet cheeks, but the fine hairs that ran between his fingers held him captive and he could not take his hand away. The soft strands caressed the roughness of his callused fingers like luxurious silk.

Steve hadn't let a woman get close to him since Cheryl had betrayed Kelly. He had kept himself aloof from to the flirting of the single women in town, and especially the married ones. He maintained a small circle of friends. The single ones he met at Casey's when he stopped in for a few beers and a game of pool, the married ones he saw mostly bringing their cars into his shop or at hockey or ball games. Some of them tried to set him up with one of their wives' friends or an unmarried sister. Steve could never get up much interest after the first date or two.

Most of the women wanted to be wined and dined in fancy restaurants that had dress codes. He hated wearing a suit and tie, always felt like a trussed up crown roast. Plus, the damn starch in the dress shirts reacted with his skin and made him itch. He would have such a rash on his neck the next day the guys would tease him about doing things he had never even gotten close to. On the rare occasion he took a girl to one of those fancy places, he would be so uncomfortable he would end the evening early just to get out of the monkey suit. Until now, he hadn't let a woman through his protective shield.

While Jenny's emotions roller-coasted, Steve continued to stroke her ash-blonde hair. After her tears were spent, he kept her safe in his embrace, content simply to hold her. So they sat in the living room, holding each other as the evening lengthened and the room became shadowed.

Jenny gathered strength, and Steve, well, he released a side of himself he had hidden for far too long. He satisfied a need foreign to him, the need to protect someone. In the quiet of that evening, he allowed Jenny to steal into his heart.

CHAPTER 29

The sun shone through the window, casting warm rays on her sleeping form, coaxing her awake. Jenny lay still, her eyes closed, enjoying the soft comfort that tingled down her exposed limbs. It was hot when she had gone to bed and she had put on a cotton nightie. During the night, the temperature had dropped, but it had been too great an effort to get up for another cover, so she lay in the darkness, chilled, not knowing if it was the temperature of the night or the frost that had invaded her body. Now she lay, basking in the soothing rays as the morning sun caressed her body.

Then thoughts drifted through the cozy fog. They came without permission, invading that place somewhere between sleep and wakefulness—that safe place, where one can hide, and escape from all the ills and evils of the world. The thoughts bulldozed through, clearing everything in their path, dissipating the misty fog, allowing consciousness to intrude. Any hint of warmth left her body as the nightmare of reality returned.

Clayton was still missing!

She let out a strangled cry. How long now? Jenny counted the days—seven of them. Where could her child be? Pushing away the visions invading her mind, Jenny got up, she had to do something. Stumbling out of bed, she pulled on a pair of shorts and a T-shirt. She laced up her runners and flew down the stairs and out the back door.

The previous night, Rhonda Fleming ran a story about the child in the morgue. He had been identified. She made latent comments about a possible connection between that child and Clayton's disappearance. Now, the media wanted Jenny's reaction.

The backyard remained empty and silent. She hurried past the vacant sandbox, past the motionless swing, and on to the back of the yard. Wanting to avoid any media lurking at the front of the house, Jenny climbed the fence and slipped across the neighbor's property to reach the street beyond. She ran.

She hadn't been aware of where she was going—she just knew she had to get out of the house, away from the media and spectators, who again kept watch on the street in front of her house. There were no spectators here.

Once moving, the feeling of escape that running had always brought came back. Jenny had been on Dresden High's track team all through high school. For most of the girls, the daily runs the coach insisted on created a constant stream of grumbling and complaints. Not for Jenny. She loved the sense of power she felt when she could force her legs to outdistance the others. Once ahead of them, she could imagine a different world for herself—an escape from her mother's constant nagging and her father's indifference. Now, she prayed to regain some control over her present world.

The physical exertion felt good. She tried to run faster than her mind could think, fast enough that she couldn't see the visions of small dead bodies. Dead children whose flat lifeless eyes would suddenly flutter open and become Clayton's. Cold, flaccid bodies whose mouths would begin to move and emit strangled cries. "Help me, Mommy. Mommy, help me."

Sometimes it was Clayton's voice—sometimes it was such tortured cries they were indistinguishable between human or animal. Jenny ran so fast that she had to almost close her eyes against the air that whipped at them. Tears coated them, but still, the visions and voices came. She made her legs move faster.

She ran until her body refused to take another step. A cramp attacked her right leg, putting her calf into spasm. Pain shot down the leg to her toes. Another pain radiated across her chest as she struggled to breathe. The humidity of the sizzling morning hurt her throat, and she experienced the pain of oxygen deprivation. Jenny tried to make her body keep going, but it refused. Stumbling to the ground, she gasped for air.

She rubbed at her leg with one hand, the other hand stretched across her ribs forcing them to be still, trying to lessen the burning pain that filled her lungs and spread across her chest. Finally, her breathing calmed. It was shallow, but came in a regular rhythm and without pain. The cramp in her leg eased, and she slumped into an exhausted heap.

It took several minutes before she noticed her surroundings. Majestic trees, manicured lawns, asphalt paths, and benches were scattered around her. The scene was familiar. She was in Springbank Park. Clayton loved to play at the activity center and splash in the children's pool.

This morning several groups of children and parents enjoyed the park. Parents clustered in two's and three's, their heads together, concentrating on the local gossip, one eye, an eye that was now more watchful since the horror of Clayton's disappearance, constantly monitoring their respective charges. The children ran around the monkey bars, swings, and climbers, their voices raised in a sharp cacophony that intensified as it hit the muggy air.

She sat at an empty park bench and leaned back against the rough wood with its fresh mahogany paint. Mesmerized by the sight of the children, her eyes brimmed with unshed tears as she watched the tiny shapes whirling to the dance of childhood.

Through the distortion of tears, the scene before her took on a mystical aura. It was as if the children were in a time and place somewhere far away. Her hand reached out to touch them then drew back quickly afraid that if she broke through the mist the children would disappear. She could only sit and watch. Maybe if she watched long enough Clayton might appear and join their dance.

Then, something distracted her. Mothers sitting on a nearby park bench were staring at her. When Jenny looked up, they quickly shifted their gaze away. Mothers, incapable of dealing with her pain. They took the easy way out, ignoring it, and her. It was easier to pretend they hadn't seen her and didn't know who she was. Anything was easier than having to deal with her loss. Admitting it and accepting it would somehow give them ownership of it. They wanted to remain in their cotton-candy-coated world where children weren't taken from their backyards. Not theirs, anyway.

The rough wood of the park bench dug into Jenny's back, but she felt no inclination to move. She stretched her head back and scanned the park. A freshly mowed lawn stretched ahead of her, lush and emerald green. Despite the July heat, the grass thrived. Flowerbeds blazed with a rainbow of colors.

A team of volunteers tended the grounds, their horticultural egos given space and productive earth. It was not uncommon to see them on their knees cultivating and weeding their designated plot. At the end of the season, the town council awarded prizes for the best arrangements.

Jenny saw a few of the volunteers stooped over their plots, trowels and rakes in hand. She let her eyelids drift almost closed, letting a partially shaded view of the vibrant colors before her filter into her consciousness. She absorbed the rainbow hues and let them fill her soul with their calming beauty. Drifting there, her body warmed in the heat of the morning sun.

Her half-closed eyes focused on a flowerbed at the far end of the park. She watched the flowers waving softly towards the sun, like flags flaunting their native lands. Then one of the yellow flowers rose above the others and seemed to leave the plot. Jenny watched as it moved away from the rest. It took several seconds for her to realize it wasn't a flower. The yellow of its petals had the distinct resemblance of the head of a blond child.

Her eyelids flew open, and she stared at the spot where a blond-haired child was moving away from the flowerbed. Jenny watched the small body with tanned, chubby arms and legs. The sight shocked Jenny out of her blissful state of semi-consciousness. The blue shorts and white T-shirt were painfully familiar.

Leaping to her feet, she began running, her shoes barely contacting the ground. She saw him just ahead. He was alone. He was moving away from the flowerbed, and away from her. She forced her legs to go faster. Park benches flew past her, their startled occupants turning to stare. She didn't stop. She had to get to the end of the park before he disappeared again—she had to get to her son.

her,His short legs moved quickly, but hers were longer and Jenny gained on him quickly. The blond head got closer with each second. Jenny wanted to call out to him. She wanted to yell at him to stop and wait for her but her energy was devoted to closing the distance between them.

The gap dwindling, Jenny slowed her steps. She was right behind him now. If she stretched out her arm, she could almost touch his blond head. Jenny tried to call his name but all that came out of her mouth was a strangled cry. She spread out her arms and wrapped them around the small body.

He let out a scream. Struggling in her arms, his chubby hands clenched and punched at her. His elbow struck her hard in the chest. Then his body spun around to face her. Jenny saw the blond hair and the frightened gray eyes that met hers. Gray eyes, not blue. Delicate tanned features on a face that was so like Clayton's, but not.

She stared at his face. Her body sagged in despair, yet her arms remained around the struggling child. She knew this wasn't Clayton, but her arms refused to let him go. Tears rolled down her face. As if the child read her pain, he stopped struggling, and his arms went flaccid.

"What are you doing?" a female voice screamed. "Leave my grandson alone!"

The woman's voice penetrated Jenny's consciousness and her hands dropped, allowing the child to escape. He ran to the safety of his grandmother, a plump, salt-and-pepper-haired woman. Tears brimming, Jenny's shoulders slumped.

"I'm sorry. I thought he was...my son," she whispered.

The woman, clutching her grandson, glared at her. "Crazy woman."

Tears tracked down Jenny's face. "My son.. he was taken...from my backyard seven days ago. He..." Jenny stretched her arm out towards the boy. She saw the woman cringe and tighten her hold.

"...he looks so much like Clayton. He was wearing blue shorts too...I'm sorry."

"And so you should be. Just 'cause you lost your son doesn't mean you can go around stealing someone else's."

"I thought it was Clayton."

"I don't care what you thought. This is my grandson and I don't need some crazy person trying to steal him. I should call the police..."

"No, no."

Abruptly, Jenny turned away. Now she could see that the child bore little resemblance to Clayton—except for the color of his hair, his size, and the blue shorts he was wearing. Yet from the back, he'd looked so much like Clayton. Tears flowed freely down her cheeks as she watched the woman rush out of the park, the child's small hand tucked securely in hers.

She swiped angrily at the tears. How could God be so cruel? How could He let someone take her child, then tease her by thinking she had found him again? It wasn't fair. Was she being punished for something?

Through her tears she saw children playing in the park, mothers staring at her. Had they seen what she'd done? Were they afraid she would try to take one of their children next? She had to get away from here, away from all the mothers sitting, gossiping on park benches, away from the children safe in their mothers' sight. She couldn't stay another minute. She had to get away.

Then her legs were in motion, taking her away from the park. At least at home, there was a chance the police might call with news of Clayton. At home, she had his toys and clothes she could hold. She could pretend that part of him was still with her.

CHAPTER 30

C layton woke with a start. The sounds of hideous screaming and vicious yapping were deafening. He covered his ears and curled his body into a tight ball. Pushing himself against the dirt floor of his prison, he cowered there. His heart was pounding. He pressed his hands harder against his ears. It didn't help. The screaming continued, rising in shrillness as the yapping mixed with low growls. His body shook and he pressed himself farther into the corner where floor met the dirt wall. There was nowhere else to go, nowhere else to hide.

The sounds continued. They seemed to be right on top of him, but he knew they weren't. He drew one trembling hand away from his ear and listened. Where were the sounds coming from? They sounded so close. Were they coming from under the cabin.

All he knew was the confines of this small, dark area. He had seen the wooden crates past the rug he sat on, but the wall had seemed to end beyond them. He remembered feeling the sticky spider webs and was sure he had felt the dirt wall behind that. Had he been wrong? Was the dirt space bigger than he had thought? What else was down here?

The animal sounds continued. His mind was racing. He'd heard sounds like that before. Where? Where had he heard anything like that before? Then he remembered.

His father liked those nature shows with the animals fighting. The ones Mommy wouldn't let him watch if she was home. But he remembered seeing a big brown dog attacking a raccoon. The sounds had been similar—the trilling scream of the raccoon as the dog made its repeated lunges, yapping and growling at the animal.

Suddenly, the yapping changed to a shrill howl, and there was a scurry of movement. Clayton heard the scuffing of paws against dirt. They seemed to come toward him. He scrunched up even smaller as dirt spattered over him.

Then, he heard a loud thud, panting, soft whimpers. It was so close. If he stretched out his hand, he was sure he could touch the animal. Was it a dog? What would happen if he did? Would it bite him?

He lay motionless, holding his breath, willing his pounding heart to be quiet. Listening to the whimpering, he thought he heard the sound of licking. He imagined the animal cleaning his wounds. How badly was he hurt? It was too dark to see where the animal was, but he knew it had to be close.

He willed himself not to make any noises that might attract the animal's attention. It had sounded vicious when attacking the raccoon. Would it attack him? He lay still for a long time. His body hurt from being in one position for such a long time. A cramp started in his left leg.

He wanted to stretch out and rub his leg. What would the animal do? Did he care anymore? The man would probably kill him if the dog didn't. Where are you, Mommy? When are you coming to get me?

A wet coldness against his leg made Clayton jump. The coldness ran along the length of his leg, alternating with blasts of warm air. The dog was sniffing him. Clayton lay still, eyes closed, afraid to move, afraid to breathe. When he let his eyes slide open, all he saw was a huge black shadow hovering over him. He clamped his eyes shut. A whoosh of warm air slapped his face, then a cold wetness. In one swipe, a large moist tongue swept across the entire width of his face. He could only imagine the size of the dog and was too afraid to open his eyes.

The licking continued, as if the animal was intent on cleaning off every speck of dirt that had accumulated on his face in the past several days. Finally, Clayton could stand no more and he opened his eyes. A large black dog stood beside him with the biggest tongue Clayton had ever seen. Gathering his courage, he pushed at the dog's neck and commanded as loudly as he could, "No more. Down boy."

To his amazement, the dog plopped down beside him and stretched out his long, furry body, leaning heavily against Clayton. His tail thumped loudly against the hard earth. Clayton tentatively put out a hand to pet the dog. The black fur felt soft and silky and warm. The dog's tail wagged harder.

Clayton spoke softly. "I'm glad you don't eat boys. Do you have a name? I'm going to call you Blackie."

The tongue reached out once more to lick his face. Then the dog yawned lazily and curled up beside him. Clayton stretched one arm out around the dog. This was the safest he had felt since the man had brought him here. His fright had tired him and he too fell asleep.

The last thought to go through his head was that if the dog could get in here, maybe there was a way for him to get out.

CHAPTER 31

S teve took a long sip of his beer. Country tunes from the local radio station filled the bar with sorrowful melodies. He relaxed into the padded cushion of one of the booths lining the side wall of Casey's Bar and Grill. Across the neck of his brown bottle, he could see the black Arborite bar that stretched along the south wall.

The bartender, Joey, was busy serving the customers. Customers occupied seven of the eight stools, their forms obscured by a haze of cigarette smoke that grew thicker as the evening wore on. Steve's cursory gaze stopped at the last stool.

Someone watching him might have noticed the twitch that creased the right side of his cheek. They might also have noted how his shoulders suddenly stiffened, or how the fingers holding his beer bottle tightened to a white death grip. The other hand clenched and unclenched, nails digging unnoticed into his callused palm.

"Want another?" Mike asked.

Steve and Mike had worked overtime fixing a transmission for tourists eager to continue their vacation. Missing supper, they stopped at Casey's for a sandwich and a couple of beers before heading home.

Casey's was the town's local hangout. Pictures of sport-related themes covered the walls and tablecloths. Waitresses wore baseball caps from their favorite teams and entertained lively discussions with the customers. Low-hung lamps in the shapes of baseballs, footballs, and soccer balls hung above each table. With its free-flowing brews and dimly lit atmosphere, it drew a variety of patrons. You could always find someone you knew to enjoy a game of pool or a round of darts. It was a good spot to observe the local color and catch up on the gossip. Little went on in Scottsville that wasn't discussed, dissected, and argued about over a pint of beer within the walls of Casey's bar.

On a Sunday afternoon, you could even bring your kids to watch whatever game was in season on the only panoramic screen in town. On Sundays, Casey controlled the drinking and opened the video game room only to children. Bert Casey knew how to milk the town. He had a constant flow of townsfolk through his doors but maintained a tight control. He'd been a heavyweight boxer in the army. No one went up against him more than once. He had few rules—fighting was done outside, no drugs, no weapons, and he decided how many drinks one might consume. If Casey thought you had had enough, then the bar was closed to you and you had to find somewhere else to tip the bottle. Casey kept the town and himself happy.

"Sure, I'll take another one," Steve answered.

Steve's empty bottle hit the table with more force than he had intended. The table shook and the resounding clunk that echoed through the room made those in adjoining booths jump. The occupant of the last bar stool turned at the noise. One side of his mouth curled into a sneer. He tipped his beer at Steve.

Steve turned his gaze quickly away and muttered a curse.

"What did you say, Steve?" Mike asked.

"I said 'damn him,' plus more that's not worth repeating." Without turning back, Steve tipped the bottle he was clenching toward the bar. "Look what a foul wind blew in."

Mike looked in the direction Steve indicated. "Shit. Sure is a foul stench to the air over there, isn't there? You'd think Casey would do something about it. Find some excuse to keep that mouthy bastard out of here."

Karen, sporting a White Sox cap, approached the table. Steve gratefully accepted one of the beers she carried. Slowly, he put it to his lips and took a deep sip. The muscle in his right cheek continued to twitch.

"Damn shame letting him in here. Makes the neighborhood go right downhill," Mike said.

"Oh, him?" Karen tipped her head toward Roberts. "Sure does."

"Maybe it'll be your lucky day, Steve. Maybe he'll leave without harassing you. Looks like he has other things on his mind."

Joe Roberts had turned his attention back to the bar. He was leaning close to Shelly Whitman, one of the new teachers in town, an attractive brunette with an effervescent smile. Steve had spoken briefly to her a few times. She had always been pleasant. He hoped Shelly had better taste and not impressed by Joe's superego. He watched the game with interest for several minutes. Roberts would lean towards her, smiling and whispering in her ear. Shelly would give a short reply, then lean toward the bar. Finally, Shelly slipped off the barstool, drink in hand, and squeezed into a booth with some people from her school.

Robert's face was a caricature of shock and disbelief as he watched Shelly escape his attentions. He must have seen Steve's wide grin out of the corner of his eye. Suddenly, he jerked around and leapt off the barstool.

Steve's grin faded as Roberts marched toward their booth. "I think, Mike, my luck just ended."

Both men tried to ignore the shadow that spread over the table. The form that followed the shadow and leaned over their table was harder to ignore.

"What were you grinning at, Townsend?"

Steve kept his gaze focused on a Casey's Bar and Grill coaster.

"You were laughing at me, weren't you?"

Steve slowly turned to look at the off-duty cop. "Nothing you do is of interest to me, Roberts."

"You were staring at me."

"It's a free world—" Steve shrugged. "—at least in here."

"You looking for trouble, Townsend?"

"Nope. It was nothing. I told you that already. Now leave me alone!" Steve raised his head and looked straight at Roberts. The air radiated sparks as their eyes locked. Steve's body tensed. He felt every muscle, every tendon, each ready and waiting to react. Roberts wasn't hiding behind his badge now. They were on equal terms. His heart was racing with an adrenaline rush, and a sweat of anticipation covered his palms.

"This is a public place, Townsend."

"And this is my table. And I don't want you here."

"Is that so?"

"I don't want you here either," Mike growled.

Roberts' lips curled into a sneer. "Shut your trap. I'm not talking to you."

His voice barely audible yet cold as steel, Steve glared at the off-duty cop. "Leave him out of this, Roberts. Now clear out."

Steve wanted to beat the shit out of Roberts. He itched to take out all his pent-up anger on the bastard, but he knew it wouldn't resolve anything. Besides, this wasn't the place. He looked away from the cop. He kept his hands on the table, his fists clenching and unclenching. It took all his control to remain seated.

"What, a baby snatcher like you giving a policeman orders? Who do you think you are?"

Anger distorted Steve's face. His eyes burned with pent-up emotion. "I did nothing wrong. Now, leave me alone."

"Is that right, Steve? Are you sure you didn't have anything to do with the Kingsley boy? Did you take him for a ride too?" Roberts taunted.

Steve catapulted out of the booth and lunged at Roberts. Roberts jolted backward. He stumbled into the partition of another booth. Steve advanced on him. Grabbing Roberts by the front of his shirt, Steve pushed it and his clenched fist into Roberts' Adam's apple. Slowly pressing upward, his knuckles dug into the man's trachea. Robert's stridorus gasp for air was amazingly audible in the suddenly silent room. Attention focused on the two men, their faces inches apart. The static between them radiated like an inferno.

Roberts struggled to free himself. Steve kept the pressure steady, allowing Roberts to draw only minimal air into his lungs. Daggers of hate shot across the inch separating them. Suddenly Roberts went still. Sweat covered his brow and his face went slack. A look of shock and fear replaced his sneer.

With Steve's emotions raging, it took seconds for reason to prevail. Slowly, he relaxed the pressure he was exerting on Robert's trachea. He slid his fist higher, pushing Robert's chin upwards. He felt Robert's feet stretching off the floor. His voice was like a taunt bow. "I told you I had nothing to do with the boy. Now leave me alone."

"Some sort of trouble here?" Casey asked.

Steve dropped his hold on Robert's shirt. With his sudden release, the cop sagged against him. In disgust, Steve pushed him away. Roberts wasn't as tough as he pretended.

"No trouble, Casey. Roberts just stopped by to say hello. Now he's leaving. Right, Roberts?"

Massaging his throat, Roberts leaned against the wall behind him, desperately trying to regain his composure. His response was slow and raspy. "Yeah. I'm going."

Steve saw Joe Roberts' eyes narrow, saw the glint of steel as his fear changed to hate, saw the promise of revenge burning. It wasn't over yet. Roberts wouldn't leave him alone, especially after this. He would find some way to make his life hell, with or without his badge.

Steve stood watching as Roberts strode away. He felt Casey's hand on his shoulder and turned slowly toward him.

"You okay, boy? Don't let that asshole get to you. He's not worth it."

Steve nodded, smiling his thanks at Casey. Easing back into the booth, he leaned his head against the backboard and closed his eyes. He waited for the tension and anger to ease out of his body.

"The next round's on me, boys. Karen," Casey yelled at the White Sox buff. "Three beers over here."

Casey lowered his considerable girth into the booth, forcing Steve to slide to the end. Karen deposited three beers on the table, gracing Steve with a grin and a thumbs-up sign. Steve grabbed a bottle and tipped it toward her.

"Let's drink a toast to Scottsville's finest. The good ones. And let's hope the assholes like him get what's coming to them."

Three glasses clinked loudly.

***

Tyrell sat in a dark corner at the back of Casey's Bar and Grill, his raccoon hat and a beer on the table in front of him. He sat alone. He spoke to no one. Through a haze of smoke, he watched. Occasionally, he nodded his head slightly at those few people he knew. He didn't invite anyone to sit with him and no one attempted to join him. Tyrell took a sip of his beer. He had time to kill. It was too early yet.

He looked around the dimly lit room, listening to the country and western tunes. Most of the booths and tables were occupied. He was glad they left him alone. There wasn't anybody here he wanted to befriend. He didn't know them and they didn't know him. Most of them were pussy-whipped gossips. They wanted to know everything about you. Then, when you trusted them, they made fun of you behind your back. They said women were bad for gossiping, but some men had the women beat hands down. At least, the women tried to veil their questions, not just blurt them out, and then make jokes about you with their friends.

He remembered the pitying looks when Patty had up and left him, taking his son with her. It reminded him of the way the town had treated him as a child—all their fake concern for the poor boy with an irresponsible drunk for a father. He didn't want their pity. He didn't want to know any of them. At least nobody had been around the cabin harassing him lately.

Looking down the row of booths, he saw Steve Townsend. He'd served with him in Iraq. Steve had been a decent sort. That was, until he made sergeant. Tyrell didn't like taking orders from anybody, but especially not from a car mechanic from his hometown.

Tyrell watched Joe Roberts approach Steve's booth. He heard the exchange between them. Smiling to himself, he took a sip of his beer. Good entertainment tonight. Too bad it ended so soon.

So, Roberts thinks Steve took the boy. Well, well, how about that? He took another sip. Good thing that he's here tonight. I hope he stays all evening. Tipping the bottle upright, he drained it. Grabbing his hat, he left quietly through the back door.

CHAPTER 32

The fourth basement window Tyrell pushed with his runners jiggled slightly. The scrape of wood against wood echoed in the darkness. He paused, had anyone heard the noise.

Silence.

He looked around. The growth of trees and shrubs along the side of the house kept him sheltered from the view of any passerby on the street. He doubted there would be any at this time of night. This was an area of town with old houses and mature families that went to bed early, turned off every light to conserve electricity, and didn't venture out past eleven.

No, he didn't expect any interruptions, not if he kept quiet. He was good at that. Lots of practice from the time he was little. Like when his pa came home in the early morning hours, falling drunk onto his bed, if he made it that far. More often, he'd only get as far as the front door. Several nights a week, he would stumble through the door and pass out on the plank floor. They would find him there, or somewhere close to their log cabin. He would be snoring gusts of air putrid with cheap whiskey, and his clothes reeking of cigarette smoke. Tyrell would have to drag him to bed, clean up his stinking vomit, settle him in his fouled underwear, and all with the least possible noise.

No, his father was not one of those quiet drunks. Roused out of his alcoholic stupor, he was prone to violent acts, acts often directed at Tyrell, whose job it was to deal with his drunken state. He had learned to work quietly, the hard way.

At first, he had tried to wake him, attempting to lighten his dead weight by making his father stumble to his bed. The blows he had received for aggravating his father's hangover had been swift and powerful. It had only taken a few belts from his muscular arms to teach Tyrell the importance of silence, and letting sleeping dogs lie. His whole family had learned to tiptoe around the two-bedroom cabin for most of the day while Pa slept off the booze.

Tyrell looked up at the sky. The sliver of a crescent moon hid behind clouds leaving the area around the house in gloomy darkness. He slipped a camping knife out of his jeans pocket, squatted by the window and fiddled with the lock. In less than a minute he was shoving the window inward.

Wood scraped on wood. Then, with a pop, the window slid on rusty hinges and disappeared into the blackness of the basement. There was a muffled thud as the window hit the floor. Tyrell held his breath. Staying crouched beside the house, he waited, alert for any sign that the sound had aroused attention.

There was no sound of footsteps, no lights turned on in this house, or in the red brick one fifteen feet away. Feeling a cocky sense of security, Tyrell took out a pencil flashlight and checked the ground he had crossed since leaving the pathway. He saw the grass and the smattering of dandelions that crept up to the house. The July heat had baked the ground to a hard crust and no footprints remained to mark his passage. He pulled a pair of latex gloves out of his pocket and slipped them on.

After another glance around, he eased his body through the basement window. He wondered how far the drop would be. Holding the window frame, he dangled briefly, bracing himself. He bent his knees to take the impact of the landing then slid down the wall. He felt the coolness of the damp concrete penetrating his black T-shirt.

Jabbing pain shot up his right leg as he landed on the basement floor five feet below. His muffled curse was no louder than the soft thud of his rubber-soled shoes meeting concrete. He waited for the pain to fade to a tolerable level. As his eyes adjusted to the darkness, he listened to the surrounding sounds. The furnace's fan hummed as it circulated air through the house. A refrigerator's compressor on its last legs squealed occasionally. Even the ticking of the kitchen clock penetrated through the darkness to ears trained to hear.

When he'd gone camping with Gramps, and later in the Gulf War, he had learned to be aware of the slightest sounds. Yes, he had always been listening, especially in the darkness, especially in the quiet of night when sounds traveled farther. When his outfit had first been stationed in the Gulf and he'd pulled night watch, it had been a game...but later...

He listened to the house, alert for footsteps, the flushing of a toilet, or the hum of a newly turned on light. There was no sound to disturb the silence. He waited. He had all night. The boy would sleep.

It had taken several minutes for the pain to settle to a dull throb. He was ready and there had been no human sound from above. There was only one person to rouse, and she was alone. He had been watching her house from the shadow of a garage down the street and watched as Jenny systematically turned out all the lights. No one had noticed him. The army trained him well; taught him how to hide in small dark spaces, taught him how not to be seen.

So far, he'd been lucky. The street stayed quiet; no pedestrians, and dogs brought in for the night. It was rare that a car even passed by. He hoped his luck would hold. Maybe he would get lucky another way. He smiled and felt the rush of blood swelling him. Maybe when he had gotten what he had come for he would find something else to come for. His smile widened.

She is a pretty piece, isn't she? All that put on innocence. I bet she's not as innocent as she pretends. Just maybe I'll find out. I wonder how she likes it?

Visions of the woman upstairs mingled with memories of Patty. When he'd come back from Iraq, Patty had changed. Demanding him to be rougher and rougher, and asking to have her hands and feet tied to the bedposts. He'd objected at first...Did Jenny like it that way? Blood rushed to fill him. He placed his foot on the first of the basement stairs.

His erection made walking difficult, but he had to go slowly anyway. Don't want to wake her till I'm ready. He grasped the handrail and used it to guide him through the darkness, one riser at a time. With each step, his pulsing organ slid between his leg and the rough denim cloth. Shivers of excitement ran up and down his spine.

Mounting the stairs was a slow process, but finally, he reached the top. The basement door was closed. He grasped the handle and turned it slowly. With a slight creak, the door swung open. He waited, listening. Silence. He stepped into a hallway between the front door and what he assumed was the kitchen. The darkness relieved by a sliver of moonlight that filtered through the Catherine wheel window on the front door.

He leaned forward and looked down the hall. Cupboards stood along one wall—the kitchen. The living room must be on the other side. It was important to know the layout of the house. He might have to leave in a hurry. He glanced to the left. Stairs lead to the second floor. Tyrell headed for them.

He began the ascent to the second level. The clouds must have drifted away as moonlight shone through windows on the floor above, making the going easier. Soon he was on the landing. He flattened his body against a wall and tried to determine the layout of the second floor. He saw four doors, probably one bathroom and three bedrooms.

Which one is the kid's room and which one is hers?

The left side of his lip curled upwards as he thought of finding her room. His member twitched. I better get what I came for first. His swollen organ ached with anticipation. Maybe he should check out her bedroom first.

He felt in his jeans pocket for the length of rope. It was still there. He could tie her up, do her, then get the kid's stuff. No, better get what the kid needs first. He laughed to himself. You might forget what you came for if you get showing her a good time. Get the stuff; then there'll be lots of time.

Keeping his body flat against the wall, he crept down the hall until he came to the first doorway. It was open. He saw the glimmer of white porcelain—the bathroom. He continued along the hallway. The next door was partially closed.

He shoved it gently with his sneaker. The beating of his heart took a quick surge. Boxes, cases, unused furniture, no beds. He left the door ajar and passed on to the next room. It was open. He crept to the opening and peered around the door jamb. In the semi-darkness, he saw a sleeping form partially covered by a sheet.

As he watched, his hand slid downwards and he stroked the bulge of his jeans, feeling his member move rhythmically to his touch. Blood that had eased out of his erection surged back, filling him until he thought he would burst. Straining against his jeans, it pulsated—ecstasy so strong it was painful. He cupped his hands around it, pushing, thrusting. Easy, boy you don't want to finish yet. He forced his hands away, forced his mind to change direction, forced himself to pass silently to the next door. Not yet, old buddy. He continued down the hall. The next door had to be the one.

It was partially open, and Tyrell slid behind it. He let his gaze roam around the room. He saw the single bed with its pile of stuffed shapes lined up by the pillow. A dresser stood on the opposite wall. In front of the window was a child's table, and beside it, a wooden toy box. Toys overflowed the sides of the box. A double-louvered closet was on the sidewall.

He listened again. No noises came from the bedroom down the hall. He crossed to the closet. Holding the edges of the mahogany doors, he slid the two pieces of wood apart. The door squeaked slightly. He waited. Nothing.

He looked in the closet, but no light penetrated its depths. Stepping inside, he blindly stretched out his hand and ran it along the rod until he felt the fleecy bulk of a jacket. He slid it off the hanger, then pulled off several other objects. He took a plastic bag out of his back pocket and shoved the clothes inside. On tiptoes, he crossed to the dresser.

There was an ornament on top of the dresser. Tyrell shoved it back and put the bag beside it. He used two hands to pull open the top drawer. It slid open with minimal noise. He rummaged through the contents, pushing some shirts into the bag. He went on to the next drawer. When the bag was bulging, he crossed to the bed. He picked up several of the stuffed animals, chose a soft furry bear, then shoved it into the bag.

He turned away from the bed. An edge of the bag caught on a drawer knob. He yanked it. Suddenly, it released itself, the dresser tipping slightly. Damn. Tyrell reached out to steady it, holding the dresser in place for several seconds. Satisfied it was stable, he crept toward the door and was almost there when he heard the crash of something hitting the floor. He froze.

Staring at the floor, he saw the broken pieces of a china ornament that had fallen from the top of the dresser.

□□

Jenny's eyes fluttered open. She stared into the darkness. A sliver of cloud-shaded moon filtered through the bedroom curtains, otherwise, the room was in darkness. She listened to the silence of the night while her eyes adjusted to the lack of light.

What had roused her? Had Clayton wakened and called her? She lay in the blissful state of semi-consciousness until the nightmare of the past few days came back. Clayton had not called—he was still missing. She turned her head and buried it in the pillow.

Then she heard it—a soft pat outside her room and then another one. Abruptly, her senses became alert. She listened, her body tense and still. Was it her imagination playing tricks on her again? Lately, it had been doing a lot of that. Between hearing Clayton's voice and every sound the old house made, and some it didn't, Jenny had begun to second-guess herself. She attributed it to her anxious state of mind and the rest to her exhaustion. She slept poorly, wakened often, and then had trouble getting back to sleep. It was taking its toll on her body and the effect was obvious. She lay in the darkness, her mind a whirlpool of swirling images.

The house seemed silent now. What had woken her? Maybe Ray had come home. But there were no noises of him shuffling about downstairs. She looked at the clock—eleven-forty-seven. Was it too early for him to return from wherever he had found to have a few beers?

Ray had fallen into a routine of walking the streets and outskirts of Scottsville looking for Clayton during daylight hours, then finding a place to drink for the evening. He would come home late; falling into an alcohol-induced slumber. He had been little support and she resented his ability to snore the night away. His sleep didn't seem disturbed by the nightmares that haunted her. How was she going to tell him she wanted him to go home?

Then the noise sounded again. A soft padding. Where was it coming from? Was it coming from outside the house, or outside her bedroom? Jenny remembered leaving the hall window partially open. Had the wind blown something over? She looked at the window in her room. The lace curtains were still. There was no breeze.

Her eyes flew back to her bedroom door. She stared into the darkness of the hall. What was it? She dragged herself out of bed to check. She had just reached the top of the stairs when she heard a commotion at the front door. Who was here? Then she heard the scrape of metal, and a key was being inserted in the lock. The front door opened. She heard muffled voices. Steve assisted an inebriated Ray into the house.

"What's going on?" Jenny demanded. Her voice bordered on hysteria.

Steve shrugged his shoulders. "I'm sorry. He was at Casey's and had a bit too much to drink. He insisted I bring him back here."

She ran down the stairs, her anger increasing with each step. "A bit too much. That's an understatement."

"Where do you want me to put him?"

"You don't really want to hear my answer to that one, do you?"

Steve chuckled. "Well, I could just dump him on the back porch. He probably won't remember how he got home anyway. What's your choice?"

Shaking her head, she threw her hands up in the air. "The back porch sounds good, especially if we get more rain." She grinned at Steve. "You'd better bring him into the family room."

She watched as Steve unceremoniously dumped the semi-conscious Ray onto the sofa. His only response was a loud moan before rolling over, curling into a ball, and beginning to snore loudly.

"I think I'll get a bucket. And, he'd better hit it or he'll be in deeper shit than he is right now." She grinned at Steve again when he raised his eyebrows in feigned shock at her use of profanity.

"If you bring me some towels, I'll cover the couch with them in case he does throw up."

Nodding, she went back up the stairs and gathered some old towels. It was an instinctive reaction to look into Clayton's room every time she passed and tonight was no exception. An evening breeze ruffled the clown curtains. She froze.

The window was wide open. She was sure she'd left it closed. She looked around the room. Her gaze stopped at Clayton's bed. Someone had disturbed Clayton's collection of stuffed animals; his toys lay scattered across his bed instead of the neat piles she'd arranged before bed. Something was wrong. Where was Frazer? Clayton's favorite stuffed bear was missing. Jenny lifted each animal, hoping to find Frazer hiding beneath one of the others. He wasn't there.

She looked at the floor. There, broken into several pieces, was the china pig her Aunt Joan had given Clayton when he was a baby. Someone had been in this room. Were they still here? Standing rooted to the spot, she screamed.

Steve bounded up the stairs. "Jenny, what's wrong?"

"Someone's been here!"

Steve glanced around the room. She was sure he was going to reassure her she was wrong. That was until his gaze stopped at the broken pieces of china on the floor in front of Clayton's dresser. He strode across the room, checked behind the door, in the closet, and under the bed. He crossed to the open window.

"Looks like whoever it was went out the window." Steve pointed to the sill where bits of old paint had scraped away. "Better call the police."

She ran to her bedroom and dialed 911. A minute later, she was back, feeling braver for Steve's presence. She walked around the room. The closet door was wide open. She remembered shutting it earlier when she had put his laundry away. Cautiously, she walked toward the folding door and peeked inside. Hangers once neatly organized, were now shoved together. Some clothes had fallen to the floor. She stooped to pick them up

"Better not to touch anything until the police get here," Steve said.

She straightened and confined herself to a visual search. Where was Clayton's red fleece jacket? Her eyes scanned the hangers. It wasn't there.

She turned her back to the closet and surveyed the rest of the room. Her eyes stopped at the window. The blue clown curtains waved slightly. Her heart was racing. Who had been here and why? Someone had taken Clayton's jacket, and his favorite toy, Frazer.

Chad Evans answered the call with Dave Charlton. They arrived within minutes and checked the room, then searched the rest of the house. Ray continued snoring in the family room. Later, Evans came to the kitchen, where Jenny and Steve were waiting.

"Whoever it was, it looks like they came in through a basement window. Someone pried the lock open and left it that way. I assume you didn't leave it open?"

Jenny shook her head.

"It looks like he left by the window upstairs. We'll dust for fingerprints, but he probably wore gloves. Charlton is looking outside now, but the ground's too hard to leave much in the way of prints."

Charlton joined them shortly and confirmed what Evans had told them.

"There's some broken branches on a shrub by the back fence. But I couldn't see any definite footprints. I'll come back when it's light and check again."

After they had dusted for prints, Jenny slammed the window and twisted the lock into place. Steve nailed the basement window shut. With Ray still semi-conscious on the family room couch, she didn't refuse Steve's offer to sleep on the living room sofa for the night. Nor did she object to the quick, reassuring hug he gave her before she went back to her own bed.

In the morning, she made him breakfast before he headed home. Ray continued to sleep. At least he hadn't used the towels Steve had tucked around him. She would let him wake on his own before she gave him a piece of her mind. Jenny had had more than enough of his drinking when they lived together. She vowed it would be the last time he would spend a night in her house. The phone lines would be adequate to keep him in touch.

CHAPTER 33

A light rapping on the front door startled Jenny. Over the past few days, the house had been quiet. With no media or spectators lining the streets, and the departure of her mother and Ray, the house was like a tomb. The phone hardly rang. She didn't know what was worse—the constant ringing of the phone in the first days, or the silence now.

She crossed to the door and looked out the Catherine wheel window. A ringer for Grizzly Adams stood on the other side of the door. Keeping the chain lock on, Jenny opened the door a crack. The man wore a rumpled khaki shirt, worn jeans, and scuffed ochre-colored work boots. He held a faded brown fedora in his large, rough hands.

"Mrs. Kingsley?"

"Yes."

"I'm Bill Clement. I just got back from a fishing trip and heard about your boy being missing. I wanted to see if I could help.

"Yes, of course. That's very nice of you."

Jenny wiped at a tear at the corner of her eye. It overwhelmed her how kind people were—people she had never met offering help, continuing to search for Clayton in their spare time, adding to the posters spread across town, questioning people they met, and manning the hotline.

The Samaritans far outweighed the few making crank calls. And, there had been crank calls—people telling her she wasn't a responsible parent, accusing her or Ray of having murdered Clayton. One caller even suggested they had sold him. Jenny didn't want to answer the phone anymore, but one day, she knew, it would be the call she had been praying for, the one that would tell her Clayton was found, alive and well. She looked at this waiting mountain man and thanked God for the kind ones.

"The police have a command post in the Community Center. They could tell you what you could do to help."

"Well, Mrs. Kingsley, I was talking to Officer Chad Evans..." he waited while she nodded acknowledgment of the name and then continued, "He's a friend of mine...he suggested I talk to you. He told me about the dog they had looking for your boy—"

"Yes." Disappointment filled her voice. She wondered if he noticed it. "The dog traced him to the street. The police think someone took him in a car from there."

Bill scratched his furrowed brow, then nodded at her. His callused hands worked the soft felt fabric of his hat. "Yes, that's what Chad told me. But—I have Missy. She's a bloodhound and she's mighty good at tracking. I'd like to have her look for the boy—if that's all right with you."

She sighed. He seemed so earnest, so willing to help. What would it hurt? Shrugging her shoulders, she slid the chain and let him into the house. She saw a floppy-eared dog sitting quietly on the front seat of his black GMC truck. Was this sad-eyed animal going to get any further than the police dog? So many days had passed. What could the dog find now?

The man perched on the edge of a living room chair; his hands worked the frayed edges of the fedora. Frequent exposure to sun and wind had weathered his face, deepening the lines around his mouth and eyes. He showed a natural grace surprising in a man so large, and despite his size, and his obvious affinity with nature, he seemed painfully shy. Jenny was afraid to voice her doubts and hurt his feelings.

"The police dogs tried." She paused. "They only got as far as the road," she said.

The man nodded several times. She was surprised by the light in his pale blue eyes. He forgot his fedora while using his hands to speak. His shyness forgotten while talking about his dog.

"Well, you see, ma'am, German Shepherds are very good, but they can only track for about eight hours. After that, they can't find a trail, whereas a bloodh ound...well...they've been able to find a trail one hundred days later."

He must have seen the look of disbelief in her eyes, for his right hand rose in front of him, asking her to hear him out. "Now, I know that sounds crazy. But it's true. I've been raising bloodhounds for thirty years now, and they're damned good trackers. Sorry Miss, didn't mean to curse. I just get a bit excited where my dogs are concerned."

"That's okay," Jenny assured him.

She was so tired. She wanted to tell him just to leave her alone, but she didn't have the energy to dampen on his enthusiasm. If the police hadn't found Clayton, how was he going to? Maybe if she just let him talk, he'd go away.

"Now, my Missy, she sure is one good tracker. One of the best I've had. She's had real success in finding people." Hands continued to dart about with his enthusiasm. It was as if he could read Jenny's thoughts and had to prove his dog's abilities. "Would you mind if I gave my Missy a try?"

Was she grasping at straws? This man was so sure his dog could find Clayton. What would it hurt? A straw was better than thin air, and right now, thin air was all Jenny had. She nodded slowly at him. "But how would Missy be able to find him? The other dog couldn't."

Passion shone in his eyes, his shyness forgotten, his hands kept up an active part in his conversation. Jenny tried to concentrate on his words.

"Each of us has trillions of cells that slough off every day..."

Jenny nodded. She remembered that from science class.

"Bacteria cause these cells to give off a gas. Each person has his or her own individual odor in their sweat—it contains urea, chlorine, sodium..."

She looked away. He was giving her more information than she wanted, or needed. Why was he wasting her time?

"They're released by our glands. The body has a layer of air around it which peaks about eighteen inches above our heads."

She looked back at her visitor. What was he talking about? Air...eighteen inches...heads... She had lost all track of his explanation.

"This current carries up the body and releases above it...this creates a 'scent trail' and a bloodhound can pick it up."

He was smiling at her now, and seemed to be finished talking as his hands rested quietly in his lap, the fedora between them. She nodded. Did he realize she hadn't heard half of what he had said?

"Do you have something of your son's, like pajamas, or underwear that I could take to scent the dog from?"

"His pajamas are still under his pillow. Detective Jarvis thought the Canine Unit might want them, but they didn't."

"Can you show me where they are?" He took a large plastic bag and a pair of gloves out of his jeans pocket. "I'll put them in here."

She led him to her son's room. Clement put on the gloves and slid Clayton's pajamas into the bag. With a slight nod, he followed Jenny back downstairs then went to the truck and snapped a leash on Missy. The dog padded beside him into the living room. Clement opened the bag and let Missy put her nose inside. Drool dripped from the dog's mouth onto the pajamas. After several seconds, the dog pulled her nose out of the bag and looked up at her owner. Jenny thought she must been imagining things, but she was almost sure the dog nodded her head as if telling him, "I have him now. Let's go." Pride evident in his smile, Clement closed the seal on the bag and gave the command. "Find, Missy, find."

Jenny watched the bloodhound circle the room. Coming to Clayton's favorite spot on the sofa, her tail rose. She sniffed deeply, walked toward the kitchen, and then to the back door. Clement loosened the leash and opened the door. Missy walked off the porch and then paced back and forth on the lawn. Her tail rose higher as she trotted over to the sandbox.

"See how high her tail is?" Clement asked Jenny. "That means she's got a good scent of him. They say 'the higher the tail the stronger the scent.'"

She watched in amazement as Missy set her head to the ground. Within seconds, she was at the gate. Clement swung it open and Missy followed along to the street in the same path the German Shepherd had taken eight days before.

"I can't believe she can still find his trail. And, it rained the other night." Whispering so she didn't distract the dog, Jenny stayed several feet behind. The dog proceeded—nose down, tail up, floppy ears swiping the ground.

"Actually, the heat of the sun burns off the scent. When it cools down, the scent can be picked up again. The moisture in the morning dew or from a rain really helps the bacteria release the scent." Bill Clement turned to Jenny and grinned. "The water wets the air and makes the scent stronger."

They followed Missy down the street and were close behind when she turned the corner and stopped at the curb. Jenny saw the gleam of pride in Bill's eyes. His smile deepened the lines by his mouth and eyes, making him somehow look years younger.

"This is where the Shepherd lost the trail, right?" His voice held an optimism Jenny didn't feel. Why was he so pleased? His dog had taken them no further than the other one. Missy paced at the curb, her tail high and still. Finally, she returned to her owner and sat quietly beside him. "I'll get the truck and we'll see where we go from here."

She wondered where he would go from here. The trail had ended, there was no place farther to go. The threesome walked silently back to the house. Clement, intent on his thoughts, seemed totally oblivious to her disappointment. She watched sadly as he put Missy in the front seat of the truck.

"I'll be in touch." He promised.

The dog sat, her sad brown eyes on Jenny, almost as if she too was saying sorry. Jenny stood rooted to the spot as the truck drove off down the street. Why had she dared to hope? But hope was all she had to cling to.

CHAPTER 34

Martha woke with a start. The flu bug that hit her several days before had kept her limited to her bed and the bathroom. This afternoon was the first time in the living room in days. Glad to be feeling better, despite a lingering headache, she made a cup of tea and sat in her favorite chair.

She didn't bother to open the heavy velvet curtains; the bright sunlight only made her headache worse. She turned on the television but kept the volume low. Martha was content to enjoy the peacefulness of the unlit room. The muted voices of talk show hosts and their guests were a welcome change from the silence of her bedroom. At one point, she drifted off to sleep. When she woke, she heard voices in the background. The room was dark...dark except for the flashing of light from across the room. Martha looked toward the light—the screen of the television set.

The six o'clock news was on. How could she have slept that long? She never slept during the day, but the flu had really given her a knock. Martha's joints protested, and she felt a wave of dizziness as she tried to rise, and she had to use the arms of the chairs to assist her. She crossed to the television. Her hand stretched out to push the off button when she saw a child's face flash on the screen. A commentator's voice rose above the other sounds.

"Have you seen this child?"

The camera zoomed in for a close-up. Martha stared at the picture of a blonde-haired child on the screen. She had seen that child before. Where? Her mind was groggy from her recent illness and she tried to focus on the face. Where were her glasses?

Putting her hand to her chest, she felt her glasses hanging from a cord around her neck. She put them on. Yes! She had seen him before. He was the child who had just moved in down the street. This must be the one Steve was looking for. Was he the same child she had seen walking with that fellow from out of town, the one with the limp? The one who wears that stupid raccoon hat all the time? No. It couldn't be. Why would the child go with him? Does look like the boy though.

"Please call this number, 1-800-541-2222, if you have any information."

Martha reached for the phone and dialed the number flashing across the screen. "It probably isn't the same child, but..." She listened to the volunteer on the other end of the hotline. "Yes, I'll be here all evening. Will a deputy come? Yes, that's fine."

Martha hung up the phone. She thought of this child, missing for over a week now, and then she thought of another child lying ill in a hospital bed many years ago. Her thoughts drifted to images of grandchildren she had never seen. She reached for the phone again and dialed another number.

Her fingers shook as she counted the rings. After the fourth one, the ringing stopped and a soft female voice said, "Hello."

"Is Cecily there?"

"Mom...Mom...is that you?"

Tears held in for decades, ran down Martha's wrinkled cheeks. Unable to speak, her head bobbed in answer.

Finally, Martha whispered. "Yes, Cecily. Please...can I see you?"

Long after the connection ended, Martha continued to grasp the phone to her chest. Tears of relief and joy flooded down her cheeks, drenching her embroidered handkerchief.

CHAPTER 35

Something was missing. At first, Clayton couldn't think what it was. His body was on fire and a throbbing pain over his eyes made it hard to think. His blanket was damp from the rain that had seeped under the cabin. Chills shook his body, and he started coughing. He coughed so hard his chest hurt, and he could hear a whistle when he took a breath. He wanted to be home in his own bed. He wanted his mother looking after him. Where are you, Mommy? Am I ever going to see you again?

Something nagged at him. What was he forgetting? He was down here alone. There was little to remember. Then it came to him. Before he had fallen asleep, he hadn't been alone. The dog, Blackie, had been lying beside him. He stretched out his hand in the darkness, wanting to touch the dog, wanting to feel his warm, silky fur, wanting to touch another living thing. His fingers reached out, but all they touched was the damp, dark air.

Then he ran his arm along the bare moist earth that lay past his mat. The area was empty. His hand groped into thin air. Still nothing. The cool dampness that coated his skin made the goose bumps grow in size and number. He tried to stop the shivering

"Here, boy," he called. "Come here. Come here, Blackie."

Clayton waited and listened. Nothing happened, no barking, no growling, no thump of a dog's tail. Blackie was gone and all that remained was the animal's scent and the heavy wheeze of his breathing.

He pulled his arm back and tears flowed down his cheeks. He needed the dog's warmth to penetrate the chill that had invaded his body. Tucking his hand back under the blanket, he curled up and prayed for the escape of sleep. Tears trickled down his blazing cheeks. He didn't even try to wipe them away. He was alone again.

When he woke, he thought about the dog. If the dog had gotten in, there must be a way out. He crept to where he thought the dog had come in. He stood, reaching his hands up along the dirt wall. All he could feel was more damp earth. Then, he remembered the wooden crates he had seen in a corner of the dugout area. He groped through their contents. Among the objects, he found something that felt like a small shovel. Dumping one of the crates, he took it and the shovel back to the wall.

He flipped the crate upside-down and climbed up on it. He stretched his hand above him and let his fingers run along the dirt wall. Suddenly his hand slid into a depression. Clayton felt his hopes rise as he explored the hole. He clawed his way up to the opening and tried to squeeze his body through.

Not big enough. The opening was too small. He should have been able to fit through the same hole as the dog. His fingers examined the depression in the wall. The hole must have filled back in. He picked up the shovel and began digging at the hole. It was dark, but he didn't need light for what he had to do.

He wasn't sure how long he had been digging. His hands hurt and he could hear his stomach growling. His body felt like a furnace, but the hole was getting bigger.

Suddenly, a glimmer of light broke through the wall of dirt. He dug harder, clawing away at the clay. His fingers, coated with mud, scraped away the loose dirt until finally the glimmering light grew larger.

A dull thud above startled him. He dropped the trowel. The cabin door was being closed. He heard the wooden length of wood being shoved into the latch. A shudder ran down his spine. He's back!

Clayton jumped off the crate, tipping it over in his haste. He had left the shovel in the space he had dug. He didn't have time to go back for it. He brushed away the dirt that covered his clothes and hands and hurried back to his mat. Lying on it, he curled his body into a ball. He knew it wouldn't be long before the man would be moving the dresser away, the mat, then he would be opening the trap door. The man always checked on him as soon as he came back.

Would he wonder how he had gotten so dirty?

Clayton wanted to hide, wanted to melt into the dirt-packed wall that made up his prison. But there was nowhere to hide. Nowhere to go. He wished he had superpowers and could become invisible. Then he could sneak out the trap door, and wait until the man opened the cabin door. He knew he could find his way home if he could just get out of the cabin. If he were invisible, the man wouldn't know if he stuck his tongue out at him, or if he whined. But he didn't whine anymore. He didn't want to be hit again.

He closed his eyes and waited. It was not long before he heard scraping above him, wood against wood, then a muffled sound as the rug was shoved aside. He tried not to tremble but his body betrayed him. Light filtered into the crawlspace, and then darkness returned as a large shape filled the opening.

Clayton heard the creak of a footstep on the first rung of the ladder.

CHAPTER 36

The posters were everywhere; taped to street signs, nailed to trees, sitting in shop windows—the kid's face plastered all over town. And people were talking about him, too. Tyrell heard them gossiping while he sat having coffee in his usual booth at the back of Stockley's. The first couple of days, the town had talked of nothing else. His mouth turned up at one corner. Just like the last time.

Then, as he remembered the last time, his smile faded.

Damn kid. Nothing but a sniveling brat. Not a good choice. Such a weakling, whining all the time. And then, that cough. Should've dropped him somewhere. Waited too long. How was I supposed to know his cough was that bad? I'm not a goddamned doctor. I told him to stop coughing. And he had.

He had only been coughing for a few days. It started with an occasional cough at night, then a few times during the day. Suddenly, it had worsened, and his small body racked with spasms of coughing. Even Tyrell's yelling and threatening to cuff him didn't make him stop. The spells would just run their course and stop when the boy was covered in sweat, or too exhausted to cough anymore.

Tyrell hated it when the kid started one of his coughing fits. They seemed to come more at night, and once he'd started, it was a long time before he would settle again. Tyrell couldn't sleep with him coughing all night.

I told him to shut up. Told him he'd get the back of my hand if he didn't. Wouldn't have been the first time. Little brat, he just curled up in a ball and kept coughing. Stopped that one morning, though. Tyrell had opened up the trapdoor to let him out to pee. He wondered why he was suddenly so quiet. Sure didn't expect to find him dead. Had to dump his body in the woods miles from town. Hunters found his body. The police never solved that case.

Better get this kid some medicine. Don't want the same thing happening to him. I made a better choice this time. This kid doesn't whine and carry on like the other one. Not anymore. Only a couple of good belts before he'd figured out how to behave. Pretty good kid. No trouble. Not crying all the time that he's going to pee himself like the other kid did. Too bad he's sick.

Tyrell recalled how hot the kid's skin had been when he led him to the outhouse. His eyes were kind of glassy, too. But he'd kept down the ginger ale he gave him. The clean clothes were better than the damp ones he'd had on, and his fleece jacket should help with the chills. A bit of Tylenol should fix him right up. The kid even smiled when he gave him that old bear.

Tyrell opened the glass-topped door of Stockley's Grocery Store. A poster of Clayton covered three-quarters of the glassed surface. He glanced at the message requesting anyone seeing the child to call this number. Smirking to himself, Tyrell stepped inside, letting the door swish closed behind him.

The store was a combination of old and new. The small restaurant area had been there for as long as he could remember. His mother used to bring him in as a boy. She would pick up her groceries and then have coffee and catch up on all the local happenings. She was gone all these years and not much had changed.

The mingling smells of apples and cinnamon filled the store. Tyrell inhaled deeply. Mrs. Stockley sure makes the best apple pies. Have to get myself a slice before I head home.

Can't stay long today. Not with the boy sick. Maybe I'll take him back a treat. Maybe he'd like some of those animal cookies.

The store was well stocked and it didn't take him long to gather what he needed. The Tylenol took the longest. Which one should I get? Not the infant. He picked up a bottle of children's chewables and read the directions. He remembered trying to give Tyson Tylenol once when he had been sick. His son had refused to chew the tablets for Patty, and he had to go buy the liquid. He put the chewable back and grabbed a bottle of liquid Tylenol.

Next, he went down the linen aisle and checked the blankets. He picked out a thick gray thermal one and put it in the cart. He added juice and animal crackers before heading to the checkout. Placing his purchases on the counter, Tyrell waited for Mrs. Stockley to calculate his purchases.

"Hello, Tyrell. How are you?"

"Fine, ma'am."

Keeping his head lowered, Tyrell looked away quickly. His muttered response was quiet and respectful. He remembered Mrs. Stockley's kindness to him and his mother over the years. Some of the town's folk had made his family an object of gossip when he was growing up, but not her. She had chided his schoolmates when they made fun of him. She had even given him bits of candy he knew his mother didn't have the money to buy. Mrs. Stockley had made a big fuss over Tyson, too.

But that was before Patty had gone and run off with their son.

A nerve twitched on Tyrell's cheek, and he felt the muscles in his face tighten. Coarse hairs on the back of his hand stood up. His fingers clenched his worn brown wallet, crushing the soft leather fabric.

"Hot enough for you?"

Tyrell looked down at the items Mrs. Stockley was ringing in. Her voice brought him back to the present and his fingers slowly unclenched, allowing the leather to unfold.

"Yes, ma'am, it's been pretty hot lately."

"That storm the other night didn't cool things down a bit."

"No," he agreed. "There's another one coming."

Mrs. Stockley looked outside. "Oh, I think you're wrong about that, Tyrell. Just look how bright that sky is. There's not a cloud in sight. It looks like it's going to be a beautiful day."

He didn't bother answering. Stupid town people. Couldn't read the weather to save their souls. He knew there was a storm coming. His leg had been telling him that since before he got out of bed this morning. He could even smell the moisture in the air. Couldn't she see the way the tree leaves curling, showing their silver undersides? Yes, sure as shooting, there was another storm coming. It would be here before nightfall.

"Now, this isn't what you want, is it?"

He glanced at the bottle of liquid Tylenol in her hand.

"This is the children's. You must have picked up the wrong bottle. I'll get the right one for you." Mrs. Stockley moved away from the counter, the Tylenol bottle in her hand.

"No." He could hear his raised voice. It sounded as if he was shouting. Damn woman. He glanced behind him. No one in the store seemed to have noticed. He lowered his voice. "No, that's what I want." He paused. "I have a sick animal I want to give it to."

"Well, if you're sure this is the one you want. Once you open it, you can't return it."

"I won't return it." He heard the gruffness in his voice and saw Mrs. Stockley's face tighten as she finished totaling up his purchases. She was shoving them into plastic bags. He hadn't meant to snap at her. She had always been kind to him. Maybe he would take time for a piece of one of her pies.

"You're pies are the best. What kind do you have today?" He saw her face soften again as she rhymed them off.

"I'll have the apple. You make the best apple pie I've ever tasted. I'll have a coffee too."

"Well thank you, Tyrell." She smiled. "I'll bring it right over to your table."

He headed for his usual table at the back of the restaurant. He was halfway through his pie when he saw her come into the store. Her ash blonde hair pulled back behind her ears, her face as pale and drawn as an invalid. He saw the way her shorts bagged on her hips. Good. Nice to see she's missing him. Like how I felt when Patty took my boy.

He watched as Jenny made her way up and down the aisles, putting a few purchases in her basket. It caught him off guard when she turned and saw him watching her. Unable to turn his eyes away, he saw her puzzlement growing as she stared back at him. Suddenly, she looked away and hurried down the aisle. When she was out of his sight, Tyrell held his coffee cup up for a refill and put his attention back to Mrs. Stockley's apple pie.

CHAPTER 37

Bill Clement was reading the Scottsville Daily News at his kitchen table when he noticed the sunlight dimming. Going outside, he saw clouds gathering in the distance and ran a tanned hand through his graying hair. Years of exposure to the elements had taught him how to read the weather. He saw their darkening bellies and knew the clouds would soon be heavy with rain. Moisture was tangible in the afternoon air. He could almost smell the storm coming. It was time to go.

The humidity would release scents burnt off by the day's earlier heat, releasing them back into the air. Missy should be able to pick up the trail they had lost this morning, but they'd better move fast. Heavy rains might obliterate the scents.

Wetting a finger, he checked the wind direction, then went back into the house. He lifted his backpack off the hook by the door and set it on the kitchen counter. Bill riffled through the assortment of supplies inside; dried fruit, cereal bars, water bottles, Swiss army knife, towel, training whistle, cell phone, and Missy's four-foot lead. He checked the side pocket. The plastic bag with the boy's pajama top was still there. He grabbed his yellow rain slicker off the hook, folded it, and shoved it inside.

He glanced at his watch and noted the time—three-fifteen. They should have a few good hours on the trail, that is, if it didn't rain too hard. He grabbed Missy's long leash, the backpack, and headed for the door.

Missy was outside, her nose pointed upward, sniffing the air. She knew it was time. Padding over to him, she shoved her wet muzzle into his palm.

"Time to go, isn't it girl?"

The bloodhound's tail thumped the ground. Yes, it was time to get back to work.

As soon as Bill opened the door of his GMC pickup, Missy jumped in. He made a vain attempt to adjust the pile seat cover to protect his new truck from the dog's drooling. Missy sat looking out the side window, panting happily, oblivious to the continuous trail of saliva hitting the brown velour seat cushion.

Bill drove to the spot just outside of Scottsville where Missy had lost the trail that morning. He stopped only long enough to fill up with gas and grab a takeout coffee from Stockleys before continuing on the road heading west. Stopping at the second crossroad out of town, he pulled the truck off the asphalt. He cut the engine and snapped the twenty-foot nylon lead onto Missy's collar. Adjusting the pack on his back, Bill pulled out the plastic bag from the side pocket. He opened the zip-lock and let the dog sniff the contents.

Missy put her nose to the bag. After a few seconds, liquid brown eyes looked up at him. He saw the imperceptible nod of her head—her cue that she had the scent, and was ready to go.

"Find, Missy," he commanded.

Missy trotted off. She circled the area around the crossroads in a fifteen to twenty-foot radius, then licked her nose to add moisture to the air. Her tail rose and her head tipped to the ground. She trotted off in the same direction she had been heading the other morning. Now though, the moisture in the air had renewed the scent. The dog went west down the side of the road. Within seconds, she had reached the end of her lead and was pulling Clement off his feet.

Her tail was high and her long legs covered the ground faster than he could. Soon, he was running.

"Take it easy old girl. I've only got two legs."

Missy slowed briefly, but her adrenaline raging, she was determined to find her target. Not wanting to restrict her efforts, Bill ran faster to keep up with her.

Several times, he tripped over the loose gravel and many ruts along the shoulder of the road. Despite being in good physical shape for his age, he finally had to give in. "Missy, wait."

The dog sat until Bill caught up to her. He patted the velvet soft fur of her neck while he caught his breath. Feeling her quivering body, he knew she wanted to keep moving. He understood her need to keep on the trail before the storm came and wasted the day.

"Okay, go."

Missy leapt to her feet and trotted along the side of the road. He followed, the lead soon taut in his hand. He tried to keep her to a fast walk. Several times, he broke into a run to keep up with her. But his stamina was no match for hers and frequently he had to stop and rest before he could continue.

"Take it easy, girl. We got a few hours before the rain comes. I'm not as young as I used to be."

Now, the houses stood farther apart, and farms dotted the roadside. Stretches of dense deciduous trees and evergreens lined the highway. Suddenly, Missy slowed to a walk. She paced in a semi-circle along the side of the road then veered toward the trees. He followed. They found an almost hidden roadway, a rutted dirt pathway, barely wide enough for one vehicle. He saw fresh truck tracks.

Who lives back here?

He tried to remember what the folks in town might have said about this place. He knew there were a couple of cabins set back in the woods and wondered if that was where Missy was going. But the dog did not give him long to ponder. Her tail high, her nose sniffing the air, she headed down the path. Her body quivered visibly.

"Missy, wait."

Again, she stopped and waited for him. Bill gathered up the lead as he approached her. Missy pulled at the leash, eager to continue. He let her go again. Tree branches that almost occluded the sunlight shrouded the path. They walked for several minutes. Missy was at the end of her twenty-foot lead and constantly pulling for more. Then he saw light filtering through a narrow break in the tree line. Raising his voice, he called out. "Missy, stop. Come. Now."

She stopped and turned, her sad eyes pleading with him. He shook his head and Missy walked obediently toward him.

He dug Missy's four-foot lead out of the backpack. Snapping the lead to her collar, he shoved the long one back into the pack, then slipped the backpack over his shoulders. With Missy at his side, he walked toward the opening in the tree line. "Okay, girl, let's go."

Missy jumped ahead, straining on the lead. He kept a tight hold. Suddenly, they were through the pines and at a small clearing. He saw a log cabin nestled in the open space. He pulled on Missy's leash and commanded her to stay. Her tail high, she whined and danced around him. Clement glanced up at the sky, darkening clouds gathered ominously above.

Missy didn't want to stop. The scent was strong and she knew she was close. She strained against the leash. He watched the cabin. Suddenly, Missy's weight jerked his arm and the leash flew out of his hand. He watched Missy trot toward the cabin, her lead trailing uselessly in the grass. He called softly. He couldn't yell. He had no idea if anyone was in the cabin, or how they would react to a trespasser.

Missy was excited. Her tail arced over her back. Then, her gait slowed. She circled the cabin, stopping to sniff behind some wild shrubs along the back of the building.

Bill pulled a small silver whistle out of his pocket and put it to his mouth. Missy lifted her head at the barely audible sound. This time, she stopped.

With a meaningful nod toward the cabin, she turned and trotted back. She sat beside Clement, her body trembling. She let out a soft whimper, her eyes shining up at her owner.

He's here!

Grasping her leash and keeping it tight, Bill retreated to the cover of the trees. He watched the cabin. Was anyone home? He saw a shed with a gray truck parked inside.

The cabin door was closed, but he would't go any closer. Taking his cell phone out of his pocket, he dialed a number.

"Chad Evans, please." Bill waited while his call connected.

"Chad, it's Bill Clement. I think you'd better see where Missy's led me."

Bill walked back to his truck, Missy at his side. It was four-thirty. He only hoped it wasn't too late for the boy.

CHAPTER 38

Jenny pushed her shopping cart to the checkout and started placing items on the counter. She felt someone watching her. Tyrell again? She turned to look at the booths that ran along one side of the grocery store. He was there, sitting in the last one. She noted the quick dip of his head when she looked his way. A shudder ran down her spine. The man gave her the creeps. Why was he watching her? Mrs. Stockley's voice distracted her.

"Odd," she said, nodding toward Tyrell. "Always been odd. Even as a boy. Kept to himself. The other kids made fun of him. Born with a hair lip. No doctors to fix it like nowadays. His mother had trouble having him. Never was right. Maybe all those beatings her no-good husband laid on her. He told her it was her fault the boy was born that way."

Mrs. Stockley continued to prattle while she rang in the groceries. Distracted by thoughts of Tyrell, Jenny wasn't really listening.

"She used to come in here with him hiding behind her skirt-tails. He didn't talk much then, still doesn't. But then it was because the other kids used to laugh at the way he looked. Couldn't talk right with his lip gaping open like that. Didn't get that fixed till he was almost nine.

"Old Watson took off somewhere and left them. Didn't come back for nearly a year. In the meantime, the county stepped in and helped the family. They sent Tyrell to one of them fancy surgeons in Smith Falls. Fixed the hair lip pretty good.

He's still got a small scar if you look close. Sent him to speech therapy for a while, but they didn't keep it up once his father came back. He told those county people his family didn't need them interfering. That ended Tyrell's speech classes.

The shopkeeper wrung her hands on her apron, then began arranging the groceries in bags.

"His speech did get better over the years, but he kept to himself most of the time. They lived out of town at the Morrison place. Little cabin back in the woods. Watson worked for farmers round here and did trapping in the winter. He used to come into town most nights, drink himself silly, then stumble on home. One day, after a weekend bender, they found him frozen in the snow."

She paused, as if reflecting on the past, then spoke again. "Mrs. Watson seemed better after he was gone. She took in sewing, and Tyrell started working on farms like his dad.

"That's where he met Patty—one of the Payne girls. Took a fancy to him. He was different from the other boys, not out drinking, and running around in cars. Guess she liked him being serious and not getting liquored up every weekend. He kept going to school. Not interested in girls till she went after him. Had to quit school though, when she got in the family way. They moved in with his mother, but she died just after the baby was born. He joined the army and was off to Iraq. Only had a couple of months to go when he got his leg shot up and got sent home. He sure found things changed."

Jenny sighed. She wished Mrs. Stockley would stop talking. But the woman had always been good to her and she didn't want to be rude and cut her off. She kept nodding while the shopkeeper filled the bags. At least Tyrell was far enough away he couldn't hear her.

"Patty went wild while he was away. Dyeing her hair lighter and lighter all the time until it was almost white. Like those Scandinavian models. That's what she wanted to be. Fat chance around here. You remind me a bit of Patty, that is before she started putting all that gunk in her hair."

"Patty went wild while he was away. Dyeing her hair lighter and lighter all the time until it was almost white. Like those Scandinavian models. That's what she wanted to be. Fat chance around here. You remind me a bit of Patty, that is before she started putting all that gunk in her hair."

Startled, Jenny squinted at Mrs. Stockley. "What was that?'

"Patty dying her hair and wanting to be a model?"

"No." Jenny swallowed. "Who does she remind you of?"

"You, dear."

Jenny felt suddenly faint. Her knees buckled, and she grabbed the edge of the counter.

"Are you okay? You look white as a sheet, girl." Mrs. Stockley hurried around the counter and put her arm around Jenny. "Come and sit down."

Jenny let Mrs. Stockley lead her to one of the side booths. She slumped onto the bench seat. Mrs. Stockley called out to her husband. "Bring us a cup of coffee and a nice slice of pie. And can you finish bagging up Jenny's groceries. She just needs to sit for a moment."

By the time Mr. Stockley brought them coffee, some of Jenny's strength had returned. She took a sip of her coffee before asking, "Why do I remind you of Patty?"

"Well, she was nice and quiet, and petite like you. That is before she went wild. Started flirting with all the men in town. Her hair was like yours—the same dark ash-blonde shade. Long too, and always falling in her face. You have the same way of pushing it out of your face. First time I saw you, I thought it was Patty."

"Where did she go?"

Jenny focused her attention on Mrs. Stockley, thoughts of her groceries forgotten.

"Oh, she moved away about seven or eight years ago. When her parents died, she sold their farm, got some money and took off. She wanted to be a model, or an actress. But I told you that already. Mrs. Stockley picked up her coffee and took a long sip.

"What happened with her and Tyrell?" Jenny asked.

"When he got out of the army and saw what Patty had done to herself, he was livid. Fighting all the time, they were. Even in front of the boy."

"They had a child?"

"Yes. I told you they had to get married."

Her voice had taken on a tone of impatience. Jenny wondered what else she'd missed while wrapped up in her own thoughts. Teach her a lesson. She should be paying attention. Clayton was still missing. She had to keep her eyes and ears open. The police had checked Tyrell's cabin when they'd searched the woods. They hadn't found anything, but maybe they needed to go back.

"Sorry, Mrs. Stockley." Jenny smiled. "I'm just not myself right now."

The storekeeper patted Jenny's arm. "I know, dear. It's terrible. All that's happened to you."

Jenny blinked several times to keep the tears away. Crying wouldn't help. She needed to know more about Tyrell. Pointing her fork to her half-eaten pie, she smiled. "Your pecan pie is delicious."

Mrs. Stockley blushed at the compliment, her gray curls bouncing as she tipped her head closer to Jenny. Her voice lowered to a conspiratorial tone. "Well, as I was saying, they had a baby. He'd have been about six when Watson came back from Iraq. Funny isn't it? Just about the same age as your boy."

Jenny was thinking the same thing. A coincidence or not? "Tell me about the boy."

"Well, he would have been about six—or maybe seven when she left, blonde hair, real shy. Don't think I ever heard him more than mumble a thank you when you gave him a candy. Like his dad in that way. Used to hide behind Patty's skirt tails. Seemed to get even more shy after his dad came home from the war."

Jenny's mind raced. Could Tyrell have taken Clayton to replace his son? What type of father had he been? If he had taken him, would he have harmed him? Her breath caught in her throat, and she could barely get the words out. "Did you ever hear of Tyrell hurting his son?"

"No, never heard tell of anything like that. But I did hear he was pretty angry at how much of a 'wimp' Patty had let him become. He wanted a real boy, not a 'sissy.'"

Jenny finished the last bit of Mrs. Stockley's pie and pushed the plate away. She smiled. "You make the best pecan pie I've ever had."

Her smile deepened the wrinkles around her twinkling blue eyes. Self-consciously, she wiped her hands on her work apron. "Just made me think of the boy today when Tyrell was in buying Tylenol."

Jenny shook her head. Had she missed something else? "He was sick?"

"No. Wanted the liquid, the children's type." She shrugged her shoulders. "I asked him if that was what he wanted. Said it was. Wanted it for a sick animal."

A sick animal, or a sick child? "Mrs. Stockley, I've got to go."

Just then, Tyrell strode past their booth and out into the parking lot. Before he reached the rusted gray truck, Jenny was on her feet. Grabbing her groceries, she hurried out the door.

She waited until he'd pulled out of the parking lot and was driving out of town. The police had talked to him, ruled him out as a suspect. She'd been with the search party when they checked his cabin. But the strange, horrible feeling wouldn't go away. How was she going to make the police go back? They didn't want a harassment suit, but if Clayton was there...

Starting the car, she drove down the same road. She had to follow him, had to know.

CHAPTER 39

J enny was running through a dark tunnel. Heavy dampness surrounded her like Beelzebub's cape. A sense of urgency and fear raged through her, pushing her forward. Destination unknown, on and on she ran through the darkness, unable to see past her face, but unable to stop. Vaguely, she became aware of a voice penetrating the darkness, penetrating the pain throbbing in her head. It sounded far away. She was on a treadmill with no shut-off switch, and she kept running.

A voice filtered through the layer of down surrounding her brain. Muffled and slurred, her words ran together. "JennyJennyareyouokaywakeupJenny..." There was something familiar about the husky, intense voice. Where had she heard it before? Who did it belong to?

As if touched by a wizard's wand, the tunnel dissipated, leaving only a cloak of darkness. Her head hurt. Jenny's steps slowed, then halted abruptly. She tried to lift her head. It was heavy and the movement made the pain worse. Everything was fuzzy.

She lay on her right side. Beneath her, the surface felt hard and lumpy. Her right side was cold, her clothes damp, clinging to her body. Jenny tried to open her eyes. The lids were heavy and unyielding. The voice persisted, getting louder.

Someone gabbed her arm. The touch increased the stinging in her arms. With a moan of pain, she tried to pull away. Hands slid around her back. She shrunk away, but the hands were strong. Through the dampness of her blouse, she felt the press of a large palm on her back. It was gentle, but firm. The hands lifted her.

What's happening?

Jenny struggled, but she was too weak, the pain in her head so intense. The hands were persistent. She forced her eyes open. A glare of bright sunlight hit her making the pain worse, and she closed her eyes again. The voice was insistent. Slowly, the sounds became distinguishable. It was a man, and he was calling her name. She pulled away. Memories seeped back through the fog in her brain.

Walking. The sound of something. Someone there. Pain in her head. Darkness.

Arms enveloped her; she was being lifted. She struggled, but the arms tightened. Unable to protest, her chest was lifted off the hard, lumpy surface and she found herself cradled against a broad chest. Her head nestled on the downy softness of a cotton shirt, soft from multiple washings. A faint lemon scent still clung to the fabric. A familiar scent.

Her eyes opened again. It wasn't so bright here. Fear tingled through her. She looked up at her captor. The angular set of the jaw was familiar, as were the wisps of brown curls at the nape of a tanned neck. It was Steve!

What is he doing here? Where am I?

Jenny looked around. A decorator's palate of greens surrounded her. Tree branches waved like fingers playing peek-a-boo with the afternoon sun. Splotches of olive-brown grass covered the baked ground. Somehow, she had fallen asleep in a small clearing surrounded by a dense growth of cedars. How did I get here? And why does my head hurt so much? She shook it to clear the cobwebs. It only intensified the pain.

Cloudy visions appeared and gradually took shape. She was walking down a dirt path, following the man from Stockleys. The images were becoming clearer, her memory coming back. She had kept his truck in view for almost a mile out of town, but when it turned onto a narrow dirt road in a wooded area, she parked her car on the side of the paved road. The truck was no longer visible. She ran to the edges of the tree line. Under the cover of the trees, she followed the dirt road.

She remembered feeling desperate, trying to remember how far away his cabin was, trying to remember the layout of his property. Then she had heard something behind her—the snap of a twig?

She froze. Waiting.

Silence. The next thing she was aware of was a resounding smack, then pain as something hit the back of her head. She felt nausea, dizziness, then blackness engulfed her.

Now, Steve was here, and she was safe in his arms. But something was wrong. She struggled to get up.

"Jenny, are you okay?"

Her forehead wrinkled in concentration. "I think so. What are you doing here?"

"Mom called. She said you were upset. She couldn't understand you—something about following someone from Stockleys."

Vaguely, Jenny remembered calling Steve and Detective Jarvis. But neither was reachable. What messages had she left? Her head throbbed with the effort. She tried to concentrate on what Steve was saying.

"I saw the car parked on the side of the road and came looking for you. What happened? What are you doing out here?"

"I was following him. He's been watching me."

"Who?"

"The man from Stockleys."

"What man from Stockleys?" he demanded.

She paused, trying to make sense of the jumble of thoughts swirling through her mind. Why had she been following him?

"I remember seeing him at Stockley's. He sits by himself in one of those back booths, drinking coffee and reading. I've never seen him with anybody. He just sits and watches. He watched Clay and me when we were in the store. But he watches other people too, so I didn't make much of it. I just thought he was creepy."

She paused for a breath before rushing on. "The police asked me if I'd noticed anyone suspicious lately. I didn't think of him. Then today, I was at the store, and he was watching me again."

Her voice took on a hysterical edge, and she struggled away from him. "That man—it's him. He took Clayton! I need to find him!"

"Who is it?"

"I can't remember his name. I've only seen him at the store. He just sits and stares. He helped me with my groceries one day." She shook her head. "But today...he was watching me again. I just got this funny feeling. I had to follow him."

Jenny shook her head.

"He told me his name." The desperation rose in her voice. "He told me his name, oh, God, I can't remember."

"What does he look like?"

She shrugged. "I don't know. Brown hair, tall, thinner than you. He wears a raccoon hat."

"Do you mean Tyrell?"

"Who?"

"Tyrell Watson. He wears one of those raccoon hats. Always hanging around Stockleys."

She shook her head again, trying to clear it. "Yes. I think that's the name."

A frown crossed his forehead and he looked toward the path between the trees. "Someone told me he lives out this way."

"He does. I was with the search party when the police checked this area. They checked his cabin. They didn't find anything."

This was wasting time. Jenny struggled to get up. She needed to find him now, she needed to confront him and ask if he had seen Clayton. The pounding in her head increased. The pain seemed to be centered at a spot just behind her left ear. Instinctively, her hand went to the spot. Her fingers touched a large swelling and she winced. The area felt cold and wet, hair matted to the spot. She looked at her fingers. They were covered with fresh blood.

"He must have hit me with something."

Steve checked her hand. "Let me see!"

Jenny turned. His touch was gentle, but it still hurt when his fingers examined her head.

"You've got a good-sized lump there. And, there's a cut. We need to get you to a doctor."

"No!" Pain shot across the back of her head with the sudden movement. She lowered her head, hoping the pain would ease. "No." Her voice steeled with determination. "Whoever he is, he may have Clayton. I have to find him!"

"It sounds like Tyrell."

"Do you know him?" she demanded. If he had Clayton, could he hurt him? Was her son still alive? "Steve," Jenny screamed. "Would he hurt Clayton?"

"I don't know him well. He's always been a loner. We were in Iraq together, but he never talked to anybody there either. He was shot in the leg just before his term finished, and he was sent home. His wife left him shortly after, taking their son with her. He became even more of a recluse then. I don't know what he might do, Jenny."

She looked up at Steve, her eyes pleading. He pulled her closer. His head tipped towards hers. She felt the warmth of his breath on her cheek. His lips were so close. She desperately wanted to feel the comfort of those lips. Instinctively, her head tipped towards him. Their lips met, briefly, softly.

Steve jerked his head away. "Sorry."

Jenny felt an odd sense of loss. She turned her head away, afraid to let him see her exposed feelings. What was she doing? Her son was still missing. How could she think of anything else?

"Did you see which way he went?"

Jenny looked around, attempting to get her bearings. She saw the trees lining the dirt pathway and the evergreens surrounding the clearing. Her gaze stopped at a spot between the trees where a narrow path had been blazed, barely visible to a casual glance. "I followed him. He was driving an old gray truck. It went down that lane." Jenny pointed toward an area in the thick clump of trees surrounding the clearing. "I was following in the woods. I didn't see him come back. He must have come through the trees and snuck up behind me."

Steve stared at the dense blanket of green. Then his eyes detected a subtle difference. About ten feet from the dirt laneway, Steve noticed the outline of a narrow path and the faint tracks had flattened the underbrush. Several branches were bent and broken off at just about the same height of a human body.

"Stay here while I check something out?"

"I want to come."

"No. Wait here." He nodded to the narrow path. "I'll check that out, see where it leads, and then come back for you."

Reluctantly, Jenny agreed. Her head still throbbed and movement made it worse. Maybe if she rested while Steve checked the path, the pain would lessen. She sat cross-legged at the base of a walnut tree and leaned against it. The sun was drying her dampened clothes, and she felt warmer.

She should go with him, but he promised he'd be right back. Steve's presence was reassuring. He had been so helpful in the days since Clayton had been missing. She couldn't believe what Joe Roberts said about him. He couldn't have hurt anyone, especially a child. Could he? No! She wouldn't believe it. Anybody who knew him wouldn't believe it...

Jenny watched Steve disappear through the cover of pine branches, then leaned back against the tree trunk, her body a jumble of frayed nerve ends. She was so tired. How many days had it been since she'd had a full night's sleep? Not since Clayton had disappeared. Her eyelids felt so heavy. The dizziness, then the blackness, returned.

CHAPTER 40

S teve followed the narrow path for several hundred feet before he saw the shape of a wooden structure through the dense growth of trees, Tyrell's cabin. Beyond the cabin, the bed of an old gray pickup protruded from a ramshackle shed. That's Tyrell's vehicle all right. Was Jenny right? Does he have Clayton?

He watched from the woods. Should he check out the cabin, or call the police and leave it to them? With his luck, if he called the police, he'd get Roberts. Damn lot of good that'd do him. If Tyrell really has Clayton, Roberts would make him out as an accomplice. No, I'll look around first. See if there's anything suspicious.

The cabin door was closed, no lights visible, but it was still afternoon. Staying sheltered by the pines, Steve circled the buildings. There wasn't much to see: a log cabin, an old shed, and an outhouse. Several dark clouds drifted across the sky.

Steve hadn't spoken more than a few words to Tyrell since they'd been back from Iraq. At first, when they ended up in the same regiment, Tyrell had been receptive to Steve's attempts at friendship. But once Steve made sergeant, Tyrell became surly. It was as if he resented Steve's promotion. Lord knows I went out of my way to look out for him. He just wouldn't listen. He was almost home free when he got caught in that crossfire and was sent home. Several men had been lost that day. Don't know how I missed getting shot. God must have been looking out for me.

The wounded were evacuated to the hospital in Germany and then sent home from there. Steve had finished out his tour. At least, I didn't have any permanent injuries. Not physical ones anyway. The mental ones, well, did anyone get out of a war Scott free?

Nightmares haunted him for the first six months after his discharge. Gradually, they lessened, and he could function again. Glad I didn't end up with a shot-up leg. I wonder if that's really why his wife left. He was a loner before Desert Storm, but he's worse now.

Steve made it around to the other side of the cabin. There was nothing to indicate a child's presence. He worked his way until he saw the back of the pick-up. The tailgate was down. He saw a spare tire, a dirt-coated shovel, a couple of dented buckets, some rags, and an old tarp. *A kid could hide under that tarp. Or, someone could hide a child's body there.*

Steve shuddered at the thought. What should he do? Maybe he could make it to the shed without Tyrell hearing him. He wanted to check that tarp. He needed to know that Clayton wasn't under it. He stepped out of the cover of trees and hurried toward the shed. He was halfway there when he heard the creak of the cabin door.

He stopped in his tracks. He knew he didn't have time to hide. He was too far from the sfety of the woods and too far to hide behind the buildings. A sweat broke out across his forehead. *Damn it. Now what? Think fast. Just what the hell are you doing out here?*

Tyrell's surprise turned quickly to anger. Steve watched him slam the cabin door before he strode off the porch. Awfully hot to be keeping that door closed. Must be like an oven inside.

"Hello, Tyrell. Didn't know you lived out here."

"Yeah, this is where I live. What do you want?" Tyrell's black eyebrows drew together in a straight line, a line as straight and menacing as his lips. His nostrils were flaring and his sun-worn face had taken on a reddish tinge.

Why is he so upset? Does he have something to hide? I'd better diffuse his anger, and fast.

"I was out fishing with some buddies at Miller's Pond and got bored. Couldn't catch a minnow today if my life depended on it. Took a walk. And here I am in this beautiful spot. Didn't know there was a cabin back here. Mighty pretty spot. Love to have a place like this...so quiet and peaceful..I thought I'd just come...and see who lives here. Wondered if it might be for sale?"

"Well, I live here. So now you know. You can just go back to your fishing. And no, the place ain't for sale."

"Well if you ever change your mind," Steve said.

The chuckle from Tyrell's curled lips held no hint of humor. "I won't be changing my mind."

"Have you lived here long?"

"Long enough."

"Do you own it?"

Tyrell's voice was low, but an undertone of contempt was evident. "What's it to you?"

"Just curious. It's nice and peaceful out here. I'd like to get a little place like this. Get out of town."

"This one ain't for sale."

Tyrell remained within three feet of the house, hands on his hips, glaring at the intruder. A vein pulsated in his thick neck.

"Bet you don't get many visitors out here."

"No. Don't want none either."

Steve took a deep breath and asked. "Did you have people out here looking for the boy that's been missing?"

A muscle on the side of Tyrell's face twitched. The fingers that dug into the pockets of his denims were drained of blood. "Yeah, they came looking, but they didn't find anything. I don't like nobody snooping round here. And I'd appreciate it if you'd get off my land."

There was cold rage in Tyrell's tone. This was a command, not a request. He reached out for a long-handled shovel resting against the cabin and leaned on the top, his fists clutching the wooden handle.

Raising his arms in compliance, Steve said, "Sure, I'm out of here. Sorry to disturb you. Let me know if you ever decide to sell."

"I won't be selling."

Trying to keep the mood light, Steve shrugged his shoulders and grinned at Tyrell. "Well, I'd be interested if you change your mind."

Steve turned and walked back in the direction he had come. He still wanted to check out that truck and the shed. Maybe Tyrell would go back into the house and he could sneak back through the trees. He didn't want to call the police without something more to go on.

Steve had only gotten about twenty feet when he heard a soft rustling in the grass behind him. But before he could turn, something sharp slammed against his left arm. The force knocked him to the ground. He hit hard, his arm searing with pain. He grabbed it and felt the gush of warm, sticky fluid. Pressing his hand against the slash, he tried to stop the flow of blood.

"What the hell."

He struggled to his knees. He was almost upright when he felt the whack of the shovel against the back of his skull. His body crumpled to the ground, and for Steve, the sun ceased to shine.

CHAPTER 41

Clayton went back to the hole in the wall and, picking up the shovel, started digging. He was tired, his body hurt, yet he kept at it. Dirt coated his hands and the shovel. He had to stop frequently and wipe the damp earth away. He used his shirt as a rag. The puppy dogs embossed there disappeared under a layer of mud.

When the man had come back that afternoon he'd given him Tylenol for his fever. He still had the cough but now he wasn't so hot and his headache had almost gone. He knew he had to keep working. He was afraid the man might hear him, might come back and check on him but he had to take the chance. He had to get out of here. He was so close. If Mommy couldn't find him, he would go find her.

It seemed to take forever but finally, the glimmer of light began to grow. Clayton dug faster. The hole grew to the size of a basketball. Hiking himself up the wall, he clawed at the edges of the cavity. Dirt embedded itself under his nails as he clawed his way through the dark, dank tunnel. Mud coated his arms and legs, spattered in his mouth, his nose, his eyes. He squinted but didn't stop. A cough was coming. He tucked his head in his shirt and tried to keep the cough silent.

Could the tunnel collapse? He wouldn't think about it. He kept going. The light was getting stronger, closer. He ignored how much his body hurt and scrambled toward the light. A few more feet. A few more. Then he was at the end of the tunnel. He squinted, but this time the reason was the bright circle of sun beyond the cabin. He scrambled out the last few feet.

Finally, he was free.

Clayton crouched by the building, checking both ways. No one. Would the man come outside? The woods were close. Could he make it there before he got caught? His heart was pounding so hard he couldn't think. Clenching his fists, he looked both ways, took a big breath, then ran. He ran as fast as he could. He didn't stop until he made it to the cover of the trees. His legs shook like Jell-O and he collapsed behind a wide oak tree.

His breath came in shallow, wheezing gasps. Then the cough started. Clutching his dirt-stained arms around his knees, he rocked slowly, letting air weave deeper and deeper into him until his lungs didn't hurt anymore. A long time passed before his breathing became easier and his heart rate slowed to normal. Tears slid down his face. With the back of his hand, he wiped at them, leaving a trail of brown earth streaking his pale skin.

He looked up at the sky. It was getting dark. So many clouds covered the heavens, and here in the woods, it was even darker. He shivered. He didn't like the dark. He didn't like storms. The woods looked dark and scary, but he knew it was the only way to stay safe. Which way should he go? How long before the man came looking for him? Could he rest for a bit? He was so tired and he was starting to feel hot again.

Clayton hid in the shelter of a pine tree but he knew he couldn't stay there. What if the man came looking for him? Even as young as he was, Clayton knew he wouldn't just let him go. How long before he knew he was missing? Which way should he go? He had no idea where he was, or how far he was from home. He only knew that if he stayed in the cover of the trees, it would be harder for the man to find him.

CHAPTER 42

S he felt cold. The weather had changed. Storm clouds hovered above, almost obliterating the sun. The wind had picked up, and Jenny shivered. Where was Steve? Her watch showed five-fifteen. Over an hour had passed. What had happened to him?

Her brain was still fuzzy, probably from the blow, but Jenny remembered him heading off into the woods. What did he say his name was? Tyrone? Tyson? No, it was a different. Tyrell, that was it. Jenny looked up at the darkening sky. The sun was making a vain attempt to break through, but was losing the battle.

Jenny scrambled to her feet. Her body, stiff from sleeping on the hard ground, protested the quick movements. Pins and needles stabbed at her feet as she tried to walk. Her left ankle, still asleep, twisted as she put her full weight on it. She stumbled, wincing as a sharp pain shot up the outside of her foot. Leaning against the tree, she waited for the pain to subside. The pins and needles faded, and she tested it. The pain was a steady throb, but bearable.

Where was Steve? He'd been gone a long time. He promised he would come back for her.

Storm clouds made it look much later and Jenny wondered how long it would be before they released their burden. Hopefully, the rain wouldn't start for a while. She had to find Steve. What could have taken him so long? Had he found Tyrell? Had he found Clayton? Maybe Tyrell had hurt him. Was that why he wasn't back? Did Tyrell have Clayton and Steve? Was Steve friends with Tyrell? Too many questions, and Jenny needed answers. She headed toward the slight break in the trees. She didn't want to take the laneway; she wanted to stay under the cover of the trees. Pushing branches out of her way, she waded through the densely wooded area. Grass and underbrush were trampled from frequent use. She followed the trail.

The umbrella of tree branches and the darkening sky hindered visibility, making it difficult to keep to the path. Pine branches slapped her, releasing a heavy scent of pine and leaving scratches on her bare arms. Her arms stung as the juice of pine nettles seeped into the wounds. Mosquitoes buzzed around her head and arms. Unconsciously, she swatted them away and kept moving. Despite the obstacles, she kept up a steady pace, trying to ignore the ache in her ankle and the stinging in her arms.

Jenny walked for ten minutes before she saw the clearing. Slowing her steps, she picked her way through the trees. At the end of the wooded area, she hid behind a huge Scotch pine. Between the thick branches, she saw a small wooden cabin, and behind that, a lean-to shed. An outhouse stood not twenty feet from the house. Tyrell's house.

Is Steve here? Clayton?

The woods surrounded the cabin. The only breaks in the tree line were the barely visible opening from the path she had just followed and a narrow lane several feet away. The lane was just wide enough for one vehicle. It led behind the cabin to the lean-to.

Jenny circled through the trees until she was behind the shed. She could see the back of the cabin. Only two windows were facing the front. From where she was, there was no view from the cabin. No one could see her until they came around one of the sides. Jenny watched from the safety of the trees.

Damn it. Where is Steve? What should I do?

She wanted to run back to town. She wanted to get Detective Jarvis. Would he believe her crazy idea that Tyrell might have Clayton? Would he come out and check? If Tyrell had Clayton, did she have time to go back to town? What if she went back and they wouldn't come? Again, her mind was plagued with unanswered questions. She knew one thing—she couldn't wait.

Taking a deep breath, she ran toward the shed. Her feet flew across the open grass.

It only took seconds, but to her, it seemed like the longest fifty-foot sprint she had ever done. By the time she reached the shed, her heart raced, and she was gasping for breath. She dove for cover behind the building. The frame was rough and worn, splintering as she grabbed onto one of the boards. She leaned her shaking body against its weathered surface and a rush of air escaped her lungs.

She looked toward the cabin. There was no one in sight, and the door was still closed. Relieved, she waited several seconds before creeping to the edge and then along the side to the front of the shed. Making it to the doorway, she slipped inside and sank to the ground.

Her breath still came in rapid and painful gulps. Each gulp of the cool air stung her throat. It was minutes before her breathing returned to normal, minutes before she was able to move.

I've made it this far. Now what?

She crept back to the opening of the shed and peeked outside. The skies continued to darken. There was no one around, but inside the cabin, a lamp had been lit. Through the dirt-covered windows, it created an eerie glow.

Had Steve found the cabin, too? He'd started along the same trail, and it was the only one she'd seen. He would have to have found it. So where was he? Was he inside? Was he there, rehashing old times from Iraq with Tyrell? Anger rose at the thought of Steve inside, while she was left to wait in the woods.

She could see Ray leaving her like that, but Steve... she had thought he was different.

Maybe she should just knock on the door and see what was going on. Would she find both men sitting at the kitchen table drinking beer and telling off-color jokes? Was Steve in cahoots with this man?

Jenny wanted to rush in and find out, but something held her back, told her to wait. Reluctantly, she listened to the inner voice and moved deeper into the shed.

Maybe she could find some sort of weapon to protect herself with. The farther she went, the darker it was. The faint sunlight didn't penetrate the back of the shed.

Then she recalled a deep, raspy voice on the end of a telephone line. 'I saw him in the ground with wood over him…it's very dark…and there are lots of trees.' Jenny's heart leapt to her throat as she remembered the middle-of-the-night call. She had dismissed the woman as a crank caller, now, as the words ran through her head: 'in the ground, wood over him, and lots of trees' Jenny wondered if this was the place. She had to check the cabin.

She edged toward the end of the shed. Her foot hit something firm. She froze. Her heart skipped several beats, then raced in a staccato tempo. Terrified, she waited for whatever she had hit to fall over or shift, or do something to create enough noise to make her presence known.

There was no loud crash, no bang; only a soft moan. Unsure of what she had heard, Jenny waited. Yes, there it was again. The distinct groan of someone in pain, but not a four-footed one; this sound came in human form. Her stomach lurched as a queasy feeling invaded her body. Her knees buckled and she leaned against the wall of the shed. Who was at her feet?

Jenny wanted to run. Her legs refused to obey. She heard another moan. She needed to find out who was lying on the shed floor. Who was moaning in pain? Maybe it was Clayton. She looked down, her eyes still adjusting to the dimness.

But it was a large form. Too large for Clayton. Thank God. "Steve?" The name was out of her mouth before she realized she had spoken. She heard another moan and dropped to her knees. Brown waves, made darker by the poor lighting, curled over the neck of a cotton shirt, Steve's shirt. Jenny whispered his name. The only response was a soft groan. Her voice became more insistent.

"Steve? Are you all right? Answer me!"

Another soft moan was her only answer. She tried to remember the first aid courses she had taken over the years. ABC. The words came back to her—Airway, Breathing, Circulation. She knew he was breathing; he was making noises. Tentatively, she touched his neck and searched for the jugular vein that should be coursing blood throughout his body. There, there it was, just below his jaw. Her fingers gently covered it and counted. It was fast, faster than she knew it should be, and weaker, too.

He must have lost a lot of blood, but from where? Jenny's fingers ran through the soft brown waves. She felt something wet and sticky and pulled her hand away. She smelled the odor of old pennies. Blood. Bracing herself, she made her hand return to the site. A soft swollen area had formed on the left side of his temple where blood and hair matted together. She felt a trickle of blood oozing from the cut.

Jenny forced herself to think rationally. The hit on the head might have knocked him out, but the amount of blood trickling from that cut shouldn't be enough to make his pulse so fast. Look for something else.

Steve lay partially on his right side. Jenny ran her hands over the rest of his body, first the right arm and leg that were facing up. Nothing. Then she checked his chest. Jenny felt a sticky hardness on the left side of his shirt. Her fingers probed the mat of soft brown hairs. No injury there.

She tried to be gentle, but sliding him onto his back caused him to moan again. She ran her fingers over his left side. Just below his left elbow, she felt thick liquid streaming down his arm. Her fingers probed further. She gasped as they sunk into a wide hole. Warm liquid flowed rapidly out of a deep laceration on his upper right arm.

She had to do something quickly. Steve could bleed to death if the flow wasn't stopped. Jenny looked around the shed, thankful her eyes had finally adjusted to the dim light. She searched for something to tie around his arm, anything to curb the flow of blood. Her eyes caught on a bit of white lying on the tool bench behind her. Jenny rushed for it. Her foot caught on something hard and she almost stumbled to the ground.

She reached out and pushed the obstacle out of her way. Her hand felt cold sticky gel on the end of a curved piece of cold metal. A shovel. Was that Steve's blood on the end of it? Swearing, she kicked it out of her way and grabbed the rag from the bench.

Fingers shaking, she ripped the rag apart, tore it into a long strip, and slid it under Steve's left arm. He moaned again. She drew the edges together, forming a makeshift tourniquet, pulling it tighter and tighter until she felt the blood slow to a trickle. Please, God, let the bleeding stop. Please let him be okay.

Then she wrapped another piece of the rag over the cut. The rag might be dirty, but she couldn't worry about infection now. If the bleeding didn't stop, there would be no need.

Jenny sat back on her haunches. There was nothing else she could do for now. He had to have proper medical attention. At least the bleeding was under control. She pulled her cell out of her jeans pocket and punched in three numbers.

Her heart stayed on pause until the operator answered. Pressing the phone to her ear, she whispered, "I need help. Need an ambulance, my friend was injured. I need Detective Jarvis. My son, Clayton, I think he's here."

She answered her questions. "Jenny Kingsley. I think Clayton's here." She tightened her grip on the phone. "I can't talk louder. He might hear me." Another question. "Tyrell." Jenny felt her shoulders tense. She closed her eyes for a half second. "Please, get Detective Jarvis here as soon as you can."

The woman was asking more questions, telling her to hold, telling her to stay on the line.

"Are the police coming? The ambulance?"

Jenny ended the call, cutting off the woman's plea to stay on the line. She couldn't wait. Right now she needed to find out if Clayton was here. If Tyrell could hurt Steve like this, what could he have done to Clayton?

No! Don't think of that now. I have to believe he's still alive.

She remembered the clothes stolen from Clayton's room. If this man worried enough to get his clothes then he must want to keep him alive. Jenny remembered what Mrs. Stockley had said about Tyrell's son. Could he have taken Clayton to replace him? She had to find out.

She leaned over Steve to check the makeshift bandage. Putting her hand over the dressing, she felt cold, sticky wetness. She waited. The wetness wasn't increasing. The bleeding had almost stopped. The slash must not have been deep enough to cut an artery. Holding her breath, she loosened the tourniquet. She kept her fingers on the bandage, expecting to feel the warm wetness of blood saturate the material. She wished there was enough light to see, instead her fingers were her only guide. After several seconds, she breathed a sigh of relief. The dressing had become only slightly damper. She checked his pulse. It was slower. Jenny wanted to believe it felt stronger.

Steve would be okay. Now she had to see if Clayton was here.

Jenny crept back to the end of the shed and peered at the cabin. Was he still inside? Jenny suddenly realized that she had been so upset over helping Steve that Tyrell could have been right behind her and she wouldn't have heard him.

CHAPTER 43

Tyrell opened the cabin door. Sweat glistened on his forehead and two large beige stains spread at the armpits of his T-shirt. He slammed the door behind him.

Shit. Everything was going pretty good, till now. Even though the kid was beginning to like me. I was going to start letting him out more. He isn't whiny, not like the other one. Shit. Just when I'd started to trust him. Now, he's gone and run away. Can't trust anybody. Never could. And, that damn Townsend. Snooping around here.

Where the hell was the kid? And how the fuck did he get out?

Tyrell slammed his fist into one of the support posts on the porch. The wood shook, and the resounding smack echoed through the cabin. Tyrell ignored the sharp pain that shot through his fist. He stomped from one end of the porch to the other, striking out every few steps at anything that came within his reach. The cedar boards beneath his boots rattled with each forceful step.

He scanned the area in front of him. The clearing showed an expanse of sparse grass and scraggly bushes, but no small child. The woods were dense and he saw nothing hiding in the spaces between the trees, and neither did he detect any movement. He looked up at the sky. The air was heavy with the approaching storm. Clouds rolled swiftly by and the sky was darkening. Visibility decreased as he watched.

Shit. Shit. Everything's getting too complicated. I better find him soon.

Tyrell tried to think. His thoughts were jumbled—too many things happening. First, the kid's mother following him from the store, having to knock her out, then Townsend snooping around. And now, the kid's gone. What else?

How'd the kid get out? And when? It can't have been long.

He checked on him when he came back from town. That must have been about three-thirty. He looked at his watch. It was after five now. How long had he been gone? Five minutes, ten, or over an hour. He had to find him, had to stop him before he made it back to town. Stop him before somebody gives him back to his mother. She's not going to take him away like Patty did. This one's mine.

Tyrell's left leg ached with the coming storm. He could feel the moisture seeping out of the clouds, seeping into his bones, his joints. He ignored the pain in his leg and glanced upwards. Storm clouds raced across the sky, obliterating the sun. The branches of the pine trees danced as the cool wind whipped at them. The air was heavy with intermingling scents of pine and dampness. The throbbing in his leg intensified. The rain would come soon.

I've got to find him. He can't make it home. Doesn't know where he is. But somebody might find him. He might tell...

He had wrapped a rag over the child's eyes when he put him in the truck. The kid couldn't know where he was or how to get home; all he had seen was the cabin and the outhouse.

Dumb kid. He'll get lost in those woods, unless he sticks to the trail. Got to get him before somebody finds him. Better do it before the rain comes. Got to check on Townsend, too. Should've tied him up. Maybe I should finish him off.

Thoughts of Townsend lying unconscious in the shed went through his mind. As his anger grew, a lump grew in his throat and the vein at his forehead began to throb.

Damn, Townsend. What the hell did he want? Was he looking for the boy or just snooping? Never liked him, not when we were kids, and not in the Gulf.

His body shook with rage. Why'd they make him sergeant? He wasn't any better. Him giving me orders while pretending to be so nice. I wasn't going to take orders from the likes of him. But I got him. Maybe I even killed him. Damn him, and damn the woman, too. Better find the boy first, then I'll do something about him. Tyrell stepped off the porch. He felt another stab of pain in his left leg. Tyrell cursed it as he began to circle the house.

He made it to the far side of the cabin before he noticed anything. He had to sidestep around an overgrown lilac bush. Unexpectedly, his bad leg caught something and he stumbled. Reaching out an arm to catch himself, he saw the fresh mound of dirt beside the house.

Before stumbling, he'd been looking at eye level, not at the ground. He would never have seen the broken branches on the lilac bush, nor the pile of dirt, nor the tunnel under the cabin. He knelt to investigate. His hand ran over the area. The clay surrounding the cabin was hard and dry but he felt the cool wetness of freshly dug earth. Well, Goddamn.

He picked up some of the moist earth and let it trickle through his outspread fingers. A wry smile flickered across his face. The boy's smarter than I thought. Tyrell's hand slid over the mound of dirt and found the hole he knew would be there. So, that's how he got out. Shit.

Tyrell eased to his feet, his left leg protested with another stab of pain. Unconsciously, he rubbed the scarred area. The pain diminished slightly. He looked at the trees surrounding the cabin. He has to be out there somewhere. He can't have gone far. He needed a flashlight. Tyrell thought of the flashlight under the seat of his truck.

His gaze continued around the clearing, eyes focusing on every detail. His body still, the hunter watching, waiting. He scanned the dense wall of green trees, then the weathered browns of the lean-to shed. His gaze went past the shed, then returned to it, and stopped. It was filled with an assortment of lawn implements, old pieces of furniture, and his hunting gear. He saw his old gray truck sticking out the end of the shed. The truck's flatbed was dotted with buckets, a tire, the old tarp, and his toolbox. A toolbox big enough to hold a large assortment of hardware. Large enough for one small boy? Or the tarp. Could he be under that?

Maybe he's not in the woods.

A sense of steely calmness came over him. He inhaled deeply, letting the cool evening air fill his lungs. As the blood pulsated through the vein in his neck, he counted the increased rate of his heart.

Tyrell headed silently toward the shed.

CHAPTER 44

Dry grass crunched. Jenny turned. The storm clouds blocked the sun; shadows lengthened and distorted. She peered through the semi-darkness. There was nothing there. Then, she heard it again. The soft crunch of a footstep just behind her. Jenny froze. "Steve?"

Silence.

Afraid to move, afraid not to, Jenny tried to think, but fear paralyzed her. Whoever was behind her, it wasn't Steve. Steve was probably still unconscious in the back of the shed where she had left him seconds before. Her heart seemed to stop. She waited, listening.

Then another crunch of grass, this time closer. Jenny started to run back to the shed. She heard footsteps behind her. They were running too. Then, they were so close she almost felt their owner's heavy breathing on her neck. She tried to run faster.

Something grazed her back. Jenny forced her legs to move faster. The footsteps were right behind her. A hand grabbed at her shoulder. It dug in, pulling her backward. She twisted sideways but Tyrell's large fingers dug into her shoulder blade with such strength she thought her collarbone would snap. The pain was intense.

She lost her balance and fell backward. Stumbling, arms flailing, she landed hard against the ground. She tried to scream but her cry was halted mid-flight as arms, like steel bands, circled her body. A hand was on the back of her head and her face was being pushed down until she could taste the coarse dry grass on her tongue. She couldn't breathe. She gasped for air but her mouth filled with blades of loose grass. Shaking her head violently, she fought against his hand until her mouth was above the ground. She spat out the mixture of grass and dirt.

Then he was turning her, pinning her arms against her chest, crushing her body with his. The breath was knocked out of her. Jenny gasped for air, then almost choked as the sour smell of his sweat filled her nostrils.

He lifted her off the ground. Jenny twisted her body, kicking out at him. Her foot made contact. He grunted in pain. Then, tightening his grip, he pulled her even closer. "Cut it out, bitch."

Jenny tried to wriggle free but she was being swung from side to side. She thudded heavily against his hip. He pressed her against his stained white T-shirt. Jenny twisted again, trying to get out of his grasp. She pounded her fists against the arms that pinned her body. Suddenly she was falling downward. Her body landed heavily on the grass. What little air she'd been able to get into her lungs; was forced out. She struggled to breathe.

Then, a knee was shoved into her back, forcing her torso deeper into the ground making it impossible to refill her lungs. The knee pressed harder and she winced with the pain that radiated down her spine. Lifting her face inches off the ground, Jenny gasped for air.

"Stop fighting, bitch. You'll only get hurt."

Tyrell grabbed her hands and pulled them roughly behind her back. She felt a thin cord wrap around her wrists. She struggled to free them. There was intense pain and then moistness as the cord cut through her skin. She felt the sting of blood ooze along her arm.

His large hand dug into her shoulder and she was flung onto her back. The hand held tight, cutting through her cotton shirt and into the flesh below. Her bound hands dug into her backbone. She stopped struggling. Instead, her scream cut through the clouded sky.

"Make as much noise as you want, bitch, there's no one to hear you."

His harsh laugh was accompanied by a smirk. Jenny saw the glint in his steel gray eyes and shivered. Her body twisted from side to side. She ignored the pain as the ties binding her wrists dug deeper into her skin.

Shaking her head from side to side, she screamed, again and again.

Tyrell raised his head and laughed. A spine-tingling laugh that seemed touched with an edge of hysteria. The tone of it hit Jenny like a bucket of frigid water. She stopped struggling and lay limp on the damp grass. She had to think. Was the man mentally ill? Physically she was no match for him, but mentally...if he was bordering on insanity...how should she deal with him? She had to find out about Clayton. She stared up at him, unable to control the trembling of her body as the harshness of his voice taunted her.

"What? You think your friend Steve's going to hear you? Think again. He can't hear anything right now." A corner of Tyrell's lip turned up as he grinned at her. "And, when I finish with him, he won't ever hear anything again."

Despite her fear, Jenny forced herself to demand. "Clayton...do you have Clayton?"

"Came looking for him like a good little mommy did you?"

Tyrell's laugh sent shudders radiating down her spine. "Police couldn't find him. What makes you think you're going to?"

"Please. Do you have him?"

"Did have."

"What do you mean? Do you have him? Did you hurt him?" Jenny heard her own hysteria. She struggled to get up. The cords cut into her wrists setting off a burning pain that radiated up both arms. Ignoring the pain, she thrashed about. The arm pressing into her shoulder increased its pressure.

"He's gone. Didn't like it here."

"What do you mean? Where is he?"

"Now neither of us has him." His giggle made the hairs on the back of her neck stand on end.

The wail that came from her body was like the cry of a banshee. When it had exhausted itself, Jenny lay limp in the grass. Her last hope vanished. Clayton was not here. She closed her eyes. Nothing mattered anymore.

"Mommy. Mommy."

Jenny heard a child's voice, Clayton's voice. Was she dreaming? She turned toward the sound. A dark-haired child was running toward her. Her heart sank. It was like the other child in the park, the one she had thought was Clayton. But this one was so familiar, except for the darkness of his hair. He came closer. It was Clayton. Dirt coated his blonde hair. This time it was not a dream, nor was it someone else's child. It was her son. He was alive!

"Well, well," Tyrell muttered harshly in Jenny's ear. "He's back."

"Clayton. No! Run away." Jenny screamed. She struggled to get up. Terror raged through her. He had to get away. "Run. Run and hide."

Tyrell's grip tightened, his fingernails dug into her flesh. She wrenched away. Jenny barely felt the sting as his fingernails cut through her skin, or the blood that trickled down her arm.

Clayton was still running toward them.

"Clayton, stop. Go and hide."

He kept running. His short legs crossed the distance quickly. He hurled himself at Tyrell. Clenched fists pounding the man's back. He was screaming. "Let my mommy go!"

Tyrell flung his arm out at the child. Clayton continued to pound his back. Tyrell turned and lunged for him. Clayton escaped his grasp by inches.

"Let her go." Clayton launched at Tyrell's back, then his teeth sank into the flesh of the man's upper arm. Jenny heard Tyrell's howl of pain, saw the imprint of his teeth and the specks of blood that oozed from the site.

"You little bugger."

Clayton ducked under Tyrell's arm and ran around behind him.

"Please, Clay, get away."

Tyrell lunged again. Jenny felt the loosening of his grip and twisted out of his hold. He jerked her back with his right hand. Using his left, he slapped her across the face. Jenny cried out. She felt the stinging imprint of his hand on her cheek. Tyrell grabbed her with both arms and shook her. "Don't try that again."

"Don't hit my mother." Clayton came at him again. He pounded on Tyrell's arms with his fists. Tyrell elbowed him away.

"Let go of my mommy."

Drawing his leg back, Clayton kicked Tyrell in his left shin. Tyrell howled with pain. He bent to grab his leg. Jenny, released of his hold, rolled onto her side and tried to get up. Her bound hands made rising difficult.

Clayton tried to pull her up. "Get up, Mommy. Get up."

Clayton pulled her arm, and Jenny struggled to her knees. Tyrell's arm shot out and grabbed her around the waist. She tried to get away but he lifted her like a rag doll. Smashing her against his hip, Tyrell lashed out for the child with his free arm. Clayton kept out of his reach. He tried to kick the man's leg again but Tyrell dodged his efforts.

At some point, Tyrell realized that as long as he held his mother, he didn't have to hold the child and he stopped trying to catch the boy. Instead, he dragged Jenny to the cabin. Storm clouds now covered the sky and a spattering of rain began to fall.

Got to get her into the cabin. Tie her up. Then decide what to do. Too many things happening. Need to think. It's getting too complicated. All I wanted was the kid. Now, what the fuck do I do with the mother and Townsend? Got to get away. Maybe I should take her.

Thoughts of Patty raced through his mind. What she was like when he first met her, sweet, innocent. Nothing like the whore he had found when he'd come back from Iraq. This one is like Patty when I first met her. Don't really want to kill her. Townsend, I don't mind. Snooping bastard.

Clayton pounded on his back.

"Stop it, kid." Tyrell's arm flung out in a wide arc toward the child.

Clayton ducked under his arm. He jumped out of his reach and then came at him again. Clayton beat his fists against any part of Tyrell he could reach. Like a flyswatter, Tyrell's arm swatted out at the child. And, like a bothersome fly, the child kept coming back. Tyrell dragged Jenny to the porch. He stumbled as his bad leg struggled with the steps. Jenny felt his grip loosen. She twisted her body. He groaned in pain but reestablished his hold.

It seemed to take forever to get her into the cabin. Without releasing his hold, Tyrell grabbed a hank of rope off the counter. He thrust Jenny onto a kitchen chair and held her with the force of one hand while his other wrapped the rope around her and the chair. Clayton kept beating at his kidnapper. Suddenly Tyrell's arm flung out, catching Clayton off guard and sending him sprawling to the floor.

Jenny screamed. "Don't hurt him. Clayton run away."

"Scream all you want, bitch. Nobody gonna hear you."

Tyrell finished knotting the rope around the chair. He leaned close to Jenny's ear and she could smell the tobacco and beer on his breath. Caressing her bare upper arm, he whispered to her. "Maybe you should come with me. We'll take the kid. We could have a real good time."

Yellow-stained teeth leered at her.

Jenny struggled at the ropes that bound her.

Tyrell grabbed at Clayton, his large hands clamping around the child's pale arm. He rubbed a hairy hand over Clayton's head.

"What do you think kid? Should we take your mother with us?"

Clayton pushed his hand away, then rubbed at the spot as if clearing away an infestation of bugs. Tyrell laughed harshly.

The wind had picked up and howled around the cabin with low mournful cries. There was a crack of thunder, then rain pelted against the windows. Jenny looked toward the front of the cabin. A flash of lightning lashed across the sky blinding her. She stared at the window; it was an effort to hold back the scream that filled her throat. A dark shadow was silhouetted in the glass.

The cabin door flew open. It crashed against the wall like a clap of thunder. A flash of lightning illuminated the room. A large figure filled the doorway. Then it was moving, advancing quickly into the room. Jenny blinked. Steve.

Blood matted the hair on the side of his head. The bandage on his arm was saturated a dark red, below it crimson fluid trickled down his arm. In front of him, he held the shovel encrusted with his blood. "Let them go, Tyrell."

Tyrell turned toward the door, his face contorted in an evil mask. His eyes were dark with fury and his cheeks flushed crimson. The tight line of his lips slashed across his darkened face. He spat his words. "You! Damn you to hell..."

"You didn't kill me after all, Tyrell. Now, you have a second chance...if you let them go."

"No way, Townsend. I'll kill you, then take them with me."

"Let them go. Nobody has to know. Jenny just wants her son back."

"He's mine now. They both are."

"Over my dead body."

"If that's the way you want it." Tyrell's laugh was like tinkling ice. He grabbed one of the wooden chairs and flung it at Steve.

Brandishing the shovel in front of him, Steve let it take the brunt of the blow. The sound of the chair shattering filled the cabin. Splinters of wood shot through the air. Jenny lowered her head to protect herself from the flying shards. Clayton, huddling at her feet, covered his face with his hands and pressed his small body against her.

A crack of thunder split the sky, intermingled with the sounds of smashing wood and thunder. Jenny thought she was hallucinating. She thought she heard the faint wail of a siren. Another flash of lightning lit the cabin. Steve advanced on Tyrell. He held the shovel like a bayonet in front of him.

Reaching out for the only other vacant chair in the room, Tyrell clenched it by the top rung. His face was a reddened mask of rage. He held the chair high above him for several seconds then, with an inhuman scream, he hurled it at Steve. While the chair was in flight, Tyrell reached under the table, groping for Clayton. Jenny kicked out at him as Clayton scurried out of his reach.

"Damn you." He screamed. "Get over here, kid."

"No." Clayton ran from him, going across the room to the wall of kitchen shelves.

The crash of the chair hitting the shovel shattered through the cabin. Then, Steve was on the other side of the table. He looked pale and wobbly, but he was still upright. Tyrell lunged at him, knocking him off his feet. Jenny watched in horror as both men wrestled, stumbled, landed hard on the floor, their arms and legs intertwining as they struggled.

Clayton slid behind Jenny's chair. She felt the pull of the twine around her wrists and twisted her head to see what he was doing.

"It's okay, Mom. Stay quiet."

"Clayton?" She whispered. A crack of thunder sounded above the cabin. Seconds later a flash of lightning lit the room and Jenny saw a shiny object in Clayton's hand. He had a kitchen knife and he was using it to saw through the twine binding her wrists. "Clayton, be careful."

She heard Tyrell's harsh laugh and turned back to the men wrestling on the floor.

Tyrell had him face down on the rough wood floor, his knee in Steve's back and he was reaching for the ball of twine.

"You're no match for me, Townsend."

Steve's face had gone ashen; his body was limp and unmoving. Blood flowed down his arm, turning the bandage bright red. His wound must have opened up and he was bleeding again. Jenny stared in horror. Tyrell yanked Steve's hands behind his back and was wrapping the twine around them. Steve did not move, even when Tyrell shifted to bind his feet together. "See if you can get yourself out of this." Tyrell laughed.

He gave Steve a shove, then turned to check them. His leering grin disappeared in an instant. "What the hell are you doing, kid?"

Tyrell leapt to his feet and lunged for Clayton. Jenny kicked out at him, landing a hit to his shin. He screamed with pain. His hand shot out, slapping her across her face. The blow was so hard her head whipped sideways, the chair jerked backward and rocked on two legs. It shuddered there for several seconds before crashing back to the floor.

"Don't hit my mom."

The tilting chair had knocked Clayton down, and the knife he had been using had clattered several feet away. He scrambled to get it. Tyrell was limping toward him, blocking his way to the knife.

"Get over here you little brat, or I will hurt her."

Jenny struggled to get free. The twine around her wrist was looser but not enough, not enough to escape. She winced as the twine cut into her flesh. She had to get free; she had to protect Clayton from this crazed man. The twine cut deeper.

Tyrell grabbed for Clayton. The boy was quick. He slid his body around the chair and hid under the table. Tyrell reached for him, stretching his arm out for the child. Clayton scooted out of his reach.

Kneeling, Tyrell swiped his arm out at the child. His shoulder bumped the table's frame. The table teetered. Jenny pushed against it. She had to keep it standing, other than her chair, the table was Clayton's only protection. Tyrell grabbed for Clayton again, his shoulder tilting the table until it hovered on two legs. Clayton scooted around Jenny's chair. Tyrell lunged for him.

The table tottered several times before righting itself, but the objects on the table continued to shake. The yellow flame of the kerosene lamp flickered as its base wobbled. It leaned precariously, then toppled. The lamp hit with a shattering of glass and rolled toward the edge of the table.

Jenny watched in horror, time suspended, as the lamp, in slow motion, rolled across the wooden table. She fought against the twine that bound her, desperate to stop the lamp's progress. Sharp pains stabbed at her wrists as the cord deepened the previous cuts. Blood stung the reopened wounds. Jenny tipped her chair toward the rolling light. Unable to reach it, she watched helplessly as the lamp made its way across the table. It lingered briefly at the edge then dropped, twirling twice before landing on Tyrell's back. He started with the sudden impact and tried to move away.

He jerked upright, knocking the lamp to the floor, but not before kerosene splashed onto his T-shirt. A minute spark tickled the fabric, then a dot of yellow-red hues glowed, kindled briefly, then spread like tiny fingers over the thin material.

Tyrell must have felt the heat. He batted at his back. The act gave the sparks the oxygen they craved. The sparks burst into a flame. The flame caught and spread rapidly across the shirt. Frantically Tyrell clawed at his T-shirt. A cry came from deep within him, and he howled like an animal in pain. Panic showed in his eyes, his mask now one of terror. The acrid smell of smoke and burning flesh filled the cabin. Tyrell stumbled out of the cabin door, his gait awkward, his back a mass of crimson flames.

Clayton rescued the metal lamp base and placed it back on the table, but already a large dark stain of kerosene had spread in an irregular circle on the floor. Hot glowing embers embedded into the rough wood, sparks caught, ignited, mushroomed.

"Clayton, get the knife," Jenny screamed. "Cut me free."

Clayton grabbed the knife from the floor and began sawing at the twine. The seconds it took to cut through it seemed like hours. Finally, she was free. She leapt out of the chair and stomped on the sparks spreading across the floor. They were moving quickly, too quickly. Tiny flames began to flicker, instantly flaring as they made contact with the kerosene-soaked wood. Jenny felt the heat climbing up her legs, watched the angry, crimson flames grasping for more air, escalating beyond her control.

Steve! She needed to check on him. They needed to get out of the cabin. "Clayton," she yelled. "Give me the knife." She ran to Steve. He was moaning: he was alive. She sliced viciously at the twine on his feet. Three swipes and she was through, then his hands were free.

"Steve! Steve, wake up. We have to get you out of here." She shook his shoulder. He moaned again but his eyes remained closed. Jenny put her hands under Steve's arms and began dragging him toward the door. "Clayton, help me." Clayton grabbed Steve's feet. He was small, not strong, but his effort aided Jenny's. They were almost to the door when she glanced back toward the table.

Flames danced in the circle of kerosene-stained wood, spread, engulfed the table and chair, jumped to the splintered chair pieces as if there were kindling, and raced across the plank floor. The heat in the cabin escalated. Adrenaline surged through Jenny's veins as she continued to haul Steve toward the door.

Outside, she heard Tyrell's inhuman screams mingled with the sounds of the raging storm. She blocked out his high-pitched cries and concentrated on getting Steve and Clayton out of the cabin. Pulling harder, she dragged Steve through the doorframe, onto the porch, and down the stairs, not stopping until she had him on the grass safely away from the now blazing cabin. Behind her, fingers of fire were groping hungrily up the curtains, into the furniture, and the log walls. Her heart was racing and her hands were damp with sweat. Between the claps of thunder, she could hear the wail of sirens approaching the cabin and let a sigh of relief escape her body.

Exhausted, Jenny slumped to the ground. She pulled Clayton into her arms, clutching him to her heart. They sat on the wet grass, oblivious to the rain pouring down around them. Tears slid down Jenny's face. Her son was safe and well. Steve was injured, but alive.

The sirens grew louder. Headlights shone through the darkness. An engine roared. And then was quiet. Jenny heard the slamming of doors, then footsteps. Berettas drawn, Chad Evans and Joe Roberts appeared amid a flash of lightning. Another police car, with two officers inside, pulled to a stop.

Jenny screamed through the rain. "Tyrell. Tyrell took Clayton...Shirt caught on fire...please help him..."

Roberts grabbed a flashlight from the police car and headed into the driving rain, heading in the direction of Tyrell's screams. The two officers followed him. Evans came to kneel beside her. "Are you okay, Mrs. Kingsley?"

"I'm okay. Please help Steve. He's hurt. Tyrell hit him on the head...they fought."

"An ambulance is on the way." He went to Steve, checking his pulse. "His pulse is strong. That's a good sign." He shook his shoulder. "Steve, can you hear me."

Steve moaned again, then he was rousing. He opened his eyes, blinked several times before focusing on Jenny's face. He whispered. "Jenny, you okay? Clayton?"

"We're okay," Jenny took his hand and reassured him. "We're both okay."

His eyes darted from side to side. He saw Clayton sitting beside him, smiled, then looked back at Jenny. "Thank God."

Then he was struggling to sit up.

Evans put his arm behind him, supporting him. He grinned at Steve. "Glad you're awake." He turned to Jenny. "We should get out of this rain,"

Assisting Steve to his feet, he helped him hobble to the police car. Taking her son by the hand, Jenny followed.

They had just reached the car when a loud boom sounded, followed by several loud crashes. Jenny turned toward the noise. The fire had spread throughout the cabin, engulfing the walls and the roof. Timbers were crashing and the walls were caving in. The cabin was now a crimson globe of hungry flames. They watched as the fire consumed the structure.

A blaze of light split the evening sky, and with one last thunderous crack, the rain ceased. The storm ended as abruptly as it had begun. In the red glow of sunset, Jenny saw Tyrell in the clearing.

The flames extinguished, he lay face down on the grass. Roberts' knee pressed into his hip, pinning him down while he snapped on handcuffs. He pulled Tyrell to his feet and shoved him toward the ambulance.

Jenny heard the wail of other sirens. An ambulance arrived, then a dark blue sedan careened down the lane and skidded to a stop on the wet grass. Strobe light still swirling, Detective Jarvis jumped out of the car and hurried over. The paramedics checked Steve over while Evans reported to Jarvis. Jenny saw Roberts standing beside the ambulance with Tyrell. Finding Steve stable, the paramedics went to attend to his burns. Roberts was delivering a memorized speech.

"Tyrell Watson you are under arrest for the kidnapping of Clayton Kingsley. You have the right to remain silent. If you give up the right to remain silent, anything you say can and will be used against you in a court of law. You have the right to have an attorney present at any time. If you cannot afford an attorney, one will be appointed to represent you. Do you understand?"

Tyrell looked up defiantly at the deputy's face. "Yeah, I understand."

The paramedics put Tyrell into the back of the ambulance. One of the officers climbed in behind him and the ambulance door slammed behind them. Roberts watched them drive away then approached the remaining group.

"I guess I've got a lot to apologize for, Steve."

Roberts extended his hand to Steve. Their eyes locked for several seconds. The rest of the group watched in silence. Visions of Kelly went through Steve's mind. He thought about Cheryl and how much of a liar she had been. And he thought about the state Kelly had been in when he last saw him. Maybe there was a lot he didn't know about his friend's death and maybe it was time to let go of the past. He could never be friends with Roberts, but he couldn't refuse his offer of peace. Slowly, he reached out and shook the proffered hand. Nodding, Roberts turned and went back to his car.

Detective Jarvis broke the silence. "Mrs. Kingsley, we'll get Watson downtown and keep him under lock and key. Don't worry. I'll be around tomorrow to talk to you. We need all of you to go to the hospital and get checked out. Looks like Steve here needs some attention. Then, I want you to go home and try and get some sleep."

Jenny clutched Clayton to her. Unable to take her eyes off the ambulance, she watched, as lights flashed, her child's kidnapper was taken away. Only then would she get in the police car taking them to the hospital.

Clayton's body clutched to hers, Jenny smiled up at Steve. Now that her son was safe, she felt a euphoria so overpowering she was lightheaded. She was thankful for the support of his arm around her and leaned against him.

All was right with the world again. And now, after what she'd suffered, she felt she could do anything. The terrible days and nights she had endured had made her stronger. They had made her realize she could depend on herself. She was strong and she would survive.

CHAPTER 45

Only a day had passed, but it was a very different group that gathered in Jenny's kitchen. Smiles and laughter replaced sad faces. Jenny's own smile was a bright light illuminating the entire room. Today, even the sunflowers on the wall behind the table glowed with brilliant yellows and rich browns. Myrtle filled teacups and refilled the plates of freshly baked brownies and oatmeal cookies. Her peaches and cream skin glowed as she watched the group crowded around the kitchen table. They were all here, safe and sporting healthy appetites.

Jenny, with Clayton squirming on her lap, sat beside Steve. His chair positioned close to hers, his arm protectively resting on her shoulders while his fingers stroked her back. She leaned toward him.

It had taken eleven stitches to close the slash on his arm and another six on his temple, but he had been discharged from the emergency department with a list of instructions. The doctor on duty had also examined Clayton. Other than a slight cold, he was sent home with a clean bill of health. The doctor had also arranged for follow-up visits with a psychologist to deal with any emotional trauma. The wounds on Jenny's wrists were cleansed and antibiotic creams applied. The lump on her head needed nothing more than cleansing and time for the swelling to go down.

Jenny had made the necessary calls, first to Ray and then to her mother. They were coming this afternoon for a celebration. In tears, Ray had promised to become the father Clayton deserved. She was willing to let him try as long as he didn't pressure her to get back together. Her mother, well, Jenny would just have to put her foot down and let her know she wanted her love but not her interference. She had plans to take computer courses and knew she could make a good life for herself and Clayton. She hoped that Steve would be a part of that life, but even if that was not to be, she knew she would be okay.

A knock at the door interrupted her thoughts.

Myrtle went to answer it and within seconds returned with Bill Clement, Missy trotting at his side.

"Excuse me, Jenny, but I just wanted to see how you and the young lad were doing."

Jenny leapt out of her chair and hugged him. "I don't know how to thank you. The police told us how you and Missy found the cabin. I'm so grateful." She hugged him again. "Please join us."

Clement sat and let Jenny introduce him and Missy to the group. Clayton didn't wait for a formal invitation and was already on the floor beside the dog. While he petted Missy, Clayton told the dog about Blackie, another dog who had come to visit him and helped him get away from the bad man.

"I wonder, Jenny—" Clement paused. "If I could have a word with you?"

"Of course."

She followed him to the front porch. They returned moments later. Clement was carrying a large box that he placed in front of Clayton.

"Someone wants to meet you."

Clayton jumped up and began to open the box. "Mommy, look. A puppy." He looked up at Clement. "Can I hold him?"

"You sure can." Clement lifted a fluffy black-haired puppy out of the box and handed it to Clayton. "Do you think you could look after him?"

Clayton nodded vigorously.

"Then I guess he's yours now."

Hugging the puppy, Clayton smiled broadly at the man. "Mommy, can I really keep him?"

"You have to learn to take care of him.

"I will," Clayton promised. "I'm going to call him Blackie." He sat back down on the floor, sharing his attention between the puppy in his lap, and Missy sprawled beside him.

The adults were just settling back into their conversation when there was another knock at the door. Steve answered this time, returning with Martha Hawthorne. She too had brought something to the celebration—a double-layer chocolate cake, and a wrapped box. She handed the cake to Jenny and the box to Clayton.

"I just wanted to say how relieved I am that your boy is back."

"Thank you. I can't quite believe the nightmare is over."

Martha took the chair Steve held out for her and Myrtle made introductions all around. Martha's face lit up as she watched Clayton open his present and hug the fluffy, brown bear. "I heard you lost your friend in the fire."

"Thank you. I'm going to call him Frazer Two."

"I think he would like that, Clayton." She turned to Jenny who was wiping a tear from the corner of her eye. "My daughter and grandson are coming to visit."

"Cecily's coming to visit?" Myrtle asked.

Martha nodded. The smile that lit her face took away ten years. "Yes, she's coming today. It's been so long…"

"Well, we're having a party to celebrate Clayton being home. Bring Cecily over. It would be nice to see her again," Steve said. He turned to his mother. "I think we need a refill on those brownies, Mom, plus some of that chocolate cake." He grinned at his mother. "We've got a few starving people here."

She smiled back at him, then her gaze traveled to Jenny and tears welled in her eyes. She could not believe it was over, but here they were, sitting around Jeeny's kitchen table begging for food. Jenny kept a hand on Clayton's shoulder while he sat at her feet with Missy and the new puppy. Every few minutes she would run her fingers through his hair or touch his cheek. Myrtle understood her need for constant reassurance. She also saw the times Steve reached out and rustled Clayton's blonde hair, the way his hand rested on Jenny's shoulder, the tender looks that passed between them, and it was all good. And finally, it was over. Hopefully, for them, it would be a new beginning.

Myrtle placed a plate, brimming with warm brownies and chocolate cake on the table. She watched as hands reached out for the food. Within moments, the plate was ready to be refilled.

Bev Irwin is an award-winning author and screenwriter. She writes children's, middle-grade, and young-adult stories—adventure, historical, paranormal, mystery, and shiver bites. For adults, she writes thrillers, suspense, and romance. Lee Child and Michael Palmer blurbed her medical thriller, WITHOUT CONSENT. Missing Clayton, In His Father's Footsteps, and Ghostly Justice have been adapted to scripts. She has garnered many awards for her scripts.

She also has published Love Remembered, a collection of poems about life and love. Bev lives in a small village outside of London, Ontario, with a Golden Retriever look-a-like and a persnickety Maine Coon cat. As a retired nurse, she likes to add a touch of medical to her writing and enjoys crafting evil villains. When not writing, she enjoys reading and spending time with her family, especially her three wonderful grandchildren."

Website bevirwin.com

BEV'S BOOKS

SUSPENSE / THRILLER
Missing Clayton

Without Consent

ROMANCE
When Hearts Collide

City Slicker

Cruising Hearts

MIDDLE GRADE / YOUNG ADULT
In His Father's Footsteps

Ghostly Justice

The Worn Bear

CHILDREN'S
Winnie's Cape

The Wooden Statue

Bumbles the Bear

Farley Goes to Market

Farley's New Home

SCRIPTS
Missing Clayton

In His Father's Footsteps

Ghostly Justice

POETRY
Love Remembered

www.ingramcontent.com/pod-product-compliance
Lightning Source LLC
Chambersburg PA
CBHW030106260626
47156CB00008B/2553